Melody

Hardman Holidays Faraday Book 7
A Sweet Victorian Holiday Romance
by
USA Today **Bestselling Author**
SHANNA HATFIELD

The Christmas Melody
Hardman Holidays Book 7

Copyright © 2018 by Shanna Hatfield

ISBN: 9781792881015

All rights reserved. By purchasing this publication through an authorized outlet, you have been granted the nonexclusive, nontransferable right to access and read the text of this book. No part of this publication may be reproduced, distributed, downloaded, decompiled, reverse engineered, transmitted, or stored in or introduced into any information storage and retrieval system, in any form or by any means, including photocopying, recording, or other electronic or mechanical methods, now known or hereafter invented, without the written permission of the author, except in the case of brief quotations embodied in reviews and certain other noncommercial uses permitted by copyright law. Please purchase only authorized editions.

For permission requests, please contact the author, with a subject line of "permission request" at the e-mail address below or through her website.
Shanna Hatfield
shanna@shannahatfield.com
shannahatfield.com

This is a work of fiction. Names, characters, businesses, places, events, and incidents either are the product of the author's imagination or are used in a fictitious manner. Any resemblance to actual persons, living or dead, business establishments, or actual events is purely coincidental.

*To those who view stumbling blocks
as challenges
and never give up...*

Books by Shanna Hatfield

FICTION

CONTEMPORARY
Love at the 20-Yard Line
Learnin' the Ropes
Rose
Saving Mistletoe
Taste of Tara

Rodeo Romance
The Christmas Cowboy
Wrestlin' Christmas
Capturing Christmas
Barreling Through Christmas
Chasing Christmas
Racing Christmas

Grass Valley Cowboys
The Cowboy's Christmas Plan
The Cowboy's Spring Romance
The Cowboy's Summer Love
The Cowboy's Autumn Fall
The Cowboy's New Heart
The Cowboy's Last Goodbye

Friendly Beasts of Faraday
Scent of Cedar
Tidings of Joy
Boughs of Holly
Wings of An Angel

Welcome to Romance
Blown Into Romance
Sleigh Bells Ring in Romance

Silverton Sweethearts
The Coffee Girl
The Christmas Crusade
Untangling Christmas

Women of Tenacity
A Prelude
Heart of Clay
Country Boy vs. City Girl
Not His Type

HISTORICAL
The Dove

Hardman Holidays
The Christmas Bargain
The Christmas Token
The Christmas Calamity
The Christmas Vow
The Christmas Quandary
The Christmas Confection
The Christmas Melody

Pendleton Petticoats
Dacey   Lacey
Aundy   Bertie
Caterina   Millie
Ilsa   Dally
Marnie   Quinn

Baker City Brides
Tad's Treasure
Crumpets and Cowpies
Thimbles and Thistles
Corsets and Cuffs
Bobbins and Boots
Lightning and Lawmen

Hearts of the War
Garden of Her Heart
Home of Her Heart
Dream of Her Heart

Chapter One

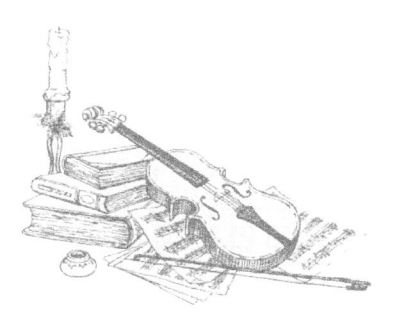

1902
Hardman, Oregon

A carpet of crimson and gold cushioned her footsteps as Claire Baker wandered along a path carrying her deeper into the woods.

The scents of autumn — of apples, spice, smoke from chimneys, and the loamy richness of earth settling in preparation of the coming winter — filled her senses and drew out her smile.

"What a perfectly splendid afternoon," she whispered to herself, afraid if she spoke in a normal tone, the birds chittering in the trees around her would silence their delightful song.

She continued walking along the trail made by deer that her nephew had shown her a few weeks ago, admiring the vibrant hues of the leaves and the sun-dappled trees surrounding her.

Fred told her as long as she stayed on the path, she'd be safe and wouldn't get lost. At times, she still had difficulty embracing the notion her nephew was a year her senior. Fred Decker was wonderful, though, and so was his lovely wife, Elsa.

Claire thought it quite romantic when Fred not only proposed to Elsa on Christmas Eve, but arranged everything for their wedding that very day. Of course, Claire and her two sisters, Ari and Bett, had helped as much as he'd allowed. Still, the very idea of how besotted he was with his bride made her heart giddy with joy.

When Claire had returned to Philadelphia with Ari and Bett after the holidays, she'd missed Hardman. For a girl who'd grown up with every luxury at hand, there was something about the rugged western town that called to her.

Although her family had planned to come for a visit in September, Fred and Elsa had instead made a trip to Philadelphia in August. They were thrilled to see the home John Baker, Claire's father, had built. They'd toured some of Claire's favorite places to visit, strolled through parks, attended parties, and joined in several elaborate dinners. All too soon, the couple left to spend a week in Boston with Elsa's family.

When they stopped on their way home, Heath, Ari's husband, and Clark, Bett's husband, both invited Fred and Elsa to stay, but they were adamant it was time to return to Hardman.

But when Elsa invited Claire to join them, she didn't hesitate to pack her trunks and travel west with the couple.

In the three weeks Claire had been in Hardman, she'd felt so relaxed and at peace. Although she missed her sisters and brothers-in-law, she loved being in the small town with Fred and Elsa.

Fred had a farm and helped in Hardman wherever he could, not because he needed the money, but because he enjoyed the work. From what she'd observed, on any given day he could be found lending a hand at the livery, lumberyard, or sheriff's office, if he wasn't at the bakery his wife owned.

Elsa had shared ownership of the bakery with her twin brother, Ethan, but after the man wed quite unexpectedly right before the holidays last year, his heart wasn't in the business. Fred and Elsa bought his share and Ethan moved to Portland with his wife in the spring.

Claire thought it best that Elsa now had full control over the bakery. She'd hired Anna Jenkins to work there through the holidays, but the girl loved it so much, she'd convinced her parents to allow her to continue working year-round. Everyone in town knew Anna and Percy Bruner planned to wed as soon as they both graduated from high school, but they had two and a half years before that happened.

Elsa had hired a widow woman who was not only good at baking, but never complained about washing the mountain of dishes that piled up each day. Claire had helped with the dishes a time or two and knew how much work that job entailed.

She glanced down at her hands, no longer silky smooth. A blister she'd gotten yesterday on her palm still hurt. Fred warned her to wear a pair of gloves if she wanted to help in the barn, but she'd hefted the pitchfork and cleaned the stalls with her usual gusto.

Although Fred said the stalls had most likely never been so clean, Claire had gotten a blister from the pitchfork handle rubbing on her delicate skin.

Ari and Bett would have had ten different kinds of fits to see her wearing britches and helping Fred around his place the last few weeks. But her nephew and his wife didn't seem bothered in the least by her tendency to want to run a little wild.

In fact, they both seemed to encourage her to do as she pleased.

That morning, after attending services at the Christian Church where Chauncy Dodd delivered an engaging sermon, the three of them ventured to Alex and Arlan Guthry's home where they joined them for lunch. Fred spent most of the time they were there playing with the couple's young son, Gabe, and enduring Arlan's teasing comments about it being his turn to increase the population of Hardman.

Once the dishes had been washed and dried, they all gathered in the parlor where Alex dazzled them with a few of her magic tricks. Alex had been a professional magician before she fell in love with Arlan and teaching.

In spite of having Gabe to care for, Alex continued to teach at Hardman School in the mornings. Lila Grove took over the duties in the afternoon. So far, the arrangement seemed to work well and the students enjoyed learning from both women. Claire offered to fill in as a substitute if they ever needed her help, although she wasn't sure she could keep the students in line as well as Alex or Lila managed.

Claire enjoyed watching Alex perform and sat enthralled as the woman made Gabe's stuffed bear disappear then reappear.

The little boy broke into his infectious belly laugh, amusing them all before his mother declared it his naptime.

Elsa took that as their cue to leave and they returned to the farm. Fred and Elsa settled on the porch in the shade with a book they'd been reading together.

Not wanting to disturb them with her pent-up energy, Claire decided to go for a walk, which is how she found herself wandering through the autumn woods on such a blissfully beautiful afternoon.

She sighed with contentment and tipped her head back, feeling the warmth of the sunshine on her cheeks while a slight breeze caressed the tendrils of dark tresses that escaped the pins she'd used to subdue her thick hair before they went to church.

Claire yanked out her hairpins and tucked them into her pocket, then shook out her wavy locks. She had such a yearning to feel free and unfettered. In Philadelphia, due to their social standing and reputation as part of the Baker Empire, she often felt confined by what was expected of her. Ari and Bett were ladies to a fault, but Claire often struggled to behave as she should. While her sisters took joy in their ability to handle domesticity with precision and grace, Claire much preferred to be out riding or practicing her archery skills.

Oddly enough, the men she'd met had no benefit in becoming involved with a woman who could outride and outshoot them.

Ari and Bett had never tried to curb her interests, but they had encouraged her to pursue more genteel arts, too. Claire had a talent for painting. She could sing quite well although she knew she'd never perform on stage. And she could spin a good story, especially if it involved romance.

Regardless, she still preferred to be outside, seeking an adventure rather than reading about one.

She inhaled a deep breath, reveling in the decadent fragrance of autumn in Eastern Oregon. The air did not smell like that in Philadelphia, of that she was certain. She didn't miss the noise or air heavy with what she'd heard Heath refer to as smog.

There was nothing quite like the peaceful,

wonderful world here in Hardman. Oh, how she would hate to go back to the city, but Ari and Bett had agreed she could stay with Fred and Elsa until Christmas unless they tired of her before then.

She knew her sisters said that last part in jest, but she was mindful of giving Fred and Elsa plenty of privacy and time alone, since they had not yet been wed a year. Their house was large and with the bakery and Fred's busy schedule, so far they'd not had anything but fun together. Fred had quite a sense of humor and Elsa did, too. Claire enjoyed their teasing banter and joined in without hesitation.

Claire continued meandering along the path, lost in the beauty around her. She kicked at a pile of leaves, sending them dancing on the slight breeze.

She watched them twist and turn in a blended blur of jewel tones before continuing on her way. As she neared a bend, she thought she could hear music. But how could that be?

She stopped and cocked her head to one side, intently listening. That was definitely music. A violin, if she wasn't mistaken. Why in the world would someone be this far out in the woods playing a violin?

She rushed ahead on the path around the bend and drew in a startled gasp. Before her was one of the most magnificent scenes she'd ever witnessed and her fingers itched to capture it on paper or canvas. A pity she'd left her paints at Fred's. If she'd been thinking, she would have at least grabbed a notepad and pencil.

Sunlight shone through a break in the tops of the trees onto a tree stump at the edge of a creek. There, on the stump, stood a tiny child with masses of golden-brown curls falling around her form. The fact she wore a pair of boy's pants with a brown plaid shirt did nothing to diminish her delicate beauty. For a moment, Claire wondered if she'd encountered a wood nymph or fairy.

But it wasn't the wild curls or choice of attire that held her attention. It was the way the child played a haunting tune on a small violin.

The little one couldn't have been more than three or four, yet she played with the skill and talent of a master who'd studied for decades.

Enthralled, Claire was afraid to breathe, let alone move, and disturb or distract the child. Silently, she sank onto a fallen log and watched the girl play. She could have closed her eyes and listened to the music all day, but she wanted to see the child. The music seemed to flow through her, become one with her, as she drew the bow across the strings of a violin polished to such a high shine, the refraction of the sunlight from it was nearly blinding.

Claire shifted a little to her left to better watch as the child bend slightly forward as she played. The song segued from slow and somewhat sad to a lively tune. The girl captured the sounds of nature so perfectly, Claire had no idea how she did it, but she could hear the rustle of the leaves, the chirp of birds, the gurgle of water trickling over stones in the creek in each note played.

The music made her want to leap to her feet and dance, to give words to the song swirling in her ears and settling in her heart.

Raw, ripe talent oozed from the child as she played, completely absorbed in the notes, in the sounds, in the world where only she and her music seemed to exist. The tempo increased, the child's fingers flew over the strings, and her little body appeared relaxed yet strangely taut, as though at any moment she might fly apart.

Claire felt trapped in the music, unable to escape even if she'd wanted to. In truth, she'd never heard anyone more talented perform than this child, alone in the woods, who played with her soul bared.

Abruptly, the song ended and quiet descended over the glade. After being so drawn into the music, to the tiny performer's web of magic, Claire felt bereft. It was as though she'd witnessed something almost more magnificent than the human mind could grasp, and suddenly it was gone.

Fearful if she burst into a resounding applause she'd frighten the little girl, Claire slowly rose to her feet and took a step forward.

She opened her mouth to speak, but a man appeared out of nowhere and swept the child into his arms.

"That was wonderful, Maddie Mae. You get better every time you play," he said, lifting the child in the air then kissing her cheek.

Claire stared at the man, not recognizing him from those she'd seen in Hardman, or even the nearby town of Heppner. His brown hair was far longer than was fashionable, growing down to his shirt collar. He sported a scruffy beard that covered his cheeks and chin. He was tall, although not unusually so, and though his shoulders were broad, he appeared very trim and lean.

He kissed the child's rosy cheek again, making her giggle and squirm "Your beard gives me tickles, Daddy."

The man growled, a sound that could have come from a bear, and rubbed his chin across his daughter's face and neck.

The child squirmed and laughed, putting a half-hearted effort into getting away.

He set her down on the stump and ran a hand over her head, letting it trail through the tangled curls. "Do you want to play another song?"

"Maybe," the little imp said, giving him a grin.

Unable to stop herself, Claire stepped forward from where she'd remained hidden by the trees. "Oh, please, won't you play another song?"

The child shrieked and the man scowled at her, both clearly startled by her unexpected presence.

"I'm sorry. I was walking on a path nearby and heard the music. You play with a rare talent," Claire said, smiling at the child. "I'm Claire."

The little girl gave her a scrutinizing look. Claire thought the child was lovely, from all that gorgeous hair to her blue eyes snapping with life and interest, to a rosebud mouth which formed into an inquisitive pucker at the moment.

"I'm Madison, but my daddy calls me Maddie." The child dipped into a curtsey then broke into a smile, showing off her milky white baby teeth. "That's my daddy."

Claire turned toward the man, expecting him to at least smile or offer a word of greeting. Instead, he stood with his hands balled into fists at his sides and a dark scowl on his face. She saw wariness in the depths of his dark brown eyes and wondered what had happened to put it there. To make him take an immediate dislike to strangers.

"It's nice to meet you, Mister..." Claire took a step closer to him, determined not to be intimidated by his gruff appearance.

"Carter." The man glowered at her as his shoulders tensed.

"Mr. Carter, it's a pleasure to make..."

"It's not Mister Carter," he said, emphasizing every syllable of the word mister. "Just Carter."

"Well, just Carter, your daughter is amazing. I have friends back East who could make sure she attends the best schools and trains with masters if you're ever interested."

"No." The man spun away, picked up his daughter, and strode off.

Maddie, charming child that she was, wiggled

around until she could look over her father's shoulder.

"Bye, Claire!" Maddie called. "I hope I see you again."

Claire waved at the child. "I hope to see you again, too, Maddie!"

Carter gave her one last dismissive look over his shoulder before he lengthened his stride and disappeared from her view behind a hulking tree.

Filled with the strangest feeling of loss, Claire turned around to begin the long walk back home. Her mind buzzed with unanswered questions about Carter and his daughter. The child was obviously being reared well and with manners. But that man was... odious. Obnoxious. Ornery.

Claire grinned as she thought up a few more names to describe him. He had no reason to be so rude to her, especially when she meant no harm. She'd merely wanted to enjoy the magic created by his daughter as she played.

In spite of her best efforts, Claire couldn't seem to find the path she'd been on earlier. She knew she was lost when she wandered in a circle not once, but twice, and found herself back at the log where she'd sat to listen to Maddie play.

She plopped down on the log and wondered how long she'd have to wait before Fred realized she couldn't find her way home. Claire hated to admit it, but she hadn't paid attention to her surroundings after she'd heard the music and lost track of where she was. Under normal circumstances, she'd never have done such a thing. But she'd gotten carried away by Maddie's performance. Otherwise, she would have made a mental note of where the path was located, or at least landmarks that would guide her in the right direction.

A longsuffering sigh to her right made her squeak in surprise.

She slapped her hand to her chest and drew in a shallow gasp, then glared at Carter.

"You are pathetic," he said as he pushed away from the trunk of a towering pine tree.

"How long have you been standing there?" she asked, rising from the log and glaring at him.

"Long enough to see you pass by this spot twice."

Claire huffed with indignation. He could have at least possessed the decency to speak up earlier instead of watching her blunder along. "It's past time for me to return home and I can't quite seem to locate the path. I don't suppose you have any idea where it's located."

The man made a noise that sounded like a grunt and walked past her. She fell into step beside him, realizing he wasn't quite as tall as she originally thought. He was probably a handful of inches taller than her, although she was considered quite tall for a woman.

"Don't you have a husband to keep track of you?" he asked as they skirted around a boulder and turned past three aspen trees that quaked in the breeze.

Claire ignored the prickly tone of his voice and shook her head. "No, sir, I do not. Right now, I'm visiting my nephew and his wife."

The man stopped walking and stared at her. She felt his perusal start at the top of her head, continue over her face and drop down to her toes before he reached her face again. One eyebrow lifted as he gave her a dubious look.

"Your nephew? How old is he?"

"A year older than me, but that's a story for another day," Claire said, smiling at the man, hoping that left him slightly confounded. "What about you? Is Maddie with your wife? Do you live here?"

"No and yes." Carter continued walking.

Claire assumed it was no to a wife and yes to living in the Hardman area, although she couldn't be certain.

They'd gone about fifty feet when he pointed to his left. "That path will take you back toward town. There's a farm across the creek where it comes out of the trees."

"That's my nephew's place. Have you met Fred?"

"No." Carter gave her one parting glance, as though she was the most helpless, brainless female he'd ever met. "Stay out of my woods."

"I don't believe you are the sole owner of them, Carter. Last I checked, God created them," she called after his retreating form.

He tossed one angry glare over his shoulder before he jumped onto a big rock and bounded out of her view.

"He's positively horrid," Claire said as she began marching down the path. She'd only gone a few yards when she stopped and glanced back toward the creek. A slow smile broke over her face. "And I'm just the girl to fix that."

Chapter Two

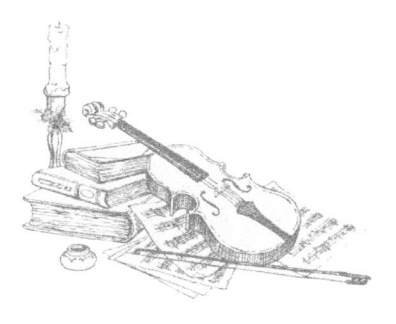

"Are you okay?" Fred asked as Claire walked around a bend in the path not far from his place.

Surprised to see him and Elsa headed her direction, she nodded her head. "I'm fine. I hope you didn't worry."

Fred glanced at Elsa and nodded his head. "Well, we were starting to get a little concerned. It's a nice day for a stroll, so we decided to look for you."

"I'm glad you did, but it wasn't necessary." Claire pecked Fred's cheek, gave Elsa a hug, and fell into step with them as they headed back toward the farm. "Is it getting late?"

Truthfully, she'd lost all track of time from the moment she heard Maddie playing. It could be mid-afternoon or heading toward evening, and she had no idea. With the canopy of trees blocking her view of the sky, she couldn't even gauge how close the sun was to setting.

"It'll be time for dinner in another hour," Elsa said, glancing at Claire. "Are you sure you're well? Your cheeks look flushed."

"I'm perfectly fine," Claire said, wondering if her tumultuous thoughts were somehow visible on the outside. She felt invigorated, irritated, inspired and annoyed. How did one express or even process such a strange mixture of emotion? She had no idea.

"Did something happen to delay you?" Elsa asked.

Claire watched as Fred placed his hands on Elsa's waist and swung her over a log, setting her down on the other side, although he left one hand at the curve of her waist as they continued onward. With her long legs, Claire merely stepped over the log and went on her way.

"Did you run into a problem?" Fred asked when she didn't respond.

"No, not a problem, exactly." Claire considered the best way to describe Carter and his enchanting daughter.

Fred raised an eyebrow as he looked at her, waiting for her to elaborate.

"I was walking along the path, admiring the beauty of God's handiwork," Claire said, then looked at Elsa. "Don't you agree the colors seem quite spectacular?"

"I do agree. I've never seen such splendid fall colors before. They seem extra bright and vibrant this year," Elsa said, bending over and picking up a ruby-hued leaf and twirling it between her fingers. "We should collect some to use in decorations at the bakery."

"Fine. Collect them as we walk home," Fred said, removing the vest he wore and holding it out like a basket.

Elsa and Claire picked up leaves as they walked, tossing them inside.

"You were saying?" Fred prompted Claire as they made their way home.

"Well, I was wandering along, just enjoying the warmth of the sun on my face and the feel of the breeze blowing around me and the marvelous colors of the season when I heard music."

"Music?" Elsa asked, pausing as she bent forward to pick up a golden leaf the size of a dinner plate. "How is that possible?"

"I wondered the same thing," Claire said with a grin. "I stopped and listened, and sure enough, it was violin music. So I followed it to a lovely glade where there was a creek. A little fairy stood on a tree stump playing the most haunting, soul-grabbing tune I've ever heard."

"A fairy?" Fred asked, unable to contain his grin. "Did she have wings?"

"No, at least none that I could see, although I'm not sure they don't exist. Only a wee one from a magical realm could make such wondrous music." Claire smiled at Fred then winked at Elsa.

"What did you really find?" Fred asked, knowing Claire's inclinations to romanticize her stories.

"I really did find a glade with a creek and there was a tree stump bathed in sunlight. A little girl who couldn't be more than four stood on it playing the violin with more skill and talent than many musicians I've heard perform on stage. She had golden brown curly hair, big blue eyes, and was dressed in boy's pants and a brown plaid shirt. If it wasn't for her hair, I might have thought she was a boy at first glance. But she truly was lovely."

Fred stopped and stared at Claire. "You didn't leave her there alone, did you?"

Claire rolled her eyes. "I'm not an idiot, Fred. If you'd let me finish my story, you'd learn that her boorish, rude, completely uncivilized father was there."

Fred frowned. "Did he say or do something he shouldn't have?"

"Not really, he just behaved rather gruffly, and he made it clear I was not welcome. He said his name is Carter. Do you know him, by chance? He was a little taller than me, lean with broad shoulders, brown hair in need of a good cut, deep brown eyes, and a scruffy beard that made him seem more like a bear than a human."

Elsa coughed into her hand to hide a giggle while Fred continued staring at her. "Carter? Carter what?"

Claire shrugged and picked up a vermillion leaf shaped like a heart. "I don't know. He said his name is just Carter. Not Mr. Carter and not Carter so-and-so. Just Carter."

"I don't recall meeting anyone named Carter. Was there a wife? Did he say if he lived in the area?"

Claire glanced at her nephew as they strode down the path. "I asked those very same questions and if I interpret his grunted answers correctly, there is no wife and he does live here. In fact, when I got turned around and couldn't find the path, he guided me to it and instructed me to stay out of his woods. Do you know if someone owns the woods, Fred? I assumed they are more like a park where anyone can wander."

"I own about twenty acres of woods behind the creek, and James Grove owns about forty on the left section, but I don't know about the rest of it on the right. I haven't heard about anyone new moving into the area, so I'm not sure what to tell you. You say he looks like a bear, acts like one, and thinks the woods are his home." Fred held a hand to Claire's forehead. "Are you sure you don't have a fever and dreamed the whole thing."

At his teasing grin, Claire shoved his hand away with a smile.

"I didn't dream anything, but I'm telling you little Maddie, that's his daughter's name, is a prodigy," Claire said with feeling. "If her father wasn't such a backward cavedweller, she could have every music conservatory in the world eating out of her hand. As it is, that dreadful troglodyte will keep her hidden away in his secret forest lair."

"Did he wear furs and carry a club?" Elsa asked with a giggle.

Claire stuck out her tongue at Elsa then couldn't help but join in her amusement.

"No, you goose. He had on brown pants and shirt." Claire stopped and thought a moment. "In fact, his daughter was wearing an identical outfit."

"How sweet," Elsa said, taking the vest full of leaves from Fred as he swung her into his arms and carried her across the creek.

Claire watched them with affection as she scurried across the bridge Fred had finished constructing a week ago. He'd built it so she and Elsa could cross the creek without getting their feet wet or waiting for his assistance.

"He did seem quite fond of his daughter. I kept my presence unknown as I listened to Maddie perform. Oh, but it was something to hear her play," Claire said, recalling how the music had moved her. "It was as though she brought the woods alive through the strings of her violin. I could hear the breeze and the birds, the water in the creek and the rustle of rabbits in the bush. It was beyond description."

"I wish we could have heard her play, too," Fred said as they made their way to the back door and went inside.

Elsa transferred the leaves to a large basket then brushed off Fred's vest before handing it to him.

"Thank you, sugar bun," he said, giving Elsa's backside a playful swat.

Claire hid her smile and turned to wash her hands at

the sink. "Anyway, when she finished playing, her father praised her and seemed quite affectionate, giving her hugs and kisses. Then he noticed me and turned into a grumbling, scowling grouch."

"Perhaps he's merely wary of strangers," Elsa said, tying on an apron and taking food out of the refrigerator to warm up for their dinner. They always ate leftovers for dinner Sunday so Elsa didn't have to cook. Claire had no idea how to cook and wasn't particularly interested in learning. Fred could fry a few things, but beyond that, Elsa was the one with a talent for transforming simple ingredients into mouth-watering meals.

"I think there's more to it than that," Claire said, taking plates out of a cupboard and setting them on the table. "Something about that man seems... I don't know. Wounded? Broken?"

"And what, exactly, do you think you're going to do?" Fred asked as he picked up the milk bucket and moved toward the back door to see to the evening chores. "Fix him?"

Claire grinned. "That's exactly what I intend to do."

"Now, Claire, maybe it's best..."

She raised a hand and interrupted Fred. "I promise I won't do anything I shouldn't. I just feel like perhaps he needs a friend."

Fred had spent enough time around her and her sisters to know when they made up their minds there was no changing it. He shook a finger at her in warning. "Just don't stir up trouble."

"I'd never," Claire said, striking a pose of innocence with her hands clasped beneath her chin as she batted her eyelashes, making Elsa laugh.

"Come on, you loon. You can slice the bread while I fry the ham," Elsa said, placing a knife in Claire's hand.

For the next week, Claire ventured out to the glade where she'd been enchanted with Maddie and both perturbed and intrigued by the child's father. A man who was so sweet and good with his daughter couldn't be as cold and stoic as Carter pretended to be.

And Claire knew, with enough time and effort, she could get the man to relax and smile. After all, the three Baker sisters were legendary for their charm in Philadelphia. When she wanted, Claire could be so charismatic, gracious, and amicable, no one was immune to her engaging personality.

However, she'd returned each day feeling less hopeful of running into Carter and Maddie again. At least she knew the path by heart, now, and had no worries of getting lost again. She'd even taken to venturing off in the direction she'd seen Carter carry Maddie, but she'd yet to find their home. Perhaps they'd merely been passing through and she'd never see them again.

Claire spent Saturday with Elsa at Granger House, assisting Filly Granger and some of the other women in town as they made a quilt for a couple who recently announced their engagement.

"What color do you think Anna would like?" Ginny Stratton asked Elsa as they sat across from each other around the quilt frame.

"Anna?" Elsa asked, glancing at Ginny. "Anna Jenkins?"

Ginny nodded. "Everyone knows Anna and Percy plan to wed as soon as they finish school. If that boy had his way, they'd already be married."

"True," Elsa said with a grin as she pulled her needle through the quilt made from autumn hued fabric scraps. Colorful calico leaves danced on a background of pale yellow muslin. "But they both are determined to finish their schooling and save all the money they can.

As for what color Anna would like, from what I've seen, her favorite color is green, but that's a question to ask her mother."

"She would have been here today, but one of the younger boys has been down with the sniffles," Alex Guthry said as she clipped her thread and glanced up at Ginny. "Are you still planning to host the ice skating party at your house this year?"

Ginny nodded. "Of course! Blake and I look forward to it. We'll be hard pressed to keep Seth out of trouble and out of the way, though."

As though the little boy heard his name, he raced into the room with his grandmother hustling to catch up to him.

"He get away from you, Mother?" Ginny asked as she lifted Seth and kissed his chubby cheek.

Dora nodded as she braced a hand on the back of Ginny's chair and caught her breath. "He's getting quite good at escaping. He must get that from his father."

Ginny gave her mother a knowing look and shook her head. "I'm more inclined to believe his uncle Luke is teaching him bad habits."

Filly laughed. "I'd defend my husband's honor if the accusations didn't bear a bit of truth. Luke is still as rascally as the day I married him."

"It's a good thing Maura and Cullen take after you, dear," Dora said, patting her daughter-in-law on the shoulder.

An unladylike snort burst out of Ginny, earning a glare from her mother before she reined in her mirth. "Cullen is exactly like Luke, Mother, and well you know it. As for Maura, she may look like Filly, but that girl is every bit as ornery as her brother."

"Perhaps she takes after her aunt Ginny," Abby Dodd suggested, then ducked when Ginny tossed a piece of fabric at her.

Claire loved these gatherings. The women of Hardman were so open, so friendly and giving and full of fun. She tried to picture sitting in the stuffy drawing room of one of Ari's friends and quilting, or tossing fabric, or even teasing to the extent these women did, albeit with love and lightheartedness.

Elsa glanced up at her and smiled, then turned to look at Lila Grove. Not only was she a cousin to the Grangers, a part-time teacher at the school, but was also married to Tom Grove, who owned the local newspaper. Between the school, the paper, and family, she usually knew most everything going on in town.

"Have you ever met a man named Carter who has a little girl?" Elsa asked Lila.

Lila appeared to mentally dig through her thoughts before shaking her head. "No, I don't recall meeting anyone by that name. Why?"

"Oh, just curious, that's all." Elsa winked at Claire and went back to making even stitches on the quilt.

"Did someone new move to town?" Dora asked as she picked up Seth and bounced him in her arms, attempting to distract him.

"I'm not sure," Elsa said, looking at Claire. "Claire met him in the woods, but Fred thinks she might have encountered fairies."

Everyone laughed and Filly changed the subject, asking if anyone had seen the winter fashions in the latest issue of *The Delineator*.

The following morning after church services, a few of the women asked Claire if she'd seen any fairies in the woods. She took their good-natured teasing and dished some back before she joined Fred and Elsa as they made their way home.

Elsa had left a chicken roasting in the oven for their lunch. When the jingle of harness alerted them to company, Claire tamped down a sigh. She'd hoped to trek back to the glade in the woods and see if Maddie and her father might be there again. She'd completely forgotten Fred had invited Tom and Lila Grove along with Tom's parents to join them for lunch.

She forgot about Maddie and Carter, though, as she played with their daughter and enjoyed the lively conversation.

By the time Monday rolled around, Claire realized she'd been acting like a ridiculous ninny, wasting her time waiting for Carter and his daughter to appear.

After helping Elsa at the bakery that morning and eating lunch with her and Fred, Claire returned home, changed into a pair of britches, a white loose-sleeve shirt with a vest, and a tall pair of brown boots that nearly reached her knees. Quickly, she unpinned her hair, pulling it back into a braid. She tugged on a pair of smooth leather gloves, grabbed her bow and a quiver of arrows, then strode out the back door toward the creek.

The air held a nip to it, a hint of winter on its way. She supposed that wasn't unheard of since October neared an end.

But the sun shone brightly overhead and she was grateful for the warmth it provided. She crossed the creek then hurried down the path into the woods. The temperature dropped beneath the canopy of the trees that blocked out much of the sun, but Claire didn't mind.

In fact, it was such a beautiful day, she was sure nothing could dim her pleasure in it.

Although she didn't intend to head there, her feet carried her to the glade she'd visited multiple times in the past week. She listened, but heard no sounds beyond the birds in the trees. That was fine with her. Although she would like to hear Maddie play again, the reason she was there had nothing to do with Carter or his daughter.

She merely wanted to get in some archery practice. If she didn't, she'd get too rusty to compete, and that would never do. She'd been the reigning champion at the tournament held for women at the club Heath belonged to the past three years running. Ari found it inappropriate for ladies to compete, but it didn't stop Bett. The two Baker girls locked in the top two spots each year. If Claire wasn't careful, Bett would edge her out of the top position and leave her in second place. Of course, at the competition, Claire wore the latest fashions, complete with a corset that threatened to cut off her air supply.

But today, she had no such worries. She'd left the corset in her bedroom and enjoyed the freedom of movement she had in the britches she'd had the dressmaker sew for her despite Bett and Ari's protests.

She leaped onto the stump where Maddie had performed and danced an impromptu jig before she pulled an arrow from her quiver, notched it in the bow, and let it fly into a tree. It hit the exact spot she'd been aiming.

Without hesitating, she grabbed another arrow and sent it zooming into the first, splitting it down the shaft.

"What are you doing, woman?" a voice bellowed behind her.

Claire spun around so fast she would have toppled off the stump if Carter hadn't been there to catch her.

With her face mere inches from his, she could see golden flecks that seemed to spark like embers from a fire in his nearly obsidian colored eyes. He smelled of winter fires and freshly hewn wood, and all man. Involuntarily, the hand not holding her bow settled on the curve of his shoulder, finding the muscles solid and hard beneath her palm.

"Careful," he said in a gruff tone, but he gently set her on her feet before he took a step back. "I thought I told you to stay away from here."

"You did, but I don't do well following orders when I find them ludicrous." She gave him one of her most charming smiles and studied his face.

Something flashed in his eyes, something she couldn't quite define, then he clenched his jaw. Even she could tell that much despite the detestable growth of hair on his face that did make him seem rather primitive.

"You could hurt someone shooting like that. What if Maddie had suddenly popped up?" he took a step away from her and scowled so hard, his eyebrows nearly met in the middle of his forehead.

"I assure you, I've been trained to handle distractions."

He gave her a pointed look. "You didn't handle me taking you by surprise well."

"That's because you bellowed like a wounded moose," she said, sliding another arrow from the quiver. Before he could blink she sent it flying to the tree where the other two had struck. "I know what I'm doing."

"I'm not sure you do, Miss Claire. For the sake of my daughter, would you please refrain from shooting that thing around here?"

At the look of true concern on his face, Claire nodded. "I promise I won't bring my bow and arrow here again."

"Add in the promise you'll stay away, and we'll call it a successful day."

Claire laughed and backed away from him. She had the sudden irresistible urge to run her fingers through Carter's hair. It was far too long, too unkempt, but something about it drew her interest, just like something inexplicable about this man captured her attention.

"Where is Maddie?" she asked, looking behind him, expecting the adorable child to appear.

"It's her naptime," Carter said, taking a step forward and closing his hand around Claire's elbow. Before she could protest, he nearly dragged her away from the glade and over to the path that would take her home. "Leave and don't come back here, Miss Claire. Please."

It was the soft, anxious way he said "please" that made her study his face, see the desperation there.

She wouldn't make a promise she had no intention of keeping, but she did back away from him. "I won't come back with my bow and arrow again. Is your home nearby?"

Rather than answer her, he spun around and marched into the trees, disappearing before she had a chance to catch up to him.

Resigned to pestering him another day, Claire headed toward home, wondering what she could do to convince Carter she didn't mean him or Maddie any harm.

Chapter Three

Grayson Carter stood in the shadows of the trees and watched the impish woman-child named Claire stride into his sun-drenched glade.

He'd hoped he'd scared her off the other day, but he knew she'd been back nearly every day the past week. Purposely, he'd kept Maddie away from the glade in the afternoon to avoid having to speak with Claire.

If nothing else, she was certainly persistent.

Had he known she listened to Maddie play the other day, he would have sent her off much sooner, but she'd caught him off guard. He'd been so immersed in Maddie's music, he'd failed to notice the interloper until it was too late.

Of course, his daughter had been thoroughly enthralled with her, asking about Claire every day.

For her sake and his sanity, he hoped she forgot about the woman soon. Her nonstop questions about Claire were about to drive him mad.

He'd been grateful for a few moments of quiet when Maddie had fallen asleep mid-afternoon. Since she'd turned four a few months ago, she'd deemed herself far too old to take naps, but once in a while sleep claimed her whether she liked it or not.

Gray used those moments while she slept to take care of tasks he preferred not to do with her close by, like splitting wood or hunting. He'd been on his way to split more of a tree he felled last week when he caught a glimpse of something through the trees.

Silently, he returned to the glade and observed Claire enter it with a force of energy and zest that was nearly palpable.

His beloved wife, gone these past four years, would never have donned a pair of britches and marched around with a bow in her hand and a quiver of arrows on her back. Laura was the epitome of a lady. The first time he'd seen her, he'd been sure heaven was missing an angel because she'd come down to earth just to claim his heart as her own. She was petite, delicate, fair, and the great love of his life even after she'd died.

Yet, the sight of Claire had so unnerved him, he'd been unable to do anything but stare at her for several moments. He'd still been fighting to chase away images of her, with that head full of luxurious black hair hanging to her waist and her smooth skin and sparkling blue eyes, from his thoughts. Seeing her in the pirate-like shirt with a leather vest and the tight britches tucked into knee-high boots would certainly not help matters any.

Today, she'd woven all that hair into a single braid that fell down her back, although wayward strands had escaped and framed her heart-shaped face. Had he not been annoyed with the woman, he might have thought her quite beautiful. He may have even said she looked like she knew how to have fun.

But she'd already gotten on his bad side and he intended for her to stay there.

However, he couldn't see any harm in watching her for a few moments, especially when she jumped onto Maggie's stump and proceeded to shoot two arrows better than any man he'd ever witnessed. Before she could send a third one sailing through the air, he'd startled her.

The last thing he wanted or needed was her falling into his arms, but he hadn't been in a rush to let her go when it happened.

Her fragrance, something that made him think of jasmine mixed with snow, ensnared his senses while he fell into the warmth of her incredible blue eyes. Her bottom lip, slightly fuller than the top, enticed him, tormented him until he wanted nothing more than to taste it.

What little sense he still possessed prevailed and he set her down. He lectured her about Maddie's safety if she came around randomly shooting arrows into the trees. While he was concerned, he could tell Claire was skilled with the weapon and wouldn't likely accidentally harm anyone.

Regardless, he wanted her gone. Out of his woods. Out of his sight. Out of his thoughts.

It was far easier to chase her away than to rid his mind of images of her, especially with the little sway in her step as her long legs carried her down the path toward her home. Although she thought he'd disappeared into the trees, he'd merely stepped behind one and watched to make sure she left. He should have just kept walking back to his cabin and Maddie.

With a sigh, Gray lifted an armload of firewood and

carried it to the cabin, leaving it stacked on the porch by the door. He gathered another arm full and went inside, quietly setting the pieces in a bin near the fireplace. He added a piece to the low-burning fire, then crossed the open room to the kitchen area, adding a few pieces to the stove so he could cook supper for him and Maddie.

"Daddy?" a small voice called from behind a closed door.

Gray reached the door in three strides and opened it, smiling at his daughter. Maddie's hair looked like a snarled nest of tangles as she sat up on her bed, rubbing her eyes.

"Hi, sweetheart. Did you have a good nap?" he asked, holding out his hands to her. She stood up on the bed, bounced twice and launched herself into his arms with a laugh.

"I did, Daddy. The sleep fairy came and got me, even though I wanted to stay awake and play." Maddie gave him a tight hug around his neck. "Did the pretty lady come back? Can we go see her, Daddy? I like Claire. She likes my music."

"I know she liked your music, Maddie Mae, but you know she can't stay here with us."

"I just want someone to play with, Daddy. Can we go to town soon? Can I see Maura?"

"Maybe in a few weeks," Gray said, hesitant for his daughter's hopes to rise. The easiest and best way to keep her safe was to stay home, hidden in these woods where no one ventured. More than a thousand acres of land belonged to him and he'd placed his cabin in the middle of the property, hoping to keep anyone from discovering it.

So far, no one had found their home, although a few people had wandered to the glade where he and Maddie enjoyed spending their afternoons.

A young man had come there more than a year ago.

He didn't say a word, but he seemed to sense he wasn't welcome when he saw Gray watching him from the trees. Thankfully, Maddie hadn't been with him that day.

Right before Christmas last year, he'd caught a couple of drifters wandering around and resorted to chicanery and trickery to scare them away. Gray had killed a bear not long after he'd bought the land. He hadn't wanted to take the beast's life, but when the bear made it clear one of them was going to die, Gray made sure it wasn't him. He skinned the bear and kept the fur out in his barn where it wouldn't terrify Maddie. A few times when people had wandered too close for his comfort, he'd tugged on that skin and pretended to be a bear, growling and snarling in the trees.

It had sent the drifters on their way in a hurry.

He grinned, wondering what Miss Claire would do if he snuck up behind her while wearing the bear hide. Today, she might have shot him full of arrows.

Perhaps the next time she appeared, unarmed, he'd drag out that old bear hide and frighten her away for good. With his luck, she'd pull a pistol from her pocket and throw a knife at his heart.

What kind of woman paraded around attired in britches? Furthermore, how could one who had appeared like a lady last week, look like such a free-spirited woodland sprite today?

Clearly, she was more child than woman from her behavior, but she certainly had filled out her clothes well, not that he noticed such things. He'd resigned himself to spending the rest of his life alone for the safety of Maddie. No matter how pretty Claire might be he wasn't inclined to change his mind.

He smiled, thinking of how easily she'd run one arrow through the other. Perhaps, if he lost every last ounce of his sense and decided to consider her a friend instead of a foe, he could ask her how she'd done such a thing.

"Daddy!" Maddie said, patting his cheeks and drawing him back to the present instead of lost in his thoughts.

"What is it, sweetheart?"

"May I please go outside to play for a while?"

He nodded and set her down. "You may, but stay close to the cabin where I can see you. I'll be watching out the kitchen window."

"Okay, Daddy!" Maddie said, then raced outside. From the door, he watched as she ran over to a pile of leaves he'd raked together. With arms outstretched and head back, she threw herself into the pile, giggling. She rolled over and waved at him, then got to her feet to repeat the process.

He really should at least think about getting a puppy or a kitten for her to play with. He knew Maddie grew lonely and bored with only him for company. The life of a fugitive was not what he and Laura had planned for their daughter.

Gray sighed. Thinking about what might have been would only cause the ache in his heart to reach unbearable levels. He needed to focus on getting a meal prepared for his daughter, doing the evening chores, and perhaps she'd gift him with one of her songs before bed.

Maddie's talent with a violin was beyond anything he'd ever seen in his years of traveling the world. Truly, God had blessed her with a gift that he couldn't even begin to comprehend. If people found out about her talent, about what she could do at just the tender age of four, he could only imagine the pressure that would be placed on her as she grew older.

He didn't want that for her. Oh, he wanted so many things for his daughter. In spite of the challenges that surrounded them, he was giving her the best childhood he could. Maddie might be stuck with him in exile, but she was loved and knew it. She was smart and funny, and had a sweetness that came from his wife, because he knew it hadn't come from him. He tended to be cynical and brooding while Maddie was full of light and goodness, just like her mother had been.

Gray had been convinced what light existed in his life had been extinguished with Laura's death. But there was Maddie, a tiny baby in need of care and love, and he'd given her all he had to give.

In return, she'd pulled him out of his all-consuming darkness and given him purpose.

Gray went out to the smokehouse and brought back a chunk of venison. He cut it into thin slices, dipped them in flour, then fried them in bacon grease he'd saved from breakfast. He added cream he strained off the milk to make gravy. He'd serve the meat and gravy over slices of bread he'd baked yesterday along with tomatoes and cucumbers from his garden.

Necessity had taught him how to cook along with a cookbook he'd picked up on one of his few trips into town. The folks in Hardman were a friendly sort and under other circumstances he would have enjoyed getting to know them. As it was, he generally went to town two or three times a year, stocked up on what he couldn't hunt, raise, or grow himself, then he'd hurry back home hoping no one would pay him any mind. So far, they hadn't.

At least until Miss Claire had shown up in the glade looking like... like... Gray didn't even know words to describe his thoughts on her appearance. A temptress? A woodland sprite? An instigator of shenanigans? A beautiful woman?

He growled, determined to chase away thoughts of Claire — of her long legs and shapely form and flowing hair the color of a raven's wing and that smile full of sunshine.

How did a grown woman have such an innocent, childish smile? And how had her eyes captured the very essence of a summer afternoon sky in their depths?

He wondered if she'd been trained musically. The look of appreciation on her face after Maddie finished her song was one he would expect to see on someone who knew the difference between a treble clef and an eighth note.

Although Claire appeared to run rather wild and free, he got the distinct idea she'd been raised with money and reared to be a lady.

But would a lady march around in britches and shoot arrows with such ease? Surely not. Then again, he hadn't exactly minded the view as he watched her take position and let the arrow fly. Long legs, long tapered fingers, long dark hair dancing in the breeze as though it called to him, dared him to come closer.

What would have happened if he'd given in to temptation and kissed her like he wanted to do? Would she have accepted his kiss? Returned it? Slapped his face and screamed for help? Run him through with one of her arrows?

He grinned, liking the idea of her kissing him back.

Gravy bubbled up in the pan, plopping on his hand and burning it.

"Ouch," he muttered, jerking his hand back and wiping off the hot liquid.

Aggravated with himself and his wandering thoughts, Gray sliced the cucumbers with more force than necessary, nearly turning them into pulp before he inhaled a calming breath.

A glance out the window assured him Maddie was fine as she played on the swing in the tree near the garden.

No matter what he wanted or wished for, the only thing that mattered was his daughter and keeping her safe, protected, and sheltered as he'd done the last four years.

He'd do well to remember that the next time he encountered the lovely, lively Miss Claire.

Chapter Four

The November wind whipped around Gray as he left Maddie with the one family in town he trusted then made his way to the bank. The doors had barely opened when he walked inside and made a withdrawal to cover his expenses for the next several months. He drove his wagon and team to the mercantile and handed George Bruner his shopping list.

The store owner and his wife rushed around gathering his supplies. While they stuffed boxes with spices, salt, sugar, candles, lamp oil, and a myriad of necessities, he wandered up and down the aisles studying each item, thinking of what his daughter might like for Christmas. He doubted he'd return to town before the holiday and wanted to make sure he had gifts tucked away for her.

She'd been too young past years to fully grasp the concept of Saint Nicholas, but she'd been talking about the jolly old man for weeks, contemplating if he might pay them a visit, even at their cabin in the woods.

He'd assured her that if she was a good girl, Santa would find his way to them. He just needed to decide what Maddie would most enjoy receiving.

A baby doll with chubby cheeks and golden hair caught his interest. Perhaps the doll would be something she could not only play with, but would serve as a friend for her to talk to when she tired of his company. He picked up the box and tucked it under his arm then made his way to a display of children's books.

A copy of *Twas the Night Before Christmas* made him grin. He recalled his papa reading the story to him and his siblings. Oh, those were such happy times when life was simple and uncomplicated and his most pressing concern was if he'd get a bigger orange in his stocking than those his brothers received.

Thoughts of his brothers made a lump rise to his throat and threaten to close off his airway, so he swallowed it down and focused his attention on finding gifts for Maddie. He started to walk past the books, but snagged the Christmas poem before continuing on his search.

He looked over the clothing selections and chose a heavy wool coat, a pair of warm boots, and pants and shirts in sizes Maddie would grow into. It wouldn't be long before she outgrew the clothes she'd been wearing. While he was at it, he selected two nightgowns, underclothes, a pair of white stockings, and a beautiful little pair of kid leather shoes that were silly to buy but Maddie would love.

While Maddie wore pants and shirts most of the time, on the rare occasions they came to town, she wanted to do it with style, donning a dress and insisting her hair be combed into a semblance of order. Even though the only place she went was the home of his friends, she wanted to look like the lovely little girl she was.

Tears, buckets of tears, generally ensued as he tried to comb out the tangles of her wild, curly hair, but he couldn't bring himself to cut it. Although Laura's hair had been blonde, she'd passed her masses of curls on to their daughter.

For the most part, Maddie looked like him, but her golden brown curls, her big blue eyes, and her fair skin came from her mother. And her laugh. Every time he heard his daughter's laughter, it made him think of Laura.

About to be sucked into the pain of his memories, he straightened and carried his selections to the counter.

"Is that everything?" George Bruner asked as he set work gloves, a new lantern, and a length of rope into a box.

"There are just a few more things I want to purchase," Gray said, adding a game of checkers, a box of chocolates, a bag of peppermint drops, and a lovely silver clip for Maddie's hair to his purchases. "That should do it."

George gave Gray the total then helped him load the wagon and cover it with a canvas tarp.

"If we don't see you for a while, Carter, have a Merry Christmas."

Gray nodded at the friendly man then shook his hand. "I plan to, Mr. Bruner. Thank you."

He'd turned to climb onto the wagon when a store window caught his eye. With a quick glance both ways to make sure no one was watching him, he hurried into the dress shop.

"May I help you?" an attractive woman asked as a little boy clung to her skirts. The toddler looked as though he was about two as he glanced up at Gray with big, curious eyes.

"Do you have any dresses for little girls?" he asked.

The woman smiled and motioned to a rack of dresses on the far side of the store near a small table that held children's toys. "I have several over here. Do you know the size? Color preference?"

"Pink and she's four, but tiny."

The woman gave him another smile then riffled through the dresses until she found what she'd been searching for. She held up a pink dress, dripping with lace and little pearl buttons that Maddie would love.

In fact, Gray could almost hear her squeals of joy at opening it Christmas morning. "I'll take it."

"Are you sure it will fit her. If you want to bring her in, I could make adjustments."

Gray shook his head. "That's kind of you to offer, Mrs…

"Dodd. Abby Dodd. I own this shop. My husband is the pastor at the Christian church. I don't think I've seen you around town before. Are you new to the area?"

Gray shook his head again and took money from his pocket to pay for the dress. A fancy red wool coat with black trim and a matching hat and fur muff caught his eye. The garment and accessories were completely unsuitable for his rough and tumble daughter, but something compelled him to purchase them. They'd certainly look cute with the little leather shoes he'd bought for her.

"Is that coat set available to purchase?" he asked, pointing to the display behind Mrs. Dodd.

She glanced over her shoulder then turned back to smile at him. "Of course. I have one in blue, if you'd rather."

"No, I think the red, for Christmas," he said.

Mrs. Dodd nodded in understanding. "Of course."

She gave him the total and accepted his money, then tried to go into the back room to get a box, but her son continued to cling to her skirts, hampering her every move.

"I can hold him, if you don't mind," Gray offered, wanting to speed things along. The only child he'd ever held was Maddie, but she'd been with him every single day for the last four years.

"That would be such a help, sir. Thank you," Mrs. Dodd picked up her son, kissed his cheek then handed him to Gray. "Be a good boy, Owen. I'll be right back."

The child stared up at him then reached out and grabbed a handful of his beard and gently tugged.

Gray playfully growled at him. At first, the little one's eyes grew wide, then he giggled and flapped his hands in the air. "Mo, do mo!"

A grin broke out on Gray's face and he growled again, then nuzzled the toddler's neck, as he often did Maddie's. Owen's giggles filled the shop and Mrs. Dodd returned to the front with a box in one hand and a big smile on her face.

"He's been fussy all morning, so thank you for making him laugh," she said. With speed gained from practice, she quickly folded his purchases and tucked them into the box among sheets of thin pink paper then she tied a red ribbon around the box. "You're all set, Mister... I don't believe I caught your name."

Gray intended to keep it that way. He tickled Owen beneath his chin then handed the boy to his mother, picked up the box, and tipped his hat to her. "Thank you, Mrs. Dodd. I appreciate your help today."

"I hope you'll come again," she said as he opened the door and stepped outside.

He quickly made his way to the wagon, hid the box beneath the tarp, and climbed up to the seat. He swung by the post office and retrieved the mail that had accumulated since his last trip to Hardman, then drove to the edge of town to collect his daughter from the home of his friends.

Granger House was a grand home, but it was the couple who lived there that Gray most admired. Luke Granger and his wife Filly had befriended him the moment he'd arrived in Hardman. Over the years, he'd shared bits and pieces of his past, although no one but him knew the full story of what had driven him from his home back East to the untamed lands of Eastern Oregon. Filly and Luke never pushed or prodded, but always welcomed him to their home.

Maddie loved playing with their daughter, Maura, and their son, Cullen, who'd turned two not that long ago.

Today, Maura was at school, but Maddie would have been able to spend the morning playing with Cullen.

Gray left his wagon parked by the barn where anyone passing by wouldn't immediately notice it then made his way around to the back door. Luke's old dog, Bart, lounged on the step and lifted his head while his tail wagged in welcome.

"How are you doing, old friend," Gray asked, hunkering down to pet the dog. He gently ran a hand over Bart's head and scratched behind his ears before he straightened and tapped twice on the door.

"Come in," a voice called and he turned the knob, stepping inside the warmth of the kitchen.

The scents of yeast and roasting meat hung in the air.

Filly smiled at him as she stirred something in a pot on the stove while Cullen and Maddie sat at a little table in the corner playing quietly together.

"Something sure smells good," Gray said, removing his hat as he shut the door behind him.

"I hope you'll stay for lunch. I made plenty," Filly said.

"Please, Daddy?" Maddie said, running over to him and wrapping her arms around his legs, looking up at him with a pout that yanked at his heartstrings.

"We'll stay, sweetheart, but only if you've been a good girl while I was gone." He removed his coat and hung it along with his hat on a hook by the door.

"She's been an angel, Carter. In fact, she even helped me bake some cookies while Owen took a little nap."

"Is that right?" Gray said, lifting his daughter in his arms and giving her a hug. "What kind of cookies did you make?"

"The good kind!" Maddie said, excitedly patting his cheeks.

He had no idea what that meant, but grinned when Filly handed him a soft molasses cookie. The smell of spices tickled his nose and cinnamon teased his tongue as he took a bite. "Mmm. That's the best cookie I've had since the last time we stopped by."

Maddie snitched a bite then wiggled so he set her down. She skipped back over to where Cullen pounded a lump of dough.

"What are they making?" Gray asked, moving closer to Filly so he could speak without the children hearing him.

"Nothing, really. I gave them some leftover pieces of dough to play with. It keeps them entertained and playing quietly, at least for a few minutes." Filly removed the pot from the stove and poured thick liquid into stemmed bowls.

Gray couldn't recall the last time he'd enjoyed a bowl of pudding. And Filly had made chocolate, his favorite.

"I hope Maddie wasn't any trouble," he said,

accepting the spoon Filly held out to him when she'd scraped the pan. He licked it, feeling like he was eight years old and had snuck into the kitchen.

Filly gave him a knowing look and set the pan in the sink and filled it with water before she scrubbed it clean and dried it. "She really wasn't any trouble at all. You know you're welcome to leave her here anytime. Wasn't the last time you came to town right before Easter?"

"Probably. I needed to stock up on seeds and such. I know I bought Maddie's birthday presents then."

"Did she have a good birthday?"

"I believe she did. I attempted to bake a cake and it even turned out mostly edible. One side got a little crispy, but the rest of it was pretty good," Gray said, rinsing the spoon and setting it in the sink. He glanced at Filly. "You and Luke are so good to us. Is there anything I can do to repay your kindness?" he asked.

"No, Carter. You ask that every time you come, but you always bring us a piece of venison, or a basket of vegetables from your garden, and I absolutely love the carved basket you left with the violets in it the last time you were here." Filly pulled two golden loaves of bread from the oven and set them on a dishtowel. She buttered the tops and glanced over at Gray.

"If you want to help, would you mind setting the table? Luke should be home soon and then we can eat. I set the plates there on the end of the counter." Filly tipped her head toward the counter.

Gray set the plates down, counting an extra one. Unless Filly had placed one too many in the stack, it appeared he wasn't the only company she expected for lunch.

Panic set in at the thought of encountering someone new and having to sidestep questions he didn't want to answer.

He glanced at Maddie playing so contentedly with Cullen and he tamped down his need to grab her and flee. For her, he'd somehow manage to make it through lunch. If luck was with him, perhaps the guest would be Luke's partner, Arlan Guthry. He'd met the man a few times and liked him.

Gray placed napkins and cutlery on the table then turned to Filly as she started to remove a beef roast from the oven.

"Need any help with that?" he offered, hurrying over to lift the heavy pan and set it on the counter where she indicated.

"Thank you." Filly set the lid back on the roast then picked up a knife to slice the bread.

"Do you happen to know a girl named Claire?" Gray heard himself ask, wondering how the words had escaped his lips when he had no intention of voicing the question.

"Claire?" Filly stopped mid-slice as she held a loaf of bread in one hand and a knife in the other. She tossed him a questioning glance while amusement danced in her eyes. "Beautiful girl, tall, dark hair, perfect skin, eyes full of mischief, and wears her heart on her sleeve. She could be dressed like a princess for a ball or in britches packing around a bow and arrow. Sound familiar?"

Gray chuckled at her perfect description of the woman he'd encountered in the woods. "That sounds about right."

Filly nodded her head. "I do know Claire. Her name is actually Clarice Baker. Her nephew lives here in town. She and her sisters came to visit him last year for Christmas. When Fred, that's her nephew, and his wife went back east to see the girls this summer, Claire returned with them and intends to stay through the holidays."

"So she doesn't live here?" Gray felt unreasonably saddened by that bit of news. He refused to examine the reasons why.

The sound of the front door opening and closing alerted them to Luke's arrival home. The sound of hushed voices trickled down the hall.

Filly continued slicing the bread. "No, she lives with her oldest sister in Philadelphia. Claire is quite…"

"Quite what?" Claire asked as she stepped inside the kitchen with Luke and gaped at Gray.

Chapter Five

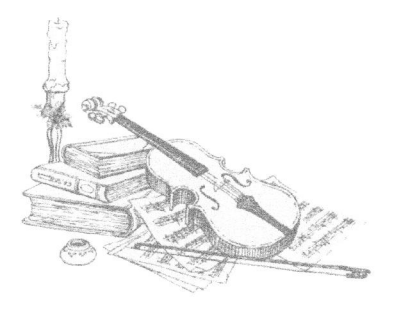

Claire couldn't believe Carter and Maddie were in Filly's kitchen. She'd gotten the idea he preferred to remain hidden away in the woods.

She had no idea he knew the Grangers, least of all enough to join them for lunch. Then again, Filly had been known to invite perfect strangers in for a meal if they looked like they were hungry.

"Claire!" Maddie chirped, jumping up from the little chair in the corner where she sat with Cullen and raced across the kitchen.

Claire dropped to her knees and wrapped the little girl in a hug before setting the child back so she could look at her. Maddie's wild tangle of curls had been combed and tied with a lopsided ribbon at the back of her head. She wore a dark blue sailor dress that made her eyes seem an even richer shade of blue. Truly, the child was lovely. And so full of energy. It fairly snapped around her as she bounced off one foot to the other.

"How are you, Miss Maddie Mae?" she asked with a warm smile.

"I'm great! Daddy comed to town for supplies and I got to stay with Aunt Filly and Cully today. We baked cookies, the very best kind!" Maddie grabbed Claire's hand and swung it back and forth. "We're going to have lunch with Uncle Luke and Aunt Filly. Can you stay, Claire? Please?"

Claire laughed and hugged the little girl again then rose to her feet. She took Maddie's hand in hers. "I am going to stay for lunch. Shall we go wash our hands so we'll be ready to eat?"

"Yes!" Maddie said, clutching Claire's hand as they left the kitchen and made their way to the downstairs bathroom.

Maddie chattered the whole time Claire helped her use the facilities then wash her hands.

"I want one of these rooms at our house, but Daddy says we can make do with the outhouse," Maddie said, giving Claire a pouty look in the mirror above the sink. "I don't like the outhouse. It scares me and its cold."

"Well, if your father said no, he knows best," Claire said, wondering if the man lacked the funds to have a bathroom installed. Then, again, living as he did in the midst of the woods, installing a bathroom most likely wasn't an option. She pondered why he lived like a hermit when his daughter so clearly enjoyed being around people.

"I know," Maddie said, sounding somewhat dejected, then her face brightened. "Guess what I saw this morning?"

"I'll never guess, so you'll have to tell me," Claire said, setting Maddie on the floor and taking her hand as they made their way back to the kitchen.

"Three deer and one of them had a baby. It was so cute. I asked Daddy if I could have it as a pet, but he said the mama deer would miss it too much." Maddie skipped and jumped her way down the hallway, holding tightly to Claire's hand. "I really want a puppy. That's what I hope Saint Nicholas will bring me."

"A puppy, is it?" Claire grinned at Maddie. "What color should this puppy be?"

"Oh, I don't care as long as he's soft and cuddly and likes to play." Maddie raced ahead and climbed into the chair her father held out for her. A little wooden seat boosted her up so she could reach the table. Cullen sat in a similar seat next to Filly.

Much to Claire's surprise, Carter hurried to pull out a chair for her between him and Luke. She settled her skirts and gave him a nod of thanks.

Grateful she'd worn one of her favorite dresses that morning, she was shocked to find the man and his daughter at Granger House. She knew for a fact Filly didn't have any siblings and Luke's only sibling was Ginny Stratton. Why in the world did Maddie think they were her aunt and uncle?

"I didn't realize you were all related," Claire said after Luke gave thanks for the meal and passed her a bowl of mashed potatoes.

"We're not," Filly said, smiling at Claire then Maddie. "But Maddie has graciously allowed us to be her honorary aunt and uncle."

"Yep, they're my aunt and uncle and Maura and Cully are my cousins," Maddie beamed at Claire then took a noisy slurp of her milk.

Carter gave his daughter a look and she picked up the napkin draped across her lap and wiped her mouth.

"Maddie said you came into Hardman to get supplies," Claire said, addressing Carter. "Do you often venture into town?"

"No."

Claire waited for him to elaborate, but he never even lifted his gaze to hers. He merely cut a bite of roast and stuffed it in his mouth. Undaunted, she wasn't yet ready to give up her efforts to pry information out of him.

"Do you plan on coming to the community Harvest festival?" she asked, sweetly smiling at him.

"No."

"Well, surely you'll join everyone for Christmas festivities. There's the ice skating party at Ginny and Blake Stratton's place, and the children's program at church, and Christmas Eve services. Oh, and the magic show during the Christmas carnival at the home of Luke's parents."

"Magic show?" Maddie asked, staring at her father. "What's a magic show?"

"A splendiferous display of prestidigitation," Luke said in a theatrical tone, spreading his hands wide in the air, as though he was a showman announcing a performance.

Carter scowled at him and then Claire. "No."

Before she could ask Carter another question, Luke jumped into the conversation. "Say, did you happen to see yesterday's paper?"

Carter wiped his mouth on his napkin and nodded his head. "I didn't have a chance to read it, but I did notice a headline about the mercantile in Helix being robbed with tools taken from right in the store."

Luke nodded. "Talk about adding insult to injury. It's bad enough the thieves broke into the store, but they used tools they found there to drill a hole in the safe. They poured powder in the hole and blew up the safe, just to steal twenty-nine dollars."

"Really?" Carter asked, looking surprised.

"I don't think the safe held the payday the men were expecting," Luke said. "The article said the robbers also stole jewelry and the owner's overcoat came up missing."

"That's terrible to rob a man and blow up his safe, but to steal his coat, too?" Carter shook his head in disgust. "That's wrong in so many ways."

"Agreed." Luke turned his attention to his wife. "Another delicious meal, Filly, my love."

"You say that at every meal, Luke," Filly smiled at him. "And you may continue to do so at each one."

Everyone laughed and Luke guided the conversation to happenings in their community and upcoming events. From the way Luke and Carter spoke, she got the idea Carter had never participated in any community gatherings, but he obviously liked to hear what was going on in Hardman.

"Did I see a new book shop open in town?" Carter asked, glancing at Filly.

"You did. It's been here about two months or so," she said. "A lovely elderly couple owns it and they have a granddaughter living with them. She's probably around fourteen or so."

"She's a sweet little gal," Luke said, "but most times I've seen her, she's got her nose buried in a book."

Claire grinned. "What else would you expect her to do?"

"Perhaps you can give her archery lessons," Carter suggested, giving her a pointed look.

She planned to silence the man with a defiant glare, but her gaze tangled with his and she struggled to recall anything beyond how much she'd like to know Carter better. To figure out what made him smile, besides his daughter, and filled his heart with joy.

"Speaking of lessons, did Filly tell you Maura is learning to play the piano? Mother has been teaching her," Luke said.

"Oh, that's exciting," Claire said, tugging her gaze away from Carter's and smiling at Filly. "When she becomes proficient at it perhaps she can play with Miss…"

Carter's leg bumped rather forcefully against hers. The look in his eyes warned her to keep her mouth shut where his daughter's musical talent was concerned.

"With Mrs. Granger. Wouldn't Dora love to play a duet with her granddaughter?" she asked, smiling graciously while fighting back the urge to kick Carter in the shin.

Filly served the still warm chocolate pudding topped with sweetened cream for dessert.

"This is delicious, Filly. Thank you," Carter said as Filly set a second bowl of pudding in front of him.

"I don't know how you do it, Carter," Luke said, dipping his spoon into the creamy pudding. "If I had to rely on my own cooking, I'd purely starve to death."

"That's not an exaggeration of the truth. He's hopeless when it comes to cooking," Filly said, giving Luke a look full of indulgence and love.

"It's a good thing I've got you around, wife."

Filly winked at her husband. "For many reasons, the least of which is my cooking."

"I've heard your peach pie has made grown men weep," Claire joked.

"Only whine a little," Filly said, with a teasing smile. "Elsa is the one who brings everyone to their knees with her baking. I still can't get my cinnamon buns to taste like hers."

"She is amazing at what she does," Claire said. "I'm so happy she and Fred found their way to each other."

"Fred is your nephew and Elsa is his wife?" Carter questioned. "And Fred is older than you?"

"Yes, that's right," Claire said, dabbing her lips with her napkin then turning to Carter. "Fred's mother was the only child of my father and his first wife. She was in her twenties when Papa married my mother, a woman much younger. They had three daughters, me and my two older sisters, but Fred's mother married and left home, venturing here. She preferred none of the family contact her so Fred was unaware we existed until after his mother passed away. I'm so glad he reached out to Papa's attorney and we found each other after all these years. He's quite special to all of us."

"He's grown into an honorable, respected man, Claire. Considering how things started for him, it's quite an accomplishment," Luke said, "One he should be proud of."

"I don't think Fred is proud, but grateful. He frequently mentions how blessed he is with his life," Claire said, feeling tears sting her eyes as they did each time she thought about her dear nephew's tragic story. At least it had a happy ending. After he fell in love with Elsa everything settled into a rightful place. "We are quite proud of him, though. Fred is so gentle and kind. It's almost impossible to think of him being raised by Mildred and her outlaw husband."

"What's an outlaw?" Maddie asked, glancing at Claire with interest.

"A person who does bad things," Carter said, patting his daughter on the back. "Finish up that pudding, Maddie Mae, then we best head for home. I don't like the looks of those clouds out there."

"It certainly looks like it could snow," Luke said, leaning back and gazing out the window. "Wouldn't be the first time we've had a snowstorm in early November."

"I noticed the temperature had dropped quite a bit this morning," Filly said, grabbing Cullen's cup of milk before he spilled it on the floor. "It feels much more like winter outside today than autumn."

"Fred said he's noticed the animals are getting thick coats early. I suppose that means a cold winter is coming." Claire looked at Luke. "What does the Farmer's Almanac say?"

"What makes you think I know?" he asked, feigning disinterest.

"Because anyone and everyone knows you study that book until you could spout the weather forecast on any given day." Filly gave Luke a teasing smile.

"I'll spout something at you, Miss Sassy," Luke said, winking at Filly. "A man can't even have a hobby around here without having it scrutinized at every turn."

"And here I thought your hobby was figuring out ways to work the word prestidigitation into every conversation," Claire said, drawing a laugh from Filly.

"That's enough out of you two," Luke said, rising from the table and carrying his dishes to the sink. "As much as I'd love to stay and allow you ladies to continue your insults, I need to get back to the bank."

Carter stood and shook Luke's hand, then Luke placed a kiss on top of Maddie's curls. "You be a good girl for your papa, Maddie. We'll see you the next time you come to town."

"Bye, Uncle Luke! Thank you!" Maddie said, hopping up in her chair and giving him a hug.

Luke hugged her and set her back down in the chair, kissed Filly's cheek and picked up Cullen, kissing his son's cheek. "You behave for your mother, Cullen. I'll see you at supper."

"Me go, too!" Cullen clung to Luke, but he handed the boy to Filly.

"You stay here, little man, and keep your mother company." Luke ruffled the boy's hair, kissed Filly one more time then waved to the rest of them. "Don't be a stranger, Carter. Come back anytime."

"Appreciate the invitation, Luke. Thank you."

Claire heard Luke's footsteps take him down the hall and out the front door. Carter stood and carried his dishes along with Maddie's to the sink. "May I wash these for you, Filly?"

"Absolutely not, Carter. With the clouds growing darker out there, you better head toward home. I'd hate for you and Maddie to get caught in a storm."

"I'd hate that, too," Carter carried a few more dishes from the table to the counter then lifted Maddie out of her chair and set her on her feet. "Go get your coat, sweetheart. It's time to go."

"But, Daddy," Maddie whined, grabbing onto his hand and swinging back and forth on it. "Can't we stay? I like it here. Aunt Filly's house is pretty and Cully and Maura are here, and they gots the potty inside the house where it's warm."

Claire had to agree with Maddie that indoor plumbing was far preferred to a cold, stinky outhouse, but she kept her thoughts to herself.

She picked up two serving bowls and carried them to the counter lest she look at Filly and burst into a round of giggles.

"Maddie," Carter said in a firm, but not unkind tone. "It's time to go now. Get your things. Please."

"Yes, Daddy," Maddie let go of his hand and scuffed her toes as she slowly walked out of the kitchen. Cullen trailed after her, jabbering a mile a minute, although Claire could only pick out about every fifth word.

"She minds so well, Carter," Filly said, tipping her head in the direction the children had gone. "You've done such a good job with her."

"Thank you. I'm never sure I'm doing what's right or best for her, but I try."

"It shows," Filly said, setting dishes in the sink.

Claire wiped off the now empty table and watched as Carter slipped on his coat. His broad shoulders filled it out well, even if he still needed a good haircut and the scruff on his face trimmed, or shaved.

"Won't you think about joining us for Thanksgiving?" Filly asked, as she filled a tin with cookies then handed it to him.

"I appreciate the invitation, Filly, but Maddie and I will stay home." Carter set the tin on the counter and pulled on his gloves then picked it up again. "Thank you for these, and for everything."

"Our pleasure. Anytime you want to bring Maddie, feel free to stop by." Filly picked up Cullen when he ran back into the room and rubbed his eyes sleepily.

Maddie skipped into the room with a scarf trailing behind her and her coat half on.

Carter started to pull off his gloves to help her, but Claire hurried to the little girl.

"You better bundle up, Miss Maddie Mae, or old Jack Frost will nip that cute little nose of yours," Claire said, helping Maddie slide her arm in her other coat sleeve then fastening the buttons for the child.

"An old man will bite my nose?" Maddie asked, staring wide-eyed at Claire.

"No, sweetheart. Jack Frost is who makes the cold air. When your nose gets chilly and turns all red, Jack Frost has made it so," Claire said, smiling as she guided Maddie's little fingers into her mittens. "But you know what? Jack Frost was once a little boy, just like Cullen there. And one day he was playing with his sister. She fell in a pond and he jumped in to save her and when he woke up, he was no longer a boy, but had turned into frost."

"I don't want frosted!" Maddie said, running over to her father. "I promise I won't play in the creek when you tell me not to. I promise, Daddy!"

"That's good, sweetheart," Carter said, giving Claire a dark scowl as he tried to comfort Maddie.

Claire decided she obviously needed to work more on the stories she shared with children. She'd only meant to entertain Maddie, not terrorize the child.

"Maybe Maddie would like to hear the story about the squirrel, Claire. Maura especially liked that one," Filly said, grinning at her from where she filled the sink with hot water and soap while holding Cullen on one hip.

"Well, there once was a lazy squirrel. He sat in his tree and waited for his family and friends to bring him food. Why should he work when they all seemed to enjoy it so much?" Claire said, going over to where Maddie leaned against her father's legs and kneeling on the floor in front of her. "Then, one day he waited and waited for them to bring him food and no one came. Morning turned to afternoon then afternoon to evening, and still they didn't come. Oh, but he was hungry."

Claire placed her hands against her stomach and pretended to be starving. "The next morning, he was positively famished. But even more upsetting than his hunger was the absence of his family. He hadn't given much thought to how much they did for him. How much he depended on them. How much he'd miss them when they were gone. So he rolled himself up and climbed out of his nest in a big oak tree and glanced around. The woods were so quiet and still, not even a bird sang."

"Where did the birdies go?" Maddie asked, moving away from her father and sitting down on Claire's lap.

Claire wrapped her arms around the little girl and held her close. "Well, the lazy squirrel wondered the same thing. Where had everyone gone? They couldn't all disappear, could they? Where were the other squirrels? And the birds? And deer? And the raccoons? They had to be somewhere, didn't they?"

Maddie nodded her head, staring up at Claire as she hung on every word.

"The lazy squirrel scampered down the tree, or at least he tried. He'd eaten so many nuts, he was kind of round and chubby and it made scampering hard to do."

Claire filled her cheeks with air and crossed her eyes, making Maddie giggle with delight. Cullen clapped his hands and laughed from where Filly held him at the sink.

"Then what happened?" Maddie asked.

"The lazy squirrel looked all around, but he couldn't see any food or any friends, so he started off on a journey. He was so hungry, every step seemed like it took a mile, but it wasn't really all that far. All of a sudden he heard a noise!" Claire glanced down at Maddie and made a silly face, looking from right to left and back again, as though she checked to see if they were being watched.

Maddie's giggles melted her heart as the little girl reached up and patted her face with her mitten-covered hands. "Who made the noise?"

"His friends and his family, and the deer, and raccoons, oh, and the birds. They were chirping and singing. He ran into a beautiful glade and found them gathered around a big tree stump covered with a feast." Claire grinned down at Maddie as she held her and touched a finger to the child's pert nose. "And you know what happened next?"

Maddie shook her head. "No. What happened?"

"Well, he ran over to his family and threw his little furry paws in the air. 'How could you leave me to starve to death? What if something had tried to eat me?' he cried. His family welcomed him to the feast and handed him a big acorn and reminded him they'd asked him to come with them several times, but the lazy squirrel hadn't wanted to leave his warm, cozy nest."

"He should have gone with them. If his daddy told him it was time to go, he should have gone," Maddie said, her little voice quite serious. "You have to listen when daddies tell you to do things."

"Yes, you do, and that's why you won't ever be like the lazy squirrel." Claire filled her cheeks with air again and Maddie reached up pressing against them until she blew the air out on a whistle. She gave the little girl another hug then set her on her feet. "Now, you better run along with your daddy before it gets too cold outside for little girls."

"I'm glad you camed today, Claire. Bye, bye!" Maddie gave her another hug then ran over to Filly and hugged her when she bent down. She kissed Cullen's cheek then skipped over and took her father's hand. "I'm ready, Daddy. Let's go before the old man tries to bite my nose!"

Carter nodded and looked to Filly. "Thank you, again, for everything."

"You're most welcome, Carter. If we don't see you before the holidays are over, have a Merry Christmas."

"You and Luke as well," Carter said, nudging Maddie toward the door. He released her hand to turn the knob and when he did, Maddie ran over to Claire for one more hug.

She lifted the child in her arms, not wanting to let her go. The little pixie was so sweet and endearing, Claire had a sudden wish to keep her with her always.

But the dark, threatening looks Maddie's father sent her way let her know that was not ever going to happen.

"It was nice to see you, Carter. Take care," she said, releasing Maddie and taking a step back as the little girl raced out the door.

"You, too. Try not to shoot anyone with that bow of yours," Carter gave her something that looked like a smirk before he hurried outside and shut the door.

Filly gave her a long, knowing look. "As soon as I put this boy down for a nap, I want to hear all about how you know Carter and Maddie."

Claire shrugged and walked over to the sink, filling a glass with water. "There's not much to tell."

Filly grinned and nudged her with her elbow. "Oh, there must be something because every time you look at him, your cheeks turn rosy red. How long have you been smitten with Hardman's mystery man?"

It was a good thing Claire hadn't yet taken a drink from the glass of water in her hand. If she had, she'd have choked on it. She set the glass down with more force than necessary and frowned at Filly. "I'm not smitten with that arrogant, overbearing, obnoxious, hairy bear-like man! Not in the least."

Filly laughed, actually laughed at her, as she carried Cullen toward the doorway. "If you convince yourself of that, let me know."

She wasn't interested in Carter. Was she?

The idea of it was preposterous. Wasn't it?

Chapter Six

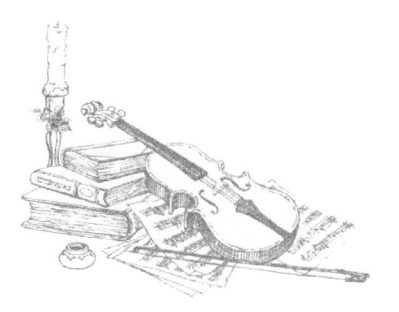

"May we go now?" Maddie asked, standing impatiently by the cabin door.

"Yes, sweetheart, we'll go now. I just need to pull on my coat and gloves." Gray gave the stew he'd left simmering on the stove another stir, set the spoon in the sink, then walked over to the pegs near the door and pulled on his coat. He wrapped a scarf around his neck, buttoned his coat, then bent down and buttoned Maddie's. He looped her little pink scarf around her neck, pulled a knit hat Filly had made her last year over her ears, then made sure she had on her mittens before he tugged on his gloves, settled a hat on his head, and opened the door.

Sunshine glistened and sparkled on the snow that had fallen the last few days. He'd barely made it home from Hardman before big, fluffy snowflakes drifted down from the sky. Maddie was thrilled, dancing in the snow like a little winter fairy while he unloaded the wagon.

Grateful for all the wood he'd chopped and hauled onto the porch so it was out of the weather, they'd stayed inside where it was warm while snow fell, covering the world around them in a blanket of white.

Maddie had mentioned several times how nice it would be to have a real bathroom instead of having to bundle up to trudge out to the outhouse or use the chamber pot. There were so many things he wished he could give her, but he didn't think she'd die if she had to use the privy instead of a nice bathroom.

It seemed each time he left her at Granger House, she noticed more and more of the luxuries available there and the lack of them at home. If things were different, if life hadn't taken the unexpected turns right after she was born, she'd be accustomed to living with every luxury available close at hand.

As it was, he was glad they lived a simplistic life. He thought it was teaching them both good lessons. Their existence in the woods near Hardman had certainly given him a lesson in humbleness. One he had desperately needed to learn.

With the sun shining around them and both of them tired of being cooped up inside the cabin, Gray swung Maddie up so she sat on his shoulders then stepped off the porch into the snow.

"It's bee-you-ti-ful, Daddy! Did fairies come and sprinkle the sparkles?" Maddie asked as he walked through the snow. Nearly a foot of it had accumulated, although if the temperatures warmed, he doubted it would last too long. Then again, it could remain cold and stay until spring.

"Do you think fairies add the sparkles to snow?" he

asked, evading her question as they headed toward the glade. He wanted to prolong her child-like fantasies for as long as he could. As quickly as the past four years had passed, he was afraid he'd blink and she'd be sixteen and daffy about a boy. Then again, if he still kept them sequestered in the woods by that time, she'd not know there were boys around.

Thoughts of her someday falling in love and leaving him made his heart ache, so he chased away the pain by pointing to where a rabbit huddled beneath the cover of a bush, nibbling on a bit of exposed grass.

"I think fairies would add sparkles to snow like they do to the water sometimes. Maybe the animals help them." Maddie glanced up at a chittering noise and watched a squirrel leap from one branch to another. "Look, Daddy. I don't think that's Claire's lazy squirrel, do you?"

He grinned, thinking of the story and the charming girl who shared it with his daughter. The last person he expected to encounter at Luke and Filly's home was Claire, but he couldn't exactly say he didn't enjoy seeing her. She'd looked lovely in a gown of deep wine that accented the rosy hue of her cheeks and the berry ripeness of her lips. He'd spent way too much time thinking of those very lips and how much he'd like to kiss them.

He should have asked Filly Claire's age. He knew she was slightly younger than her nephew, but never meeting the man, he had no idea if he was twenty or thirty. There were times Claire seemed barely old enough to wear long skirts. Then she'd give him a look that made it perfectly clear she was a grown woman. A woman who intrigued him more than he wanted to admit any woman had for a long time.

Perhaps his fascination with her rested in the fact he hadn't been around women the last four years, unless the few trips to town counted, when he generally only saw Filly Granger, Aleta Bruner, and perhaps a few females in passing on the street.

He'd vowed when he lost Laura he'd never wed again, and he planned to stick by that promise. But Claire was definitely a temptation.

If the woman wasn't so silly and full of fun, he might have been able to ignore her and her undeniable beauty. However, it was hard to discount her ability to connect with Maddie and her lighthearted nature. It was as though she was just brimming with light and goodness and he'd had far too little of either in the past years.

"What's that, Daddy?" Maddie asked as they entered the glade. She pointed to something sitting on the stump where she often played her violin when the weather was cooperative.

"It looks like a basket," he said, hurrying his step. He brushed the snow off a section of the large stump with his arm then set Maddie down. A wicker basket with a lid sat on the snow. A red ribbon tied to the handle with an envelope attached to it caught his attention.

"What's it say?" Maddie bent down until her nose nearly touched the basket.

Gray grinned at her as his fingers fumbled to untie the ribbon so he could open the envelope. He finally slid out a sheet of expensive parchment and unfolded it.

For Carter and Miss Maddie Mae —

These cinnamon buns are one of my favorite treats from Elsa's Bakery. I hope you enjoy them. And I hope the bears don't beat you to them.

With warmest regards,
Claire

Carter looked up and glanced around, hoping to catch a glimpse of Claire. He noticed tracks in the snow coming and going from the other side of the glade. They had to belong to her. No one else would have been out here.

The woman couldn't have left too long ago, or something surely would have disturbed the basket by now. Part of him longed to race after her, to thank her for the unexpected treat, to see her smile, and ensure she made it home safely.

"I'll have to tell her about bears hibernating," he muttered as he slipped the note in his coat pocket along with the ribbon and lifted the lid on the basket. The scent of cinnamon and sweetness wafted around him, making his stomach rumble with hunger.

Maddie giggled and edged closer to him. "Your tummy is talking to you, Daddy. It said 'feed me!'"

He chuckled and removed his gloves, stuffing them in his other coat pocket. "Sit on my lap, Maddie, and we'll share one of the treats Miss Claire left for us."

"Claire brought them? Where is she?" Maddie looked like she was ready to jump off the stump and chase after the woman. Gray grabbed her around the waist and settled her on his thigh as he sat on the stump next to the basket.

"She left these goodies for us. Her niece makes them." Gray pulled out one of the sticky cinnamon buns and his mouth started to water. "Take your mittens off, Maddie, and I'll share this one with you."

The little girl didn't have to be told twice to remove her mittens. It was a good thing they were fastened to a string that ran up her sleeves and around her back or they might have been lost until spring with the way she cast them off, eager for the treat.

With both little hands held up, ready to accept the pastry, Maddie's smile broadened as Gray set a piece of the cinnamon bun on her hands.

"I don't have a fork, Daddy," Maddie said, looking from the gooey bun to Gray.

He smiled and lifted the cinnamon bun he held to his mouth. "I think, just this once, you can eat with your fingers."

"Oh, goodie!" Maddie dove into the cinnamon bun and by the time she finished eating what Gray had given her, she had icing nearly stretched from ear to ear. It was a good thing he'd attempted to braid her hair or she'd most likely have gotten it in her curls, too. Frosting rimmed her mouth and both hands were a sticky mess.

He ate the last bite of his share of the bun then picked up a handful of snow and cleaned Maddie's hands.

"That's cold," she complained, but didn't try to pull away from him.

"I know it's cold, sweetheart, but this way you won't get your mittens all sticky." Gray finished cleaning her hands and his, then he opened his coat, wrapped it around Maddie, and pulled her close against him. "Are you getting warm?"

"Yes, Daddy. I'm gonna smufercate."

Gray leaned back and glanced down at her. "You aren't going to suffocate, Maddie Mae. If you have enough breath to talk, I promise you have enough to breathe."

"I'm warm now," she said and started to jump down, but Gray held on to her. He hesitated to let her get down in the snow and get cold and wet, but she was wearing boots and pants. She needed to run off some of her energy or she might never settle down and go to sleep tonight.

"Put your mittens back on first and stay close to me."

"Okay, Daddy." She tugged on her mittens so fast,

she missed getting her thumb in the proper hole, but didn't seem bothered in the least and she ran and hopped, leaped and danced through the snow.

When she spun around and around with curls escaping her braid, he just sat and watched her, his heart overflowing with love for his precocious, precious daughter. He didn't know what he would have done without Maddie, if she'd died along with Laura.

Emotion threatened to overwhelm him, so he stood, pulled on his gloves, grabbed the handles of the basket and motioned for Maddie to come to him.

"Since Claire was nice enough to bring us a gift of cinnamon buns, do you think we should make a gift for her in return?"

"Oh, yes, Daddy! A present for Claire," Maddie said, clapping her hands together. "What kind of present?"

"I don't know. What do you think she would like?" Gray asked. What did one give a woman-child who obviously came from money, had no immediate needs, and was as hard to pin down as it was to catch a butterfly in full flight twenty feet up in the sky?

"Flowers!" Maddie said, staring at him like he had suddenly dropped a notch in her hero status.

Of course his daughter would choose flowers. She was fascinated with them. Her favorite storybook was full of colorful paintings of flowers and a princess. Even before he could come up with another suggestion, Maddie was yanking on his coat and giving him an excited look.

"Claire is a princess, Daddy. And a princess needs lots and lots of flowers. We need flowers for Claire!"

"Flowers for Claire," he grumbled, wondering how his child expected him to magically make flowers appear when it was below freezing outside.

"Maybe we could find..." Gray stared at the pine

cone Maddie picked up. If one looked at it just right, it rather resembled a flower, something like a rose in bloom. An idea quickly formed in his thoughts and before he could tamp it down, he smiled at his daughter.

"Pick up more pine cones just like that one, sweetheart. I have an idea for a gift even a princess such as Claire will like."

"Okay!" Maddie raced around, grabbing pine cones until her hands here stuffed full.

Gray ended up taking off his hat and letting her use it to hold the pine cones as they made their way back to the cabin.

By the time they got there, she'd filled his hat with pine cones.

"What are we going to make, Daddy?" she asked, and followed him inside the warmth of the cabin.

"A surprise for Miss Claire." Gray smiled at Maddie. "One unlike any she's received before."

Maddie's squeal of delight made him laugh as he set the basket of cinnamon buns on the table, removed his coat, and got to work.

Chapter Seven

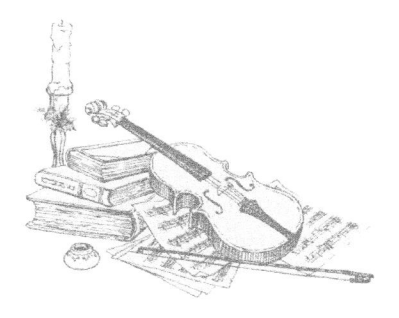

"Where in the world did you find these?" Claire asked as Fred handed her a pair of wooden skis.

"Oh, I was helping the Nilsson family pack up the last of their things today and they had two pairs of these skis out in the barn rafters. They didn't want to haul them to Portland, so they said I could have them. I thought you might enjoy them," Fred said, setting two sets of skis down on the snow near the porch steps. "Have you ever used them before?"

"No, but it can't be that hard to learn, can it?" Claire asked, studying the buckles a moment before she stepped onto the skis and bent to fasten them around her boots.

Fred stepped onto the other pair and buckled them on. "Shall we give this a whirl?"

"We shall," Claire said with a giggle. She slid one foot forward, then the other, then suddenly everything seemed to be sliding at once and she fell over in the snow.

A shout from Fred drew her gaze to him as he tumbled into a pile of snow near the front walk.

"Are you hurt?" Fred asked as he tried to disentangle himself and get to his feet.

"I'm wonderful," Claire said, laughing as she looked up at the blue sky above them. In a playful mood, she lobbed a snowball at Fred.

He shot one back at her and they both were laughing, still stuck in the snow with the skis twisted together when Elsa stepped outside and glanced from one of them to the other.

"What are you two doing?"

"Learning to ski?" Claire's statement sounded more like a question and caused Fred to snicker.

"Oh, for Pete's sake," Elsa said, stepping back inside the house and soon returning wearing her coat, hat, scarf, and gloves. "Let me see if I remember how to do this."

"You've been on skis before?" Fred asked, removing the skis on his feet and straightening them for Elsa.

"My grandmother taught us how. We used to go to a park and practice," she said as she buckled on the skis. "But I haven't done this in years. Do you have poles?"

Fred went back out to his wagon and retrieved two sets of poles. He handed a set to Elsa and gave the other to Claire once he helped her to her feet.

With a pole in each hand, Elsa pushed off and was soon gliding across the pasture with Fred and Claire watching.

"I think she remembered how to ski," Claire said to Fred as he watched his wife in awe. "Your Elsa is full of surprises."

"She certainly is." Fred beamed with pride as he watched Elsa. When she came back to where they waited, he gave her a big hug and kissed her quite passionately.

Claire had grown accustomed to their displays of affection at home. In fact, she thought it sweet and romantic that Fred was so besotted with his bride.

Face red and hat askew, Elsa pulled back from Fred and motioned to Claire. "Come on, I'll show you how this works."

Twenty minutes later, Claire kept stride with Elsa as they glided across the pasture together.

"This is such fun!" she said as joy bubbled out of her in the form of a laugh.

"It is fun. I'd forgotten how much I used to enjoy this," Elsa said as they circled around and returned to the house. Fred waited for them there and helped them both remove the skis. "You might need to get a third pair, Fred, if you want to join us because I'm claiming one of them."

"For now, I'll let you girls play with them. Maybe Santa will bring me a pair if I'm a good boy."

Elsa patted his arm with her mitten covered hand. "You're always good, Fred. The very best man I know."

Fred pecked her cheek then gave her a playful swat on her bottom. "You two get inside and warm up while I finish the chores."

Claire followed Elsa inside and helped set dinner on the table. As they ate, they discussed current news, like the sheriff of Pendleton catching the men who'd blown up the Helix mercantile safe, and a woman from Portland who was offering a $500 reward for the return of her husband who'd suddenly disappeared.

"Maybe the husband ran off for a good reason," Fred mused as they finished their dinner.

"What possible good reason could there be for a husband to abandon his family?" Elsa asked, narrowing her gaze at Fred.

"Well, maybe she got too cheeky with him, or stole the skis he just brought home," he teased.

Elsa tossed her napkin at him, but he ducked then pulled her onto his lap and tickled her sides. Claire shook her head at the two of them then began clearing the table. She didn't know what Fred whispered to his wife, but Elsa's face turned bright red and she swatted his arm before she jumped to her feet and carried dishes to the sink.

Later, as Claire snuggled into the warm comfort of her bed, she thought about Fred and Elsa and how happy they were as husband and wife. She'd known the first time she'd seen the two of them together, when she and her sisters arrived a year ago, that they were meant to be married. Fred practically followed Elsa around like a puppy and the woman was clearly in love with him.

The love, respect, and friendship they shared reminded her of the affection her sisters held for their spouses. Ari absolutely adored Heath and the feeling was clearly mutual. Bett and Clark weren't quite as openly affectionate, but their love was deep and abiding. She just hoped to someday find someone she could love that much, to be loved that much by a good, kind man.

Claire had adored her father and because of the wonderful relationship they'd enjoyed, the bar was set high for any potential suitors that came along. She had no intention of settling for anyone just to be married. Rather than do that, she'd remain a spinster all her days. Until she found someone who was even half as interesting and fun as her father, she'd remain blissfully single.

Thoughts of Carter made her smile in the darkness. For certain, he was an interesting, intriguing man. She had no doubt at all that if he got past being gruff and standoffish, he'd be loads of fun to know. In the few moments she'd caught him unawares with Maddie, she'd seen a lightness in his spirit he hid from the world. She had no idea why, though.

Her efforts to pump Filly for information were wasted. The woman was tight-lipped when it came to Carter and his daughter. Claire got the idea Filly really didn't know much more than she did about the "mystery man" as the banker's wife referred to Carter. Filly did say he'd been in the area since Maddie was a tiny baby, but Claire found it quite strange no one knew who he was or anything about it.

Regardless, she was still determined to befriend him. Not because of some ulterior motive on her part, but because she sensed he needed a friend.

Besides, she was daffy over Maddie Mae. Unwittingly, the child had twined her tiny little fingers around Claire's heart.

After the last snowstorm, she'd been so antsy to get out of the house and do something, she'd pulled on her britches and boots, talked Elsa out of a basketful of cinnamon buns, which really took no coercing at all, and marched out to the woods. She'd hoped a wild animal wouldn't get to the treats before Carter and Maddie found them, but it was too cold for her to linger in the glade waiting for them.

Tomorrow, if the weather held, perhaps she'd try out the skis and return to the glade to see if the basket was still there.

It was four days later before Claire was able to strap on the skis and make the trip out to the glade. She'd awakened to bitterly cold temperatures the morning after she left the goodies for Carter and Maddie. After two days of snow, she'd helped Fred at home and Elsa at the bakery. Only at Elsa's insistence she take in some fresh air did she return to the house, change into her britches and warmest coat, and strap on the skis.

Thanks to Elsa's instruction, she'd picked up quickly on how to use them. With a pack on her back, and adventure waiting ahead, she quietly slid across the snow, thrilled at how quickly she made it from Fred's house to the glade on the skis.

As she approached the stump, she could see her basket sitting on it, but it had been recently placed there, because no snow covered it.

She stopped next to the stump and reached out for the basket, untying the ribbon holding down the lid. When she pushed the lid open, she gasped in pleased surprise.

Inside, nestled on a bed of soft moss, were a dozen red roses. Only they weren't real roses, but pinecones cut and painted to resemble roses. The bright red of the rose she held in her hand provided a brilliant splash of color to the world of white around her.

Reverently, she ran her fingers over one petal, amazed by the clever craftsmanship.

She glanced inside the basket and noticed an envelope. Quickly pulling it out, she set the rose she held back in the basket then removed a note written in a childish print.

We made you roses.
Love,
Maddie and her daddy

Below that, a distinctive masculine script made her smile.

Thank you for the cinnamon buns. They were delicious and much appreciated, even if you were traipsing around in my woods again. And bears are in hibernation, so you only have to worry about the wild cats.

Carter

Wild cats? Was he teasing or serious? She'd heard about Blake Stratton shooting an enormous cougar a few years ago, but she'd been assured that big cats didn't normally roam close around Hardman.

Claire glanced cautiously around then cocked an ear to listen. She could hear birds chirping in the trees. If they were making noise, then all was safe in the world.

She tucked the note back in the basket then considered her next move. The tin of cookies she'd brought to leave for Carter and Maddie would keep on the stump until he found them. On the other hand, though, it would be easy enough to follow their tracks through the snow to their cabin.

Would Carter welcome her or shoo her away? Would her presence infuriate him?

Willing to test his ire, she picked up the basket, tied it to her pack so she had her hands free for her ski poles, and set out toward the cabin, following the path made by Carter and Maddie.

She smiled at the tiny little footprints that bobbed in and around the large set he made. It was easy to picture Maddie flitting about in the snow, chattering nonstop.

It didn't take long once Claire left the glade to come through a break in the trees to an open space where a sizeable cabin stood in the woods. There was a sturdy barn, a smokehouse, and a few other outbuildings all tucked next to a stream.

Smoke curled like gray wisps of cotton toward the pale blue winter sky while icicles and frost rimmed the cabin like icing on one of Elsa's fancy cakes. The setting was lovely and something Claire desperately wanted to capture with her paints. But first, she'd warm up if Carter would allow her into the cabin.

The skis made no noise as she moved across the snow. She unfastened the buckles and left them at the bottom of the porch along with her poles and made her way up the steps. About to knock on the door, she heard a sound that piqued her interest. Not just any sound, either, but the notes of a violin. She removed her pack and left it with the basket on the porch before she stepped back into the snow and walked around the cabin. The music stopped, so she waited, listening for it.

Musical notes trickled into the stillness of the afternoon from a log building set back away from the others. Smoke lazily drifted upward from the chimney there. Did someone live there?

Uncertain, but curious, Claire made her way to the door and admired the thick logs of the structure. Filmy curtains kept her from being able to see inside, but the music grew louder, beckoning her forward. She rapped three times on the door and waited.

The music abruptly stopped and she heard the rumble of a deep voice followed by the sound of footsteps. The door opened a crack and she looked into the scowling face of Carter.

"Hi," she said, feeling unsettled by the gold sparks snapping in Carter's dark eyes.

"Hi," he said, not moving to let her enter, but not slamming the door in her face either.

She took that as a sign of encouragement. "May I come in?"

"If I say no, will you leave and never come back?" he asked in a gruff tone.

Claire might have been upset, had she not noticed the teasing grin he offered her.

"What do you think?" she asked, taking a step forward.

He shook his head. "You're persistent. I'll give you that," he said. "Give me just a minute."

The door quietly clicked shut. She heard him say something and Maddie's squeal of excitement.

In seconds, the little girl raced outside, straight into Claire. She had to take a quick step back to keep from toppling into the snow as she picked up the child and gave her a hug.

"Claire! You comed to see us!" Maddie squeezed her tightly. "Did you find your present?"

"I did find my present, Miss Maddie Mae, and I love it. Roses are my favorite flower."

Maddie leaned back and clapped her hands together. "I knewed it. I told Daddy we had to give you flowers."

"You chose quite well." Claire kissed the child's cheek and then glanced up as Carter stepped outside and closed the door quickly, blocking her view of whatever was inside the building.

"Were you playing the violin?" Claire asked as Carter settled a hand on her elbow and guided her back to the cabin.

"I was playing one my…" At Carter's look and the slight shake of his head, Maddie snapped her mouth shut.

"What are you doing all the way out here and how in the world did you find us?" he asked as they rounded the cabin and approached the porch steps. He noticed the skis and pointed to them. "Yours?"

"Yes. Fred brought home two pairs the other day. We were going to try them out and failed miserably, but Elsa, it seems, is an expert at them. She gave me a few pointers before it snowed again, but today is the first day I've been able to try them out." Claire grinned. "I love them. I may never walk on the snow again."

Carter grinned, stamped the snow off his feet and opened the cabin door. "Come on in."

Claire wiped her feet on a rug made from braided

strips of rags and walked inside before she set Maddie down. Her gaze roved over the neat interior. She hid her surprise at seeing a wooden plank floor and she'd not noticed before but glass sparkled from the windows. A fire crackled in the fireplace on one end of a large open room and the other held a cook stove. There was a good sized table with four chairs, although she doubted anyone had ever been to the cabin besides her. Shelves lined the top of the walls and held an assortment of items. There were more open shelves in the kitchen area where she could see dishes, bowls, and crockery. Through an open doorway, she could see a small bed covered with a pink and white quilt.

"Come see my room," Maddie said, grabbing her hand and pulling her forward.

"Let's get you out of your coat first," Carter said, unbuttoning the coat Maddie wore and grabbing the scarf she tossed on the floor.

Claire was surprised when he held her coat as she slipped out of it. She unwound the scarf from her neck, removed the knit hat she'd donned, and ran a hand over her hair to smooth the flyaway strands.

"Hurry!" Maddie said, clasping her hand and tugging her into the room that was clearly her domain. Shades of pink and white and green created a decidedly feminine backdrop for Maddie's space. There were a few toys, a small desk with a tiny carved chair where sheets of paper and crayons had been left scattered across the surface, and a carved chest that matched the chair and desk.

"It's lovely, Maddie. Did your daddy make the furniture for you?"

"Yep. He's good at making stuff," Maddie said, picking up a stuffed white rabbit that had been well loved. She clutched the toy to her chest and hopped up on her bed. "Daddy gave me this quilt for Christmas last year. Isn't it pretty?"

"It is pretty," Claire said, running her hand over the delicate rosebud pattern. "What's your favorite toy?"

"Flopsy." Maddie held out the rabbit toward her. "He's my bestest friend, besides Daddy."

"Friends are good to have," Claire said, gently rubbing the rabbit's worn head before handing it back to Maddie.

"Would you like a cup of tea?" Carter asked, suddenly appearing in the doorway.

Claire admired the breadth of his shoulders as he stood there, arms crossed over his solid chest. "That would be nice, thank you. There's something in my pack that might go well with tea."

She stepped outside and retrieved her pack from the porch then rushed back inside.

"What did you bring?" Maddie asked, bouncing around her like she had balls attached to her little feet.

"Elsa made the most delicious butter cookies this morning. I thought you might enjoy some." Claire took the tin of cookies from her pack and set it on the table.

Maddie wasted no time in climbing up on a chair and reaching for the tin.

A look from her father stopped her and she hopped back down, ran over to the sink near the stove and held up her arms. He lifted her up and pumped water over her hands as she washed them. She haphazardly slapped them against a towel he held for her then raced back to the table.

Carter set a glass of milk in front of her. "You wait until I have the tea ready, Maddie Mae."

The child nodded obediently and placed her hands on her lap, although she couldn't quite manage to sit still as she wiggled and squirmed in her seat.

Claire hid a smile as she took out a second tin and carried it over to the slab of counter opposite of the stove where Carter made two cups of tea. "I also brought some sweet bread. It's quite good for breakfast."

"Did you make it?" he asked as he handed her a cup of sweetened tea.

Claire couldn't contain a laugh. "No. I can barely boil water without burning the pan. If anyone was dependent on my cooking talents for survival, I'm afraid they'd perish."

He gave her a look that held amusement as he followed her back to the table. "I've learned necessity can teach you most anything."

She shrugged. "I suppose that's true, but I have no intention of being in a position of needing to learn."

"What, exactly, do you intend to do with your future?" Carter asked, helping himself to a cookie after Claire gave one to Maddie.

"I haven't decided yet. I enjoy archery, as you know, but last I checked, there's not much of a future in that for women."

Carter smirked and nodded. "True."

"I enjoy painting, but I'm not museum-quality good."

"Few are," Carter bit into a cookie, ate it in two bites, and helped himself to another. "These are delicious."

"Elsa never makes anything that isn't scrumptious." Claire handed Maddie a second cookie.

"I'd like to see your paintings sometime." Carter snitched a third cookie.

With a look of scrutiny, she tried to decide if he was serious and concluded he was. What could a backward woodsman know of art? Then again, she had a feeling Carter was far more than he appeared to be at first glance.

"I might just show you one or two sometime," Claire said, sipping the tea then taking a cookie.

"What else do you enjoy?" he asked.

"I love to sing, but I'll never perform on the stage."

"You sing?" Maddie asked, leaning forward. "Would you sing to me?"

"I'd love to sing to you, Maddie. How about I sing something after we finish our little tea party?"

"Yes, please!"

Claire turned to Carter with a smile only to find he'd once again withdrawn into himself while a dark look hovered on his face. Uncertain what she'd said that upset him, she changed the subject.

"Do you have plans for Thanksgiving? I can hardly believe it will be here so soon."

"No plans."

She studied Carter. "Are you going to have a turkey? Will you bake pies? Cranberry sauce? How about sweet potatoes? Will you have those?"

He shook his head. "No."

"Then I suppose you should plan to join me at Fred and Elsa's home. They said to extend an invitation to you."

"No."

Claire wasn't surprised by his refusal, but chose to ignore it. "We'll eat promptly at one. Maddie could provide the entertainment if you'd like to bring her violin."

"Absolutely not," Carter said in a growl that might have frightened Claire if she wasn't growing accustomed to his surly ways.

"Well, then, I guess just having you join us will be enough of a gift." She turned to Maddie and smiled. "Will you have a Christmas tree for the holidays?"

"Yes. Daddy and I picked it out forever ago."

Claire glanced at Carter. "You already cut down a tree?"

"No. We just looked for a perfect one back in

October when the weather was still nice. We tied a pink ribbon on it so we could find it when we're ready to cut it down in a few weeks." Carter took a long sip of his tea. He looked as though he was about to say something, then thought better of it.

Maddie asked Claire about things Elsa made at the bakery and the two of them carried on a conversation with Carter sitting sullen and quiet while they conversed.

Claire finished her tea, wiped her mouth on the napkin Maddie handed to her, then rose to her feet. "I should go. I don't want to try and find my way home in the dark."

"I can take you back to the glade," Carter said rising to his feet. "Maddie will be okay here for a few minutes on her own."

"No, I'll just follow the tracks. From there, I know my way."

"But what about my song?" Maddie asked, throwing her arms around Claire's legs and looking up at her with tears filling her eyes. Her little mouth formed the most adorable pout.

Claire felt her heart melting as she knelt and smiled at the little girl. "One song, then I better go. Do you have a favorite?"

Maddie looked to her father and shrugged.

Claire launched into "My Wild Irish Rose." Her clear soprano filled the cabin and left Maddie staring at her in mute astonishment.

Finally, the little girl lunged forward and wrapped her arms around her again. "Oh, thank you, Claire. Will you sing to me again?"

"The next time I see you, I promise to sing another song."

Claire hurried to pull on her coat and gloves. She gave Maddie a long hug before she straightened and smiled at Carter then picked up her pack. "I'll see you for Thanksgiving if not before."

"I never said…" He sighed and ran a hand through his already tousled hair.

Claire wanted so badly to do the same, she opened the door and bounded down the steps, then remembered the basket of roses and retraced her steps to grab it and fasten it to the back of her pack.

"Thank you, again, for the roses. I will cherish them always. And thank you for the tea. It was quite appreciated."

"You're welcome." Carter leaned against a porch post and watched as she fastened the buckles of the skis around her boots then grabbed the poles.

"Goodbye!"

"Bye, Claire!" Maddie hopped up and down and waved.

As she glided across the snow, she heard Maddie begging Carter for her own pair of skis. She wondered if he could so easily tell his daughter no as he had her.

Chapter Eight

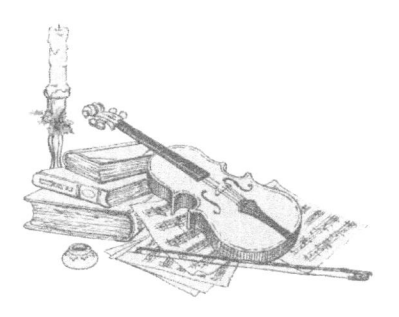

"You'll pace a hole in the rug that you sent poor Murtag all the way to Heppner to drag back here last year," Fred teased as he stepped behind her in the parlor.

Claire sighed and turned away from the window where she'd been watching for Carter and Maddie for the last hour. She'd so hoped he'd get past whatever stubbornness kept him from wanting to associate with the rest of the world and join her at Fred and Elsa's for Thanksgiving.

Elsa had been bustling around the kitchen for hours and the divine smells were making Claire's stomach growl with hunger in a most unladylike fashion, but she didn't care. She'd just wanted, so badly, to share the day with Carter and Maddie.

"I'm sorry, Fred. I just thought, perhaps, Carter

would…" She sighed again. "It's not important."

Fred pulled her into a hug and patted her back comfortingly.

Even if he was her nephew, Fred seemed more like the brother she'd always longed to have. Not that she didn't adore Heath and Clark, but Fred was different. He was blood of her blood and she felt as though the two of them had a bond because of their close ages.

"It's important to you and I'm sorry if you'll be disappointed. He's got fifteen minutes before we sit down to eat. Perhaps he'll arrive yet." Fred released her and turned her toward the kitchen. "Come help me torment my wife. If we gang up on her, maybe she'll let us have a taste of that golden brown turkey or at least a snitch of pumpkin pie."

Claire laughed and leaned her head against his arm. "Thank you, Fred."

"For what, auntie?"

"For being so kind and good." Claire kissed his cheek then rushed ahead of him into the kitchen. While Claire distracted Elsa by threatening to carve the middle out of the turkey, Fred snuck over to where his wife had left three pies, two pumpkin and an apple. He cut a wedge out of the pumpkin pie, divided it in half, then gave a piece to Claire before slipping out of the kitchen.

Elsa fisted her hands on her hips and raised her voice. "I saw that Fred Decker and if I didn't love you so much, I'd beat you with my rolling pin. I've told you a hundred times already today, stay out of my kitchen until the meal is ready!"

His chuckles floated down the hall from the front of the house.

Claire giggled and ate the last bite of the pie he'd given her.

Elsa shook a finger at her. "You're no better than he is, Clarice Baker!"

"It must be a family thing," she said, trying not to giggle again as she wiped the corner of her mouth with her thumb and caught a few crumbs of pie. "Is there anything I can do to be of help?"

"Besides keeping yourself and my husband out of the desserts?" Elsa asked on a feigned huff then smiled. "If you wouldn't mind filling the water glasses, we can start placing the food on the table.

The clock in the entry struck one as Fred held out Elsa's chair, then seated Claire. He'd just taken a seat when a tap at the back door drew their gazes that direction. He jumped up from the chair with Claire on his heels.

Fred opened the back door and smiled in greeting at Carter and a blanket covered bundle with a tiny face peeping out from inside the folds.

"You must be Carter. I'm Fred Decker, Claire's nephew. Welcome to our home." Fred stepped back so Carter could come inside. He carried Maddie on one arm and held a burlap sack in his other hand.

"Thank you for having us. Maddie has been excited since Miss Claire extended the invitation." Carter knocked the snow off his boots before he stepped inside. Claire took Maddie from him and removed the blanket he'd wrapped her in then divested the child of her coat, hat, mittens, scarf and boots.

"There's our pretty girl," Claire said, giving Maddie a warm hug. Maddie wore the same dress she had on the day she'd run into Carter at Granger House. Her hair had been combed and pulled back with a ribbon, and her eyes sparked with excitement.

"Hi, Claire! My daddy tried to smofercate me so I wouldn't get cold." Maddie gave her a hug then glanced over at Fred and Elsa. "Hello."

"Hi, Maddie. I'm Mrs. Decker. It's nice to meet you." Elsa knelt down and smiled at the little one. "Are you warm enough?"

The child nodded.

"Are you hungry?"

Maddie nodded again.

"Well, let's fix that, shall we?" Elsa held out a hand to Maddie.

The little girl glanced at her father. At his nod, she followed Elsa to the table and climbed into the chair where books had been stacked to give her a boost.

"This is very kind of you. Thank you," Carter said, handing the burlap sack to Fred. "It's a smoked venison roast. I thought perhaps you'd enjoy it on a cold wintery day."

"Thank you, Carter," Elsa said with a warm smile. "We most certainly will enjoy it."

Claire thought Carter appeared nervous as he nodded at Elsa and then Fred. He removed his coat and hat, and hung them on the rack by the door.

"I hope we didn't keep you waiting. The snow was deeper in a few spots than I anticipated and it took a little longer to get here than I planned." Carter glanced from Elsa to Fred.

"We'd just sat down to eat when you arrived, so your timing couldn't have been better," Fred said, motioning for Carter to take a seat next to Maddie, and across from Claire.

When everyone was seated, Fred bowed his head and offered a heartfelt prayer of thanks for their bounty of blessings. Elsa handed him a sharp knife and long fork and he began carving the turkey.

"That's a beautiful turkey, Mrs. Decker," Carter said, watching as Fred cut into the golden, crispy skin. "Claire mentioned you own the bakery in town. The cinnamon buns and cookies she shared with us were excellent."

"Thank you. I love to bake. My grandparents came

from Sweden and started a bakery in Boston. My parents and older siblings are still there," Elsa said, smiling at Maddie as the child took a sip of her milk then dabbed her mouth with her napkin.

Claire was impressed with the manners Carter had obviously instilled in his child. His past mystified her, but at the moment, she was far more interested in the fact he'd walked all the way to Fred and Elsa's house to join them for Thanksgiving.

The meal was lively with Fred drawing Carter into a conversation that put him at ease. Maddie tucked into her food with enthusiasm and ate until Claire thought the little one might burst. When she finished, she sat quietly by her father, waiting to be excused.

Claire gave Elsa a look and the woman nodded, tipping her head toward the kitchen doorway.

"Maddie Mae, would you like to see the rest of the house? I can take you on a tour and show you my room," Claire said, rising to her feet and stepping around the table. She held her hand out to the child.

"May I go, Daddy? Please?" Maddie asked.

"Of course, sweetheart." Carter kissed his daughter on top of her head. Claire noticed his smile as he watched Maddie skip along beside her out of the room.

Claire walked Maddie through the house, showing her the various rooms. In her bedroom, Maddie climbed up on the bed and looked out the window at the view of the pasture below. If it hadn't been so cold, she would have taken Maddie out to the barn to play with Maude, the barn cat, but she didn't think it was a good idea for the child to be out in the frigid air more than necessary since she'd have a long trip home in the cold.

"Do you spend a lot of time out in the building where I found you the other day when I came to your house?" Claire asked, hoping to get Maddie to tell her something that would satisfy her curiosity.

"Yes. Daddy works out there, so I go, too." Maddie slid off the bed and walked over to the desk where Claire had left her sketch pad.

She'd started a drawing the other day and hadn't yet finished it. She hadn't even given a thought to anyone seeing it, but it was too late to hide it from the inquisitive child.

"Is that my daddy?" Maddie's index finger traced over the drawing, outlining Carter's eyes and nose.

"Do you think it looks like your daddy?" Claire asked. She knelt beside the child and wrapped her hand around the little girl's shoulder.

"Oh, yes. That's his eyeballs and his nose. You need his smile. My daddy has the bestest smiles." Maddie looked up at Claire and grinned. "But sometimes he does this, too."

Maddie crossed her arms over her chest, stuck out her bottom lip and scowled so hard, her eyes all but disappeared while her eyebrows nearly met in the middle of her forehead.

Claire bit back a laugh and picked up Maddie, giving her a hug. "He does, indeed, look exactly like that sometimes. I call that his grumpy bear face."

Maddie giggled as they made their way downstairs. "Grumpy bear, grumpy bear, with scratchy hair," she said in a sing-song voice.

Hard pressed to keep from laughing aloud, she took Maddie into the parlor and sat near the fire in a rocking chair where she sang softly to the child. In no time at all, Maddie had fallen asleep. Claire gently laid her on the couch, covered her with a blanket, and brushed the hair back from her face.

"Sleep well, little angel," she whispered, then returned to the kitchen where Elsa was pouring cups of coffee and serving slices of pie.

"Did you save a piece of pumpkin for me?" Claire

asked, returning to her seat.

"You and Fred already had your share," Elsa teased as she set a piece in front of Claire. "What did you do with Maddie?"

"She fell asleep, so I left her on the couch."

Carter rose to his feet and left the room, but soon returned and settled back into his seat. "She's sleeping soundly," he said, then picked up his fork and cut off a bite of pie.

Elsa gave Claire a look, then turned the conversation to the upcoming holiday season. All three of them invited Carter to join them for the various festivities.

He didn't bark out "no," so Claire took that as a good sign that he might actually consider attending something.

"I apologize if this question seems obtuse, but I don't believe I know if Carter is your first or last name. Which is it?" Elsa asked so sweetly, Claire wanted to dare Carter to refuse to answer.

He glanced from Elsa to Fred and to Claire, as though he gauged if she'd put Elsa up to asking the question.

Since she was innocent, he seemed to read the truth on her face and took a long sip from his cup of coffee before he sat back. "Carter is my last name, my first name is Grayson."

"That's a wonderful name, Mr. Carter," Elsa said, offering him another charming smile.

"Please, just call me Carter, or Gray. That's what my friends call me." He returned Elsa's smile and cut another bite of apple pie. "Everything has been delicious, Mrs. Decker. Thank you for extending your hospitality to me and Maddie."

"You're welcome anytime, Gray, but only if you'll call us Elsa and Fred."

Gray nodded his head and took another bite of pie. "Perhaps you can give me some pointers on making pie crust, Elsa. I've tried many times, but I never seem to be able to get it right."

Claire hid her grin behind a cup of coffee and listened as Elsa gave Gray her best tips for making flaky piecrust. While they talked, Claire sat back and rolled his name around in her head. Grayson Carter. It fit him perfectly. The name sounded refined, yet also a bit rugged.

Now that she'd discovered his name, she wondered if she could ever get him to shave that mess of hair off his face so she could see what he really looked like. Would he be as handsome as she imagined?

Once they'd finished eating, Fred insisted on doing the dishes since Elsa did all the cooking. Gray offered to help him. The two men didn't seem interested in Claire's assistance, so she joined Elsa in the front parlor where they both stood over the couch and watched Maddie sleep.

The child was even more adorable lost in her dreams than she was awake, if that was possible.

"I want one of those," Elsa whispered and squeezed Claire's hand.

"Me, too, but I think I'll have to agree to let a man catch me first."

Mirth twinkled in Elsa's gaze as the two of them took a seat on the other side of the room and picked up an embroidery project they'd been working on together. Elsa had wanted to make something for Ari and Bett for Christmas. Claire suggested she stitch decorative pillows for them. Somehow, Elsa convinced her to give her a hand with the detailed stitching.

It gave them something to do with their hands in the evenings while they sat near the fire and Fred read to them from the newspaper, a book or an entertaining magazine called *Puck* he'd recently subscribed to. The colorful cartoons were mostly political in nature, but nearly always humorous.

Twenty minutes had passed when Maddie yawned and stretched. She opened one eye then the other, and looked around. When she saw Claire, she smiled and held out her arms to her. Claire picked her up and settled into the rocking chair, cuddling her close.

"Did you have a nice nap, Maddie?"

"Oh, yes. I dreamed about Santa bringing me a puppy. He was brown and white and so soft and fuzzy. I named him Bear 'cause he felt like Daddy's face." Maddie looked up at Claire. "Have you felt my Daddy's face? It's soft, but sometimes it's scratchy, too."

Claire heard Elsa's choked laughter and refused to look at the woman, knowing they'd both start giggling and not be able to stop. "I have not felt your daddy's face, so I'll have to take your word for how soft it feels."

"He won't mind," Maddie said, looking over Claire's shoulder. "Will you Daddy?"

Claire glanced back to see Fred and Gray standing in the doorway. Gray looked like he wanted to bolt from the room. Fred turned away and coughed, trying to hide his laughter.

"I think it's probably about time for us to bundle up and head home," Gray said, stepping into the room.

"But, Daddy, I dreamed about the puppy Santa's going to bring me and he was so soft, just like your cheeks." Maddie snuggled against Claire. "'Sides, I just woked up and I'm not ready to go."

At her father's frown, Maddie gave him a pleading look, turning those big, persuasive eyes up to him.

Claire certainly would have been hard pressed to tell her no and wasn't surprised in the least when Gray took a seat on the sofa.

Maddie leaned back against Claire and sighed

contentedly. She remained silent for all of a minute before she looked up at Claire. "Will you sing for us? Pretty please?"

"I think I can do that," Claire said, tapping her finger on the end of Maddie's nose. "Does anyone have a request?"

"I'd love to hear 'Beautiful Dreamer,'" Elsa said, nodding with encouragement at Claire.

She handed Maddie to her father and moved to stand behind the rocking chair. The room remained silent as she sang. When she finished, Maddie clapped enthusiastically.

Claire sang a few more songs she knew Fred and Elsa liked, then she sang one she'd made up herself. She hadn't performed it in front of anyone, but today seemed like a good time to share it.

"What's the name of that song?" Gray asked when she finished. "I didn't recognize the words or the tune."

"It's one I made up. I'm still working on it," Claire said, trying not to worry whether his interest meant he liked it or hated it since his expression was unreadable and he'd not made a comment either way.

"It was lovely, Claire. You should publish it," Elsa said, in her typical, encouraging fashion.

"I agree. I think you did a wonderful job with it," Fred said.

Claire blushed, but wrapped their words of praise around her. She knew neither of them would offer idle words of flattery.

"Does anyone need more pie? I have cake, too, or cookies." Elsa stood and held out a hand to Maddie. "Do you think you might like a cookie and a glass of milk?"

"Yes, please, Mrs. Decker." Maddie jumped off her father's lap and followed Elsa to the kitchen.

"I'll go see if Elsa needs any help," Fred said, leaving the room, but not before winking at Claire.

She hoped Gray hadn't seen it. It surprised her how quickly she'd gone from thinking of the man as simply Carter to Grayson Carter.

At least one mystery surrounding him had been solved, thanks to Elsa. Perhaps if she enlisted the woman's help, they could get him to divulge all his secrets.

A grin brightened her face as she thought about coercing Gray to the bakery where Elsa would ply him with sweets and they'd charm him into talking.

One look at his dark scowl, however, chased away her mirth.

"Oh, for heaven's sake! Can't you put away that gloomy expression for one whole day?" she teased. "You look like you've had a bushel of rotten persimmons for lunch instead of the tasty feast Elsa prepared."

He grunted and glared at her before the slightest hint of a smile tipped the corners of his mouth upward. "It was a wonderful meal and I appreciate you forcing me to come."

"I did no such thing!" Claire stood above him as he continued sitting on the couch and pointed her index finger at him in a gesture of accusation. "Admit it. You're glad you came today."

"I'm not admitting anything," he said, pulling her down on the couch beside him.

Caught off guard, she gaped at him with her mouth open and a look of utter astonishment on her face.

"If it was summer, you'd start catching flies," Gray said, gently pushing up on her chin and she closed her mouth. A light of devilment danced in his eyes as he leaned closer to her. "Now, I believe my daughter made an offer on my behalf and I feel as though I must deliver."

"An offer?" Claire whispered as he leaned closer to

her. The masculine, woodsy scent of him filled her nose while his warmth surrounded her.

"Mmm, hmm. She said you needed to feel my face, didn't she?" Gray took both of Claire's hands in his and placed them on his cheeks. "Do you think I feel like a soft, fuzzy pup?"

Claire couldn't have articulated what she felt in that moment if her life depended on it as Gray continued leaning closer to her. His mouth looked so tempting, so inviting, and his eyes glowed with something she couldn't even begin to describe or define.

Suddenly, her limbs felt languid and her stomach fluttered, as though a hundred butterflies prepared to take flight.

"What do you think?" Gray asked, turning his face slightly, so her right hand cupped his cheek. The hair was soft, not bristly as she expected, and she still couldn't help but wonder what he'd look like clean-shaven. She imagined he'd be quite handsome, for even with the bushy beard she found him more attractive than any other man who'd caught her eye.

"Still not ready to share your opinion?" Gray smiled. "I don't think I've yet encountered a moment when you lacked words. Are you not feeling well, Clarice?"

Hearing him say her name, caressing it in his deep voice, caused her temperature to rise to the point she felt feverish. Maybe she was coming down with something. Maybe she should go lie down on her bed and rest awhile. Or maybe she should press her lips to his and see if they felt as soft as they looked.

Before she could put her thoughts into action, Gray wrapped his arms around her, pulled her close and rubbed his whiskery cheek against her neck.

Claire wondered what Fred and Elsa would say when they returned to the room to find she'd fainted on the couch right there in Gray's arms. She'd never fainted in her life, but the woozy and lightheaded way she felt made her consider the possibility of it happening soon if Gray nuzzled her neck again.

He pulled back and let her go, then leaned against the couch with a self-satisfied look on his face. "What's wrong, little songbird? Cat got your tongue?"

Claire was saved from trying to formulate a reply when Maddie raced into the room and climbed on her father's lap.

"Mrs. Decker let me have cake and a cookie, Daddy. It was yummy yummy in my tummy."

"Was it?" Gray smiled at his daughter. "That was nice of her. Did you say thank you?"

"I did, Daddy. And know what else?" Maddie wiggled her feet, unable to sit still.

"What else, sweetheart?"

"Mr. Decker said I can come visit them anytime. Did you know they know Uncle Luke and Aunt Filly and Maura and Cully, too?!"

"Well, how about that." Gray gave Claire a concerned look.

She struggled to pull herself together, but his proximity and the longing she felt to be back in the circle of his arms left her nearly witless. With sheer determination, she sat up, straightening her spine, tucked in a few loosened hairpins, and subtly slid away from Gray.

When Elsa and Fred returned to the room a moment later, she hoped they wouldn't be able to detect her disconcerted state.

Gray stood with Maddie perched on one arm and smiled at Fred and Elsa. "I thank you both for your warm hospitality, but I really should head for home now."

"Oh, must you go so soon?" Elsa asked as she

leaned against Fred. "We've so enjoyed your company today."

"Thank you, but I need to get Maddie Mae home while it's still light out and before it turns any colder."

"I could hitch up the horses and take you home," Fred offered.

"No, that won't be necessary. We'll make it just fine," Gray said, stepping past Claire as she continued to sit on the end of the couch.

She wasn't certain her legs would hold her if she stood, but when Gray carried Maddie from the room, she hopped up and followed them down the hall with Fred and Elsa close behind her.

Claire bundled up Maddie while Gray pulled on his things. Elsa packed food into two tins and tucked them into a knapsack for Gray while Fred ran out to the barn and returned with an old pair of snowshoes.

"These might make it easier to get home," he said, handing them to Gray.

"I've never used them before, but I'll give it a try."

They watched as Gray buckled on the snowshoes then took a few tentative steps. He walked out to the pasture and back, then reached to take the sack Elsa held out to him as they all stood on the porch.

"Thank you for everything. It really was the nicest Thanksgiving we've had in a long time." He settled the pack over one shoulder then held out his hands to Maddie.

The little girl gave Elsa and Fred each a hug. Claire hated to see her go, but she dropped to her knees on the chilly floorboards of the porch and held the child in her arms for a long moment.

"I'll see you another day, Maddie Mae. Be a good girl for your father."

"I will, Claire. Come visit us soon!" Maddie kissed her cheek then bounded across the porch and launched herself into her father's arms.

Claire walked down the steps and wrapped the blanket Gray had brought around Maddie, tucking it in so no cold air could sneak in to chill the little girl.

"Ready to go, sweetheart?" Gray asked, glancing down at his daughter.

"Yes. Let's go, Daddy." Maddie couldn't get an arm free to wave, but she smiled broadly at Fred and Elsa. "Thank you!"

"Stay warm and be safe," Elsa called.

"I'll get your snowshoes back to you soon," Gray said to Fred.

"No rush. Keep them as long as you need them," he said.

Gray fixed his gaze on Claire and she felt her temperature rising again, in spite of the bitter chill in the air. "I trust you'll stay out of trouble, songbird. Thank you for practically insisting I come today. It was nice." He gave a smile full of such warmth, Claire wondered if it might melt the snow all around them.

"I'm glad you came, Gray, and I'm happy to finally know your name."

"Oh, what's in a name, anyway?" he asked, turning away on the snowshoes, then glancing back at her. "Although I think Clarice is a beautiful name for a beautiful girl."

A flush burned her cheeks at the way he'd said her name, almost like a caress. Then he was gone, laboring along the trail with Maddie securely held in his strong arms.

Claire wished she could know the joy of being held in them again, too.

Chapter Nine

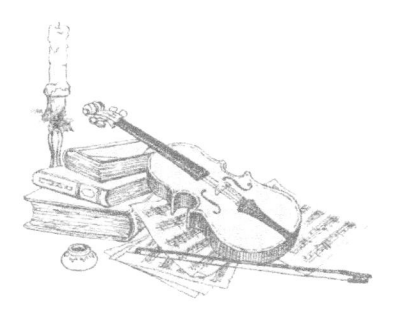

Gray lambasted himself the entire way home from Fred and Elsa Decker's place. He shouldn't have gone. Shouldn't have let them know his real name. And he most certainly should not have snuggled up so close to Claire, teasing her about his beard.

The feel of her soft, silky skin and the scent of her fragrance had nearly pushed him beyond the edge of reason. Even now, that delicate, feminine scent of hers threatened to swamp his senses.

Everything in him wanted to turn around, run back to the house, take her in his arms and...

Gray gave himself a mental shake. Thoughts like that would not serve any purpose other than to leave him upset and frustrated.

He needed to focus on his reason for isolating

himself in the woods, and that was Maddie. Nothing mattered but keeping his little girl safe.

He couldn't help but question if he'd endangered her by spending Thanksgiving with Claire and her family.

Yet, even as his mind worried over the possible bad outcomes, he couldn't bring himself to regret spending the day with such good, kind people. Other than Elsa charming his name out of him, they'd not asked any probing questions or made him feel uncomfortable. On the contrary, they'd gone out of their way to make him and Maddie feel welcomed.

Along with the wonderful friendship, the food was superb. Other than the few meals he'd eaten at Granger House, he couldn't think when he'd had any finer than the bounty that was set on the Decker's table.

Maddie had eaten until he wondered if her little tummy might pop. It wasn't any surprise to him she'd taken a long nap after the meal.

He wished he'd been in the room to watch Claire rock his daughter to sleep. He'd discovered from Fred while they washed and dried the dishes that Claire was twenty-one. For a woman so young, and often given to flights of fancy, she had a strong maternal streak he couldn't deny. Maybe both her feet weren't tripping over the clouds, as he sometimes envisioned her.

In truth, Clarice Baker seemed like a well-rounded person with a big heart. He thought she most likely looked for the best in people and probably trusted others more than she should. But he couldn't deny those character traits were among the things he admired the most about her. It was as though her heart was out in the open for anyone to see.

And what he could see was a beautiful young woman with a lovely spirit.

Which was exactly why he needed to stay away

from her. Although he was only twenty-eight, he felt decades older than Claire. Then again, he'd suffered much loss and pain in his lifetime. Pain that most people would never know or be able to endure.

Gray glanced down at his daughter. She'd chattered like a magpie as they started toward home along the path, but her eyelids fluttered, as though she fought sleep. Bundled into the blanket as she was, he figured she'd be asleep before long.

With a nap earlier, though, he hoped she wouldn't be hard to get into bed tonight. Regardless of a second nap, he anticipated her being wound up as tight as a top and spinning just as quickly after her adventures of the day.

The only people she'd been around in the past four years were the Granger family. He worked hard to instill good manners in her, so she'd know how to behave when they were around others, but he worried about the isolation he kept her in. Would it end up harming her? Damaging her spirit in some unseen way?

Should he think about reentering society, at least here in Hardman?

Had enough time passed that the dangers he'd worried about were no longer a threat?

The questions ate at him as he trudged home, grateful for the snowshoes Fred allowed him to borrow. He'd have to order a pair because they made getting around in the snow so much easier. He'd almost asked Claire if he could try her skis the other day, but managed to keep from blurting out the request. They looked like great fun, but he had no idea what he'd do with Maddie if he had a pair. At least the snowshoes left his hands free for carrying her.

The possibilities shifted his thoughts from his past to ideas for the future. Somehow, though, a vision of Claire, as she looked today in a lovely watered silk gown of blue that accented the hue of her mesmerizing eyes, infiltrated his mind. He'd noticed she and Fred had the same eyes, same mouth, and were both tall. While Fred had lighter hair, Claire's was the delightful mass of dark, wavy tendrils that practically begged Gray to run his hands through it.

He'd nearly ripped the pins from her hair and indulged in winding the strands around his hands when they were seated on the couch, but he'd held onto his control with a tenuous grasp.

For four years he'd managed not to think about women, other than grieving the loss of his beloved Laura. Why, now, did he have to find himself thinking more and more frequently of Claire?

Probably because the woman wouldn't leave him alone.

He couldn't help but question if he was merely one of her projects. He'd learned from Fred that Claire and her sisters loved to have projects to work on, especially if they helped others. They truly sounded like good people, but he didn't like the idea that Claire merely saw him as something broken she might be able to fix.

He wanted to be much more than that, yet the very notion that he did indeed want more left him angry at himself and thoroughly disturbed.

By the time he crossed through the glade and reached home, Maddie had become a dead weight in his arms and he was grateful to set her down inside the warmth of their cabin.

"Daddy!" she said, coming fully awake after rubbing her eyes.

"What, sweetheart?" he asked, helping her out of her coat.

"I had fun today. Can we go back to see Claire and Mr. and Mrs. Decker again soon? Please, Daddy?"

He removed her scarf, made sure her mittens on

their string remained tucked in the sleeves of her coat, and hung it with her little hat by the door. He balanced her on his bent knee while he removed her boots, trying to decide what to tell her. It was hard to give her an answer when he hadn't yet decided if he'd take another step forward toward a normal life, or continue to keep them hidden away from the world. "I'll think about it, Maddie. Mrs. Decker sure made a lot of delicious things to eat, didn't she? What was your favorite?"

"Cake!" Maddie said. She jumped off his leg, and then ran into her room. She returned with the slippers he'd purchased from an old Indian trader on her feet. Made of rabbit fur and leather, they kept her feet warm inside the cabin.

"How about you look at one of your storybooks while I see to the chores? Okay?"

Gray lifted her up and settled her in the rocking chair and handed her two of her favorite books. "You'll stay right there until I come back." He didn't ask it as a question, but said it as an order he expected her to follow.

"I'll stay right here, Daddy. I want to look at the princess book. She's pretty like Claire."

A sigh almost rolled out of him until he swallowed it back as he handed Maddie the book with a princess on the cover. That's all he needed — another reminder of how much his daughter liked Claire and how attracted he was to her.

Maybe while he was out seeing to the evening chores, he should stick his head in a snowbank for a minute or two. Perhaps if he did, it would chase his wayward thoughts back on track.

He kissed Maddie's cheek, exchanged the nice wool coat he wore for an old chore coat and grabbed his work gloves from the pockets, then headed outside.

They had chickens, pigs, a milk cow, and two

horses that needed to be fed. Gray knew Maddie wanted a puppy for Christmas and if he could figure out how to get one, he decided he would. He wouldn't mind having a dog around the place and the puppy would be good company for his daughter. Hopefully, it might even help keep an eye on his active little girl.

Maddie was feisty and full of spunk, but she knew when he meant business and she needed to mind him. Truly, he'd been blessed with his daughter in more ways than one.

He tried to count them all as he milked the cow and fed the livestock.

When he returned to the cabin with a bucket of milk in one hand, he was in a better mood and frame of mind.

In the next few days, he kept himself so busy he didn't have much time to think of Claire or the myriad of questions that plagued him. Even so, the song Claire said she'd made up pervaded his thoughts and he found himself continually humming the tune. It would make a beautiful Christmas song, if she ever cared to add a little polish to it and publish it.

On the Monday after Thanksgiving, he left a pot of chicken simmering on the stove to make stew then went out to his workshop with Maddie. While he lost himself in his work, Maddie practiced her violin then sat down to color, only to remember taking her crayons into the cabin.

"I need colors, Daddy," she said, tugging on the leg of the denim pants he wore.

He glanced down at her, both hands full of his current project and not at a place he could stop. "If I let you go to the house to get them, do you promise to run straight back here?"

"I promise, Daddy. I'll run fast and get my colors and run right back, just like the bunny we saw yesterday."

He smiled, recalling how much Maddie had enjoyed watching a rabbit race across the snow. He didn't bother to explain the only reason it would run that fast is because something dangerous pursued it. Maddie had intently observed it until it disappeared beneath a snow-shrouded bush on the other side of the glade.

"Okay, sweetheart. Run fast as you can."

Maddie opened the door to the workshop, hurried out, then slammed the door. Gray leaned over to watch out the window and saw her round the corner of the cabin.

Knowing his daughter, she would grab the crayons, then decide she needed more paper, and she'd probably think about grabbing a storybook, and maybe snitching one of the cookies they had left from those Elsa had sent with them.

Gray had been truly thankful for the food the woman sent home with them. They'd eaten ham and turkey along with the light bread and delicious rolls for three days. He'd enjoyed slices of pie and a moist, delicious spice cake while Maddie munched on the cookies.

They had one slice of cake and three cookies left, then he'd have to think about attempting to make something.

Elsa had given him enough pointers on how to make pie crust, he might just try his hand at it again. He had a barrel full of apples he could use to make pie. Or maybe he'd just cook the apples with cinnamon and sugar and they could eat them right out of the pan.

He glanced at the clock on the wall, and wondered what could be keeping Maddie. Maybe she made a side trip to the outhouse that she hated so much.

Chapter Ten

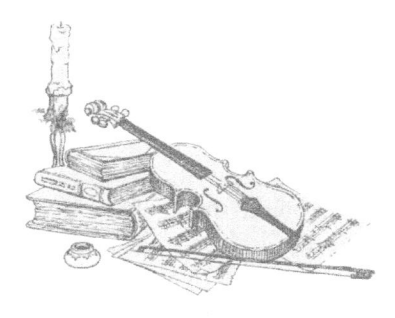

Claire exhaled a long breath as she used her ski poles to stop next to the steps of Grayson Carter's cabin. She hoped he wouldn't mind her unexpected visit.

While she'd wanted to come see how he and Maddie were faring the day after Thanksgiving, she'd remained at home, trying to decipher her convoluted feelings for the man. His name had rolled over and over in her thoughts until it had almost become like a song that played continually.

Grayson Carter.

Grayson.

Gray.

A man full of mystery and secrets. She sensed a darkness in him that battled with the light that was evident in his eyes and his smile, especially when he looked at his daughter.

Maddie was another reason Claire's heart felt like it had been run over by a team of racing horses. She felt far too young to have such maternal feelings springing up in her, out of seemingly nowhere. But she loved Madison Mae Carter with a fierce emotion that somewhat unsettled and frightened her. How could she have fallen so deeply in love with this child and her father, if Claire cared to admit it, which she did not, in such a short time?

She hardly knew Gray at all. Other than Maddie, she had no idea what made him smile or brought him joy. What drove him to hide in the woods? To live a life secreted away from the world?

Possessed of fine manners and speech, she knew he didn't acquire either of those things in some rustic cabin far removed from society. She'd bet every last penny she owned, which was a considerable sum, that Grayson had, at some point, been raised well, most likely with money. Something about him smacked of culture and wealth, in spite of his long hair and bushy beard.

Thoughts of his beard made a shiver roll down her spine. He'd nearly rendered her unconscious with his teasing on the couch Thanksgiving Day. Claire had never allowed anyone to get that intimately close to her before and she wasn't sure she would again. At least not someone who wasn't her husband. The feelings Gray stirred in her, the longings and yearnings, were so foreign to Claire. Yet, they weren't entirely unwelcome.

What would it be like to belong to a man like Gray? One with such broad shoulders and strong arms?

She'd likely never discover such bliss because of all the men she'd encountered, the dozens who'd attempted to court her, Gray was the only one who commanded her attention and interest, even if he did it without knowing. But he'd made it clear he was not interested in opening his life, let alone his heart, to anyone except his daughter.

Regardless of what he would and wouldn't accept, Claire was here to spread a little holiday cheer. After all, Christmas was three and a half weeks away and she didn't intend to let him ignore the holiday. Not if she had anything to say about it.

Claire untied the rope she'd fastened around her waist that pulled a sled behind her then removed her skis.

She picked up the two bundles she'd packed into the child's sled then marched up the porch steps.

With both her hands full, she was about to set down one bundle to knock when she heard a happy squeal and the door swung open.

Maddie raced out and plowed into her, wrapping her little arms around Claire's britches-covered legs.

"Claire! I'm so glad you're here!" Maddie practically pranced around her as she raced inside the cabin and motioned Claire to come inside.

Claire wiped her boots on the rug in front of the door then stepped into the welcoming warmth of the cabin. On the skis, it only took her about thirty minutes to get from Fred's house to Gray's, but the frigid air had left her fingers, toes, and nose tingling from the cold.

"I'm glad I'm here, too, Maddie Mae. What are you and your daddy doing today?" Claire set the two bundles she carried on the table, tugged off her gloves, and looked around, expecting to see Gray glowering at her from the kitchen or over by the fire.

The cabin remained oddly quiet, though.

"Is your daddy okay? Where is he?"

"In the workshop. I needed my colors." Maddie held up a fist full of crayons.

"Oh, I see." Claire felt relief flood over her that Gray was well and Maddie hadn't been left alone.

The scent of chicken soup filled the air, making

THE CHRISTMAS MELODY

Claire wonder if Gray would allow her to stay for lunch or if he'd send her on her way. She'd told Fred and Elsa her plans for the day, so they wouldn't worry or expect her back until later that afternoon. Now, if Gray would just go along with them, all would be well.

Claire stepped over to the stove, lifted the lid on the simmering pot of soup and gave it a stir before settling the lid back in place. She couldn't make soup that smelled half as good, but she did know enough about cooking to stir it. The bread she brought along would go well with the soup for lunch.

"Do you think your daddy would mind if I go to the workshop with you?"

Maddie shrugged then hopped over to the door, clearly eager to go. "I'm not s'posed to tell anyone about the workshop, but you already knowed about it from last time."

Claire smiled and took the hand Maddie didn't have full of crayons in hers. "I certainly did. Let's go see what your daddy is doing." She opened the door and hurried outside with Maddie. Together, they skipped along the path to the workshop. Claire opened the door and Maddie rushed inside.

"Daddy! Guess who camed to visit us!"

Claire stepped inside the building, too awed to notice Gray's head snap up from where he was bent over a workbench, his eyes wide in shock.

Quietly, she shut the door behind her and looked around the open building where violins in various stages of completion filled the space. Violin backs and necks with intricately carved scrolls hung on hooks from the ceiling. Pegs, strings, bridges, tailpieces, scrolls, and chin rests were neatly stacked on shelves and filled drawers that sat partially open beneath a massive workbench. Carving tools lined the wall above the workbench. A drafting table held stacks of papers, presumably with designs. Bits of wood and sawdust covered the floor around Gray while the scent of freshly shaved wood filled the air with a decadent, Christmassy scent.

She noticed bolts of rich velvet used for lining cases and a stack of cases and crates in the far corner of the room.

And there, nearest the big stove that heated the workshop, was a small table with a tiny chair that was clearly Maddie's domain.

Claire had no idea, none whatsoever, that Gray, the gruff woodsman, turned his hand to creating such works of beauty. From what she could see these were not violins for beginners or those with limited funds to purchase. No, each piece was an individual work of art crafted by a master.

No wonder Maddie could play as well as she did.

Claire turned and looked at Gray, wondering if he, too, possessed the talent to play.

The furious scowl on his face let her know she wouldn't find the answer to that question today. In fact, as he set down his tools, brushed off his hands and headed toward her, Claire wondered if perhaps she'd make it back home in one piece.

Gray looked positively livid, but it was too late to undo whatever damage he perceived had taken place. She was already in the workshop and couldn't unsee the wonder of it all.

"What are you doing here?" he asked on a growl as he grabbed her upper arms in his hands.

For a moment, she worried he might give her a shake or, at the least, toss her out in the snow.

Instead, his grip loosened while his brown eyes pinned hers. Suddenly unsure and definitely unsettled, she tried to take a step back, but she bumped into the door.

"Answer me!" he commanded in a harsh whisper.

Claire tried to speak, but her thoughts all jumbled together. "I... I... um... it was..."

"You'll speak of this to no one. No one! Do you understand me?" he asked, his grip tightening on her again as he yanked her against him so roughly, Claire took a gasping breath.

His eyes snapped with anger and his jaw clenched tightly as though he held back a torrent of words that would most likely sear her ears. His shoulders were tense and his nostrils flared in his fury.

Slowly, she nodded her head up and down in agreement.

Immediately, he dropped his hands and took a step back. "Why did you come?" he asked, in a much softer, gentler tone.

"I wanted to bring Christmas cheer to Maddie. Elsa sent cookie dough that we can bake and I brought a few craft projects she can work on," Claire explained. She started to place a hand on his arm then thought better of it. "I didn't mean anything by it, Mr. Carter. I merely wanted to bring a little joy to your daughter."

He studied her for the length of several heartbeats. Claire felt like squirming beneath his scrutiny. But he appeared to have calmed himself and no longer looked like he might rip her in two with his bare hands.

"I'm sorry," he said, brushing the backs of his fingers over her cheek, wiping away a bit of moisture. Claire hadn't even realized she'd started crying, until he brushed away the salty drops from her skin. "I didn't mean to frighten you, Claire, you just caught me unawares."

"Obviously, I won't do that again," she said, offering him a lopsided smile as she drew in a shuddering breath and attempted to lighten the strained atmosphere between them.

"Since you're here anyway, would you like to see the workshop?" he asked, stepping back and waving a hand to encompass his work.

"Yes, please."

He showed her a violin he was nearly finished making and talked about the different types of woods he used to create them. When he showed her the spruce wood he'd been carving when she walked in, she grinned.

"That's what smells like Christmas," she said, running her fingers over the piece of wood.

"I use maple and spruce for most of my work," Gray said, lifting a finished violin from a case lined with dark green velvet.

"Oh, it's beautiful," she said, afraid to touch it and mar the high shine of the wood. The back, rib, and scroll bore detailed carvings of leaves and vines. Even the pegs and front plate had been carved. "It looks too pretty to use."

Gray chuckled. "I hope not. The whole point of an instrument is to be played and loved."

"But what do you do with them all? Sell them?" Claire asked, uncertain how he could have a business when he rarely ventured to town.

He set the violin back in the case and closed the lid. "I do sell them. Whenever I go into town I take a load of orders and ship them back East. I have a… contact that makes sure they are delivered."

"Gray, they're just wonderful," Claire said, placing her hand on his forearm and giving it a squeeze. He glanced down at her fingers then raised his gaze to hers. Claire felt drawn to him, to something shining in his eyes, but she stepped back and walked over to where a small violin carved with flowers and fairies rested on an equally detailed stand. "Is this Maddie's?"

"Yes. In another year, she'll have outgrown it,"

Gray said, rubbing his fingers along the strings of the instrument.

"May I play for Claire, Daddy?" Maddie asked, skipping over to them from where she'd been coloring at the table.

"You may," he said, lifting her up to stand on top of a large table. He handed her the violin and she expertly tucked it against her neck, settling her chin on the rest and lifting the bow in her hand.

Maddie closed her eyes and stood perfectly still for a moment before she touched the bow to the strings.

Claire felt not just absorbed by the music the child performed, but also completely swallowed into it. To watch Maddie play was one of the most magical, incredible things she'd ever witnessed.

With sunlight streaming in the filmy curtain over the window, it created an almost ethereal glow around the little girl that made her seem more fairy than human child. Just to watch Maddie play, with her eyes closed and her whole body attuned to the song, was beyond description. The ability for the heart and spirit to encapsulate emotions and dreams in mere words wasn't a possibility.

But Claire felt each note the child played, right down to the depths of her soul. If she wasn't mistaken the piece was one written by Beethoven, but she'd never heard it played with such depth and skill before.

It boggled her mind to think the person giving a performance worthy of royalty was a four-year-old girl full of gaiety and giggles.

When the last note faded away, Claire started to clap, but Gray grabbed her hands and gave her a silencing look. Maddie then began to play a lively tune that made Claire want to spin and dance and sing. Her toes tapped, her fingers thrummed as she held her hands at her sides.

Gray must have been similarly moved by the music, because quite unexpectedly, he took her in his arms and swept her around the table in a lively dance.

Claire laughed and threw back her head, full of such joy she thought her heart might burst with it. Around and around the table they went, feet keeping time to the rhythm of the song.

When she finished, Maddie giggled and pointed the bow at them. "Do it again!"

Claire gladly complied as Maddie played another tune brimming with life that defied anyone listening to sit still.

By the time Gray had danced her through the song, Claire could hardly catch her breath. Gray seemed equally winded as he plopped onto the table by Maddie.

Claire sank onto a chair and fanned her face with her hand. It wasn't until she glanced down that she realized she wore britches. Oh, how she wished she had on one of the dozens of ball gowns she had stored at Ari's house.

Gray hadn't seemed to mind, though, and the britches were far more practical than skirts out in the snow.

Maddie set her violin and bow on the stand then climbed onto Gray's lap. "How was that, Daddy?"

"That was wonderful, sweetheart. What did you decide to call the last song you played?"

"I think I'll call it *Claire's Visit*," Maddie said, grinning at Claire.

"Oh, I'm very honored, Maddie Mae, to have a song named for me. I'll cherish this moment and memory forever and ever," Claire said, reaching out to the child. Maddie jumped up from her father's lap and sank onto Claire's, cuddling against her.

She kissed the top of Maddie's tangled curls and sat quietly for a moment before setting Maddie down and rising to her feet. "Shall we go see about baking some cookies and decking your halls?"

Maddie's excited squeal was answer enough as she yanked open the door and raced toward the cabin.

"Thank you, Claire." Gray took her hand between both of his and held it before he raised it to his lips and kissed the backs of her fingers. "If you don't mind, I'll finish what I'm working on then be in shortly."

"That's fine," she whispered, wondering how her languid limbs would carry her out the door and to the cabin. Somehow, she made it, although once she was inside, she leaned against the door while Maddie buzzed around like a drunken bee, excited for something new and different in her day.

"Come on, Maddie Mae. Perhaps between the two of us, we can bake a decent batch of cookies." Claire pushed away from the door and opened one of the packs she brought.

She and Maddie rolled out the gingerbread dough Elsa had sent and baked it without burning a single cookie. They'd had fun sitting at the table and frosting the cookies, snitching a few bites.

Gray came in close to noon and served the soup with slices of the airy bread Elsa had made and insisted Claire take along.

After the dishes were washed and put away, Claire dug oranges, cinnamon sticks, and twine from the supplies she'd brought along. She and Maddie bundled up and went outside to collect a basket full of pine cones, then returned inside.

While Maddie tied the cinnamon sticks in little bundles, Claire cut two of the oranges into thin slices then threaded the slices on the twine with pinecones and the cinnamon stick bundles. She hung the garland on the mantle above the fireplace where the heat accented the fragrances.

"That smells good," Maddie said, sniffing the air.

Claire found an empty bowl and set it in the center of the table then filled it with the oranges she'd brought along. She cut a few greens and brought them in, draping them around the bowl for a centerpiece.

"What else can we make?" Maddie asked, leaning with her elbows on the table, trying to peer into the depths of the pack that held Claire's supplies.

"How about paper chains?" Claire asked, taking colorful sheets of paper, scissors and a pot of paste Elsa had made from the pack.

"What are paper chains?" Maddie asked, picking up a piece of red striped paper that looked like a peppermint stick.

"Only the most fun things in the world to make," Claire made a silly face that caused Maddie to giggle.

She cut strips of paper then showed Maddie how to glue the ends together to form a chain. The little girl made one to hang above the window in her bedroom, then one for the kitchen and another for Gray's room.

As Claire hung the chain above the window in Gray's room, she couldn't help but notice the photograph on the dresser of him with a beautiful woman. The curly, fair hair definitely looked like Maddie's wild locks, and she thought the woman's nose and Maddie's quite similar. Claire assumed the woman's eyes were blue since Maddie's were and Gray's were such a deep shade of brown.

"That's my mommy. She's in heaven with the angels. Daddy said she was the sweetest person he ever met."

Claire knelt down by Maddie and gave her a hug. "She looks like she would have been a wonderful mommy to you."

Maddie shrugged in the way of children who don't embrace the full notion of death and loss and smiled. "I gots Daddy and he's wonnerful."

"Yes, he is," Claire said, taking Maddie's hand as they returned to the kitchen to clean up the mess their creative efforts generated.

A quick glance at the clock on the wall assured Claire she would need to leave soon, even though she wished she could stay. It was fun, for a day, to pretend she belonged there with Gray and Maddie. But that's all it was, pretend.

"Will you sing me a song?" Maddie asked, looking sleepy, although Claire could tell the little one would fight against taking a nap.

"I'd love to. How about we sit in that nice chair there by the fire?" Claire settled into the rocking chair and Maddie climbed up on her lap. Claire pushed with her toes to set the chair in motion and sang a soft lullaby. Maddie's eyelids fluttered shut, but she popped them back open.

Claire heard a click that sounded like the door and felt a cool blast of air, but she didn't look up. Instead, she drew Maddie closer to her and continued rocking and singing. When the child drifted off to sleep, Claire kissed her temple then started to rise to carry her to her bed, but Gray was there, lifting his daughter from her arms. He carried her into her bedroom and tucked her in, then closed her door most of the way shut.

"Thank you for making today so special and fun for her," he said, walking with Claire toward the door where she'd set her things. "I'm sorry about earlier when I was rather... um..."

"Surly. Cranky. Grumpy. Unforgiveably rude. Impossibly mean."

Gray grinned and cupped her chin. "All of those, apparently. I'm just not used to anyone being here except me and Maddie. I would ask that you not mention what I do or who I am to anyone. I have to keep Maddie safe."

"From what? From whom?" Claire asked, wishing he trusted her enough to tell her what had happened in his past to send him into exile in the woods of Eastern Oregon.

"That's a story for another day, songbird. You better get started home or you'll end up trying to get there in the dark." He held her coat as she slipped it on then carried her packs back out to the little sled. He'd tucked Fred's snowshoes in it, too.

"Please tell Fred how much I appreciated the use of those. They made it so much easier to get home the other day."

"I'll tell him. He wouldn't mind if you want to keep them," Claire said, bending to buckle on her skis. When she finished, Gray handed her the rope to tie the sled around her waist.

"That's a brilliant idea, by the way. I might steal it for hauling around Maddie."

"Feel free," Claire said, tugging on her gloves then looking up at Gray and getting lost in the golden light glowing in the depths of his eyes. "I... um..."

"Better go," he said, leaning down and kissing her cheek. "Thank you, Claire, for being a friend."

"My pleasure. If you don't object at all, I'll plan to come back Thursday. I have some other things I can bring for Maddie to work on I think she might enjoy." Claire picked up her ski poles and prepared to leave, hoping Gray would agree to her return.

"If I tell you no, I don't really think you'll listen anyway, so you might as well come." His teasing smile warmed her from the inside out.

She pushed off and glided forward, but glanced back at him over her shoulder. "You do know me well. I'll see you Thursday."

Chapter Eleven

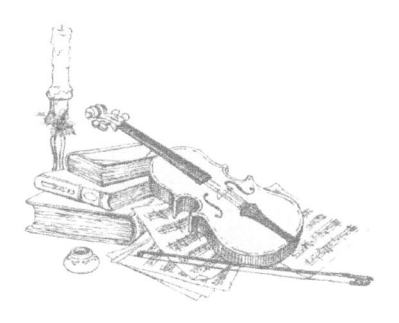

Gray glanced at the clock for the third time in fifteen minutes. Annoyed with himself and the way he'd spent the past hour listening for the sound of someone outside, he ran a hand through his hair in frustration, heedless to the wood shavings on his hands.

"What's wrong, Daddy?" Maddie asked, tugging on his shirtsleeve to get his attention.

"Nothing, sweetheart. Did you finish practicing your letters?" Since his daughter was as smart as a whip, he'd been giving her school lessons in the mornings. She knew the alphabet and several numbers, could count to forty, and was learning to write. So far, she'd perfected her letters up to Q.

Maddie ran over to her table and picked up a piece of paper, bringing it back for him to see. "You did a good job, Maddie. Next time you make a Q, just move the little squiggle on the other side and you'll have it down."

"I like the squiggle better over there," she said.

"We all have things we like and don't like, but that doesn't mean that's the way they must be done," he said, hunkering down and wrapping his arm around her. "If you want to make a Q so others know what it is, you have to do it with the squiggle over here." He tapped the paper and handed it back to her.

"I don't like it, but I'll do it," she said, then leaned against him and looked into his face. "Are you okay?"

"I'm fine. What makes you think something is wrong?" he asked, playfully tweaking her nose and making her smile.

"'Cause you did this," she said, shoving her fingers into her hair and making a face like she'd eaten something sour.

Gray laughed and picked her up, tossing her into the air. "I think you look like sour lemons," he teased.

"You look like rotten 'matoes," she said, giggling as she patted his face, then wrapping her arms around his neck and holding on tight.

It was hard to be upset with the love of his child filling his heart. Gray breathed in her sweet little girl essence then set her down. "How about I finish up what I'm working on and we go for a walk. It's not horribly cold right now and we could see if the birds found the bread crumbs you put out for them."

"Yes, please!" Maddie said, clapping her hands and skipping in a circle around the big table.

Gray chuckled and forced his attention back to the neck he was sanding. When it was finished, the scroll on the end would look like a swan's head.

He'd just picked up one of his small carving tools and nearly sliced through his palm with it when a loud rap sounded at the door and it swung open.

Claire walked in, bringing a burst of sunshine with her despite the gray skies overhead. Her eyes glowed with vitality and excitement while her smile dazzled him.

"I thought I'd look here first before I knocked at the cabin," she said, closing the door and picking up Maddie when his daughter ran over to her. "How are you, Maddie Mae?"

"Great! Daddy and me are gonna go for a walk. Wanna comed with us?"

"I'd love that. Where are you going to walk to?" Claire asked. She sidled over to the stove and shifted so the heat warmed her back as she held Maddie.

"We put out crumbs for the birds. I wanna see if they gobbled them up," Maddie said, pretending to be a famished bird as she puckered her lips then smacked them together.

"Why don't we give Claire a few minutes to warm up before we go out, sweetheart?" Gray suggested, purposely avoiding looking at Claire. He was fearful to do any actual work lest he cut himself or ruin the violin. Instead, he wiped off his tools and put them away. "Maybe you'd like to play a song for her?"

"Oh, yes," Maddie said, climbing up on the table, as though it was her stage. Claire handed his daughter her violin and bow then returned to the stove where she held her hands over the heated surface.

Gray watched from the corner of his eye as Maddie took a deep breath and closed her eyes. He never knew, exactly, what she'd play. He'd given her lessons, not through reading notes, but to play by ear. Sometimes she played what he'd taught her from Bach, Beethoven, and Vivaldi. Other times, the music just flowed through her as a gift from the heavens and he took it as such. Maddie was a miracle in so many ways, not the least of which was her rare talent at playing the violin.

A soft note, followed by another, like the hint of autumn breeze wafted around him. Gray set down his tools, turned to face his daughter and waited. This performance would be one Maddie made up as she went and he wouldn't miss a single note of it.

He glanced over at Claire to find she looked equally enraptured with Maddie's skill. He closed his eyes to better hear the music.

As Maddie played, he could almost smell the apples and wood smoke and spice in the air. Deer drank from the creek. Leaves changed color and fell to the ground where they crunched and shattered beneath feet in the forest. Birds chirped and trilled. Squirrels fussed and chattered as they gathered nuts. Then the air changed. Autumn had fled and winter arrived in a blustery storm of snowflakes. A blizzard coated the forest in a world of sparkling, glistening white. Trees, frosted like icing treats on a cake, sighed. A rabbit scampered beneath a bush of holly. Horses neighed. Sleigh bells rang with silvery, clear tones. And a dove cooed from the rafters of a warm barn. A child giggled and slid on a spot of ice.

Gray grinned, knowing the child was Maddie.

The tune then carried the scent of gingerbread baking in the oven. Of Christmas in the air. Of animals gathering around the manger for a lowly birth. And the encompassing glow of love unlike any the world had ever known. The notes, low and sweet, faded as Maddie finished her song.

Moved beyond words, Gray opened his eyes and smiled at his daughter as she bowed with great theatrical flair.

A glance at Claire left him quite surprised. The woman had sunk to the floor as though she'd lost the ability to remain upright. He rushed over to her and pulled her to her feet.

"Are you well, Claire?" he asked, keeping a hand on her waist for support. He worked to ignore the tingles that raced up his arm and how good it felt to touch her.

"I'm... I... that was..." She looked at him as though she couldn't begin to articulate the emotions Maddie's music stirred in her. "I can't believe a tiny little person can hold such wondrous music inside her. Did you teach her that?"

He shook his head, pleased Claire enjoyed Maddie's music as much as he did. "No, that's all Maddie Mae."

"Well, she's wonderful, Gray. Positively marvelous."

"May we go outside now?" Maddie asked as she hopped off the table and ran toward the door.

"Yes, we may," Gray said, still holding his hand at Claire's waist although she seemed capable of walking without his help.

Maddie yanked on her coat and hat then raced outside. Claire caught up to her and wrapped the little pink scarf around Maddie's neck before taking the child's hand in hers.

He watched as the woman held his daughter's hand and they skipped along the path to where Maddie had left crumbs for the birds. In that moment, he couldn't quite stop from thinking about Laura. Would she have liked Claire? Approved of her?

The two women were so different. Laura was quiet, reserved, always comported herself as a lady. She'd been petite and delicate and doted on Gray as though nothing in the world mattered beyond him.

Claire was tall and graceful, but fairly brimming with vibrancy and life. He was sure she didn't possess a single shy bone in her body, spoke her mind, and was, from what he'd observed, incredibly independent. She was also beautiful and big-hearted, and generous both with her heart and her time.

And Maddie adored her.

That was definitely in Claire's favor.

Although why any of it mattered, he tried not to consider. After all, he would never again marry. Never again give his heart away. Never again suffer such agonizing loss.

If he had even the tiniest grain of sense left in his head, he'd send Claire on her way and make sure she never returned. But he couldn't. He enjoyed her company too much. For the last four years, he'd deprived himself of the companionship of others and he missed it. He missed friendship and fellowship, a sense of kinship and caring.

Specifically, though, he would miss Claire terribly if he did refuse to see her again. She was such a bright, joyful spot in his sometimes rather dreary days. When she'd visited on Monday and said she'd return on Thursday, he'd practically counted the minutes until this morning, then he'd been no better than a green boy, watching out the window for her, waiting for her arrival.

Now that she was here, the last thing he wanted to do was think of a way to make her so upset or angry she'd leave him alone for good. No. Not when he wanted her to stay.

Gray refused to listen to the voice in his head shouting that he was a fool. It warred quite often of late with the voice in his heart telling him that Claire was the one who could bring healing to his broken heart and give Maddie all the mother-love his daughter craved.

He smiled as Claire picked up Maddie and showed her an empty bird's nest in a nearby tree. Torn by his doubts and longings, he set them aside to examine later and caught up with Claire and his daughter.

On the way back to the cabin, Claire gathered pine cones and cuttings from a fir tree, berry-laden branches and red twigs which Gray carried for her.

"What are you going to do with all this?" he asked.

"You'll see," she said, winking at Maddie as though the two of them conspired against him.

After lunch, which Elsa had sent and Gray heated on the stove, Claire told him she'd keep Maddie with her in the cabin while he worked.

He left the two of them with heads bent over a spool of red ribbon Claire had brought with her and the pile of nature treasures the woman had collected on their walk.

An hour went by, then two. No longer able to stay in the workshop, since he hadn't been able to focus on his work anyway, he returned to the cabin to find a wreath on the door, made from the fir branches. Tucked among the greenery were pine cones, berries and twigs. A big red bow festooned the decoration.

The sight of the wreath made him smile and reminded him of all the holiday traditions he'd missed the last few years. He wiped his feet on the rug then opened the door and breathed in the scent of chocolate.

"Is that hot chocolate I smell?" he asked as he removed his coat and hung it by the door. "I haven't had hot chocolate in years."

"It is hot chocolate," Claire said as she stirred liquid in a pan on the stove. "It's one of the few things I can make. Elsa even lets me make it at the bakery sometimes."

Gray fought the urge to plant a kiss on the smooth skin of Claire's neck as he brushed past her to wash his hands at the sink. "Where's Maddie?" he asked.

"Asleep. I think I wore her out." Claire grinned at him over her shoulder. "We baked more cookies, thanks to the sugar cookie dough Elsa sent, and then we cut out some snowflakes and made paper angels. Maddie nearly fell asleep with her hair in the paste."

Gray cringed, imagining how hard it would be to get the sticky mess out of her hair.

"Not to worry. I cleaned her up and tucked her into bed."

He placed a hand on Claire's shoulder, unprepared for the jolt that shot up his arm at the touch. "Thank you for being so good with my daughter. She is so fond of you."

"Well, I just love that little girl of yours," Claire said, offering him a soft smile as she poured the chocolate mixture into three mugs. She handed one mug to Gray, took one and left the third on the counter for Maddie when she woke up from her nap. "She's so smart and sweet and funny, Gray. Not all children are like her, you know."

"I assumed not, from the few I've been around, and recalling my own childhood years. Maddie is special, and I don't say that just because I'm a proud papa."

Claire gave him a knowing look. "Oh, you most certainly are a proud papa, but with reason." She slid a plate of cookies toward him.

It looked as though a drunken goose had walked through a bowl of frosting then stomped all over them, but he didn't say as much. "Maddie frost these?" he asked, holding one up in his hand.

Claire laughed. "She did."

He bit into the cookie, raised his eyebrows, then took another bite. "It doesn't affect the taste."

"Well, I'm glad to know that. Elsa would be terribly upset if her good cookie dough went to waste."

"Are you having a party without me?" Maddie asked as she marched over to the table, rubbing sleep from her eyes as her lip rolled out in a pout.

"Not at all, Maddie Mae," Claire said, hopping up and getting the mug of chocolate she'd poured for the child. Gray noticed she took a sip of it then added a bit of milk before setting the mug in front of his daughter as she climbed into her chair at the table. "We were just waiting for you to wake up."

"I'm uped." Maddie took a sip of the chocolate and her eyes grew so wide, Gray thought they looked like saucers. "I love this!"

"I see that little apple hasn't fallen far from the tree," Claire said, motioning to Gray's nearly empty cup. She held her mug out to him. "Would you like mine?"

"No, that's quite alright. You drink it. It'll warm you up before you have to head back." He could think of several more interesting ways to warm her up, none of which were appropriate for a man determined to remain unwed, and with an impressionable daughter watching his every move.

"Are you planning to attend the Stratton's skating party?" he asked, in need of a change of subject.

"Of course. Blake and Ginny have the most perfect pond behind their place. And then there's the Christmas carnival at Dora and Greg Granger's home, and the Christmas Eve services and children's program." Claire glanced at Maddie as she took a bite of cookie and smeared frosting on her chin.

Gray handed Maddie a napkin then looked back at Claire. "Are your sisters planning to come for Christmas?"

"Yes, at least last I heard that is their plan. It will be such fun to have them here for the holidays again. We came to meet Fred last year, and then Elsa was kidnapped, and Fred asked her to marry him, so we ended up staying until the New Year. It was a very memorable month of December." Claire smiled at him. "I'm hoping for less excitement this year."

Gray shook his head. "I have a feeling excitement floats around you, no matter where you are."

"I'll take that as a compliment, Grayson Carter."

Claire rose from the table and set her mug in the sink then looked outside. "Oh, no!"

"What is it?" Gray leaned around her and saw snow falling in what appeared to be the beginnings of a blizzard.

"I need to hurry home. Thanks for a lovely day," Claire said, taking long strides toward the door. She reached for her coat, but Gray grabbed her hands, pulling her around to face him.

"Claire, there is no possibility I'm going to let you go home in that snow. I'd take you myself, but I don't want Maddie out in it. You'll just have to stay here until the storm blows over."

Indignant, she fairly spluttered at him. "I can't stay here! It wouldn't be proper at all. Why, people will think that I… that we… I'll be fine." She reached for her coat again, but Gray stepped in front of it.

"You are not leaving in this storm. I won't even entertain the idea of discussing you going home right now. Besides, Fred and Elsa know you're here and they'll understand if you have to stay. No one else knows you came out here, do they?"

"Well, no, but it still isn't proper for me to stay here with you." Claire frowned at him and took a step back.

"You can sleep in my room and I'll make a pallet on the floor out here."

She took another step away from him and shook her head.

"If it makes you feel better, Maddie can sleep with you."

"Claire will stay all night?" Maddie asked, practically flying out of her chair to race over to them. She yanked on Claire's hand. "Will you let me sleep in the big bed with you? You can read me a night-night story and sing to me and it will be wonnerful!"

While Gray might never have convinced Claire to

stay, the pouting, pleading look on his daughter's face did the trick.

Claire nodded once and sighed. "Fine. I'll stay, but if there's a shotgun wedding in our future, let it be noted I'm not encouraging it."

"Shotgun wedding?" Gray asked with a grin. "You really think Fred will force us to wed. I don't see him being a big supporter of such nonsense especially when nothing is going to happen."

Claire shrugged and turned away from him, as though he ordered the blizzard to trap her at the cabin on purpose.

She helped him make dinner, although she didn't say much, then played with Maddie after they'd eaten while he took care of the evening chores. He'd strung a rope that went from the cabin to all the outbuildings, so he could easily find his way. With the snow swirling in the darkness around him, he was grateful to have it to hang onto as he staggered through the wind to the cabin with a bucket of milk.

When he opened the door and stepped inside, his heart thudded to a stop at the sight of Claire's dark head bent over his daughter's curls as she combed out Maddie's tangles. Apparently, Claire had melted snow while he was out and given his daughter a bath. Maddie wore her nightgown and slippers and sat on a little stool in front of the fire while Claire knelt behind her, gently combing the snarls out of her long, untamable hair.

The two of them looked so perfect there by the fire, looked like they belonged together, it made his chest ache with longing.

"You look like a snowman, Daddy," Maddie said with a giggle.

Gray glanced in the mirror near the sink and saw he did look half frozen with snow coating him from head to toe. He set the milk bucket on the counter then stepped back outside, brushing off as much of the snow as he could, before returning inside. Claire strained the milk while Maddie wielded a rag, soaking up the rapidly melting snow he'd tracked across the floor.

"Aren't you two industrious," he commented, hanging up his coat and hat and removing his boots.

"What's dustrus?" Maddie asked as she blotted at snow.

"It means you are quite a little worker bee and I appreciate your help," Gray said, picking up his daughter and tossing her in the air, making her giggle.

Maddie couldn't seem to settle down after that, flitting around the cabin like a bird that had supped on fermented nectar.

Part of him was glad because it distracted him from noticing how enticing Claire looked as she sat in the firelight with her long legs stretched toward the fire. Her skin fairly glowed and the urge to touch it was nearly more than he could resist. Thankfully, he had his hands full with Maddie as she cuddled on his lap with her favorite blanket and her worn bunny toy.

Claire watched them without saying anything for a while then moved into the rocking chair and held out her arms to Maddie.

His daughter didn't hesitate as she bounded off his lap and onto Claire's. She settled against her with a contented sigh. Claire brushed a few wayward tendrils away from Maddie's face then began rocking her and humming.

"Sing, please?" Maddie asked in a tired voice.

Claire smiled down at her and sang a Christmas hymn, one Gray was quite familiar with. In spite of the woman's protests that she'd never perform on stage, with the right training, she could have quite a lucrative career, but he couldn't picture Claire enjoying it.

And the thought of sharing her, sharing her lovely

voice, with the masses wasn't a notion he cared for at all. Not when he preferred to keep Claire all to himself. At least for a little while longer. The wind had died down and the snow wasn't falling quite as hard the last time he'd checked. By morning, she should be able to get home without any trouble.

While Claire sang, he got up and made two cups of tea, set a few of the ugly cookies on a plate, and carried them over to the small table by the rocking chair.

Maddie was fast asleep, even though Claire continued to sing softly as she rocked her. When he reached out to take her, Claire shook her head. "I've got her," she whispered, then rose to her feet. "Let's put her in her own bed. I'm sure she'll sleep better there."

He led the way to Maddie's room and pulled back the covers while Claire settled her on the little bed. She stood back as he tucked the blankets around his daughter and kissed her cheek.

"I love you, Maddie," he whispered, then moved back.

Claire bent down and kissed Maddie's forehead and whispered something he couldn't hear then walked out of the room. He left Maddie's door partially open so heat would get into the room. Before he went to sleep, he'd push it all the way open, but for now, he wanted Claire to be able to talk without fear of waking Maddie.

"Would you like some tea," he asked, holding out a mug to her.

She took it and settled back in the rocking chair. Quietly, she sipped the hot liquid then picked up a cookie and looked at it. Finally, a smile broke out on her face. "These are truly the saddest Christmas cookies I've ever seen. Elsa would be appalled."

"But Maddie had fun with you frosting them, so that's more important to me than how they look," Gray said, helping himself to one. "Besides, they taste fine and you didn't even burn them."

"Maddie kept reminding me to check on them." Claire gave him a teasing grin. "She's very vigilant about baked goods."

He chuckled softly and relaxed. From the moment he'd told Claire she wouldn't be able to leave, an uncomfortable tension had settled between the two of them. He didn't know what to do or say to lift it, but as they sat by the firelight laughing about the cookies, he could see Claire was no longer upset. Perhaps she was just resigned to the fact that she had no other options with a blizzard raging outside.

"Will you really not take Maddie into Hardman for any of the Christmas events?" she asked.

Gray sighed and sat forward, leaning his elbows on his knees as he held the mug of tea in one hand. "I don't know. Part of me wants to take her to everything and let her enjoy the joys of the community. But her safety is far more important than fun."

"I just don't understand what keeps you hiding here in the woods. Surely, no one in Hardman means you any harm," Claire said, setting down her mug on the table and studying him. "Have you spoken with the sheriff?"

"No. There's nothing to tell him at this point. As far as I know, Hardman should be safe for us, but I don't want to take any chances."

"Chances for what?" Claire frowned as though an idea suddenly came to her. "Are you an outlaw on the run? A bank robber? A murderer? Is Maddie really yours?"

Gray rolled his eyes and forked a hand through his hair, discovering a few wood shavings lodged there. He shook them out and glared at Claire. "Of course I'm not an outlaw, a bank robber, or whatever other despicable things you can dream up. And yes, of course Maddie is my daughter. I was there when she drew in her first breath, had her first bath, and even changed her first diaper. In case you haven't noticed, she not only looks like me, but is definitely the child of my heart as well as my blood."

Claire didn't say anything, but she picked up her mug and took another drink.

"Look, Claire, if I could tell you everything, I would, but then you might not be safe either. It's just better for you not to know."

"Know what?" she asked. "That you make the most amazing violins I've ever seen? That your daughter should be performing on stage? That she got her musical talent from someone, and I'm assuming that is you."

Gray remained silent.

"Can you play the violin?"

He nodded, hoping Claire would leave it at that.

"Are you as good as Maddie?"

"No. I'm not that good. I don't know anyone that plays quite like Maddie," he said honestly.

Claire set the rocking chair into motion and leaned back. "So what do you plan to do with that sweet little girl, Gray?" She pointed toward Maddie's bedroom door. "You can't keep her here forever. She needs to be around other children. She'll be ready to go to school next year. She needs to live a normal life. Hiding her here in the woods with only you and her toys for company isn't good enough."

What Claire said wasn't anything he didn't already know, hadn't considered thousands of times, but it irked him to hear her point out what she saw as his failings. "Maddie's doing just fine with the way things are. I can't keep her safe if she's in town, but I can here."

"Safe from what?" Claire asked, clearly exasperated with him.

"From my past."

He stood and walked over to the window, trying to

look out into the inky darkness, but couldn't see anything beyond the porch steps.

A hand on his arm made him slowly turn around to look down into Claire's earnest, concerned face. "I'm sorry, Gray. It's none of my business and I shouldn't interfere. My apologies."

"Accepted," he said, taking her hand in his and raising it to his lips, pressing a light kiss against her fingers. "If I could tell you everything, I would."

"I know," she whispered.

He felt so drawn to her, he scrambled for a distraction of any sort. "Would you sing for me, Claire? You have a beautiful voice and I'd love to hear again that song you said you made up."

"Oh, it's just a silly song," she said, glancing up at him. "Wouldn't you rather hear something else?"

"Not particularly." He squeezed her fingers tenderly. "Please? Won't you sing it? It's a perfect Christmas melody."

Claire nodded then softly sang the words she'd made up to a melody that had haunted him since the first time he'd heard it.

When she finished, he kissed her fingers one more time before letting her go. "You should think about publishing your song. It's very good."

She shrugged. "I don't know about that, but it makes me happy." She looked at the clock then back at him. "I think I better get some sleep. If you give me a blanket, I can sleep by the fireplace."

He shook his head and pushed her into his bedroom. After lighting the lantern on the table near the bed, he crossed the room to the dresser. He took out a clean shirt and handed it to her. "It's not a nightgown, but maybe that will work for you. I'll be by the fire if you need anything. Good night, Clarice. Sleep well."

Before he gave in to the urge to kiss her, to love

her, he backed out of the room and shut the door.

He didn't even attempt to make a pallet by the fire, knowing with Claire in his bed in the other room, sleep would never come.

Chapter Twelve

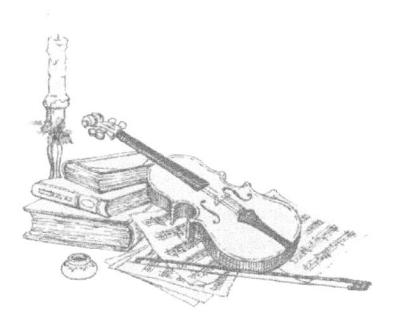

Claire bit back a giggle as she looked down at Gray as he sprawled in a chair with his hair falling over his face. His mouth hung slightly open and he made a slight snoring sound. She had no doubt he'd have a horrible crick in his neck from sleeping like he had with his chin on his chest and his feet propped up on the rocking chair.

When she'd stepped out of his room into the main room of the cabin, she'd expected to find him awake, or at least curled up on blankets by the fireplace. But here he was asleep in a chair, arms dangling over the sides, looking uncomfortable, yet entirely appealing. In sleep, he'd lost the worried, haunted look he so often carried and appeared truly relaxed. He'd mentioned his age to Fred, but he seemed so much older than his twenty-eight years.

However, in slumber, she could see glimpses of a playful, energetic boy that was probably quite similar to Maddie.

Lest she wake Gray, she quietly tiptoed across the floor and checked on the little girl. Maddie was still sleeping soundly, so Claire left her to her dreams and stoked the fire, making as little noise as possible. She tried to peer outside, but since it was still dark out, there wasn't much to see.

She filled a cup with water from the kettle on the back of the stove, made a cup of tea, and settled into a chair at the table with the sketchpad and pencil she'd brought with her.

The firelight cast enough amber light she could work. With purposeful strokes, she began drawing a scene from yesterday. Of Maddie performing what Claire thought of as her song of the woodlands. She'd heard the wind, the birds, the sleigh bells and horses. She'd felt the snowflakes whispering against her face, and tasted spice in the air. Through the notes so masterfully played by the child, she could see the deer at the stream, and smell the gingerbread baking in the oven.

Astounded and awed by Maddie's talent, she had to sit on the floor before her overwhelmed senses toppled her. Both Maddie and Gray had closed their eyes, but Claire kept hers wide open. She wanted the scene of Maddie playing out her little heart with Gray listening in the background branded into her memory so she could capture it in a painting.

It still left her bewildered that a child so small could create such wondrous music, but she'd witnessed it three times now and had no doubt that Maddie could play like no one else she'd ever heard.

She still couldn't stop thinking about what had driven Gray into hiding. It happened after his wife died, but while Maddie was a newborn, she'd at least pieced that much together. Had his wife died in childbirth? What could have possibly sent him running from his past?

And what, or whom, did he fear finding him and Maddie. One question just led to a dozen more, so she gave up trying to puzzle them out and focused on creating a rough sketch.

She jumped when something bumped against her arm and looked down into Maddie's smiling face.

Maddie pointed to where Gray still slept on the chair and placed a little finger against her rosebud lips, motioning for Claire to remain silent.

Claire nodded and watched as Maddie crept in exaggerated tip-toe fashion back to her room and reappeared with a feather in her hand. Maddie's grin broadened as she slowly made her way toward Gray.

With interest, Claire watched as the little one climbed up on the arm of the chair then brushed the feather across her father's nose.

Gray's nose twitched and he made a grumbling noise, but didn't stir.

Maddie brushed the feather over his nose again and his hand came up, brushing at his nose. When the little troublemaker turned to wink at Claire, she had to place a hand over her mouth to subdue her giggles.

The third time Maddie brushed his nose with the feather, Gray suddenly growled like a hungry bear, and grabbed his daughter, making her squeal. "What mischief are you making, Maddie Mae!"

"I woked you up, Daddy! I got you with my feather," she said, giggling as he held her upside down and tickled her.

He glanced over at Claire and smiled at her. "And did you encourage her tomfoolery?"

Claire shook her head. "I did not, sir. She handled it

well without any assistance from me."

"Is that so?" Gray rose from the chair and tossed Maddie over his shoulder, although he kept a hand on her back to keep her balanced there then ambled toward Claire, albeit stiffly.

"If you two are going to be ornery, I should send you out to do the chores then insist you make me breakfast."

"I'll do chores," Maddie chirped, squirming to get down.

"No, sweetheart, I'm just teasing," Gray said, kissing her cheek before he set her on her feet. "You get dressed in warm clothes, though, then we'll see about some breakfast."

Claire watched as he gave her a nudge toward her room. "You're very good with her," she said as she closed her sketchpad and stowed it back in her bag along with the pencil.

"What were you working on?" Gray asked as he raised his hands over his head and stretched.

Claire tried not to stare, but found it difficult when he stood just a few feet away from her. With his hair tousled and sleep lending a husky tone to his voice, she hoped the storm had blown over because it wasn't safe for her to stay in the cabin a moment longer than absolutely necessary.

It wasn't that she didn't trust Gray. No, the one she was uncertain about was herself. Oh, how she wanted to bury her fingers in his thick hair and see if those tempting lips of his were as soft and commanding as she imagined.

Before she did something utterly preposterous, like throw herself into his arms and plead with him to love her, she turned and walked over to the window near the door and looked out. Unable to see anything in the darkness that had yet to lighten with the arrival of morning, she stood with her cheek against the cool glass for a moment.

"Are you well, Claire?" he asked, placing a hand on her shoulder.

She was anything but well when the very nearness of him sent her into a feverish state. Rather than admit the truth, she pasted on a smile and turned away from the window. "Quite well, thank you."

He gave her a long, questioning look then backed away. "I'll feed the animals then make breakfast. If you wouldn't mind checking on Maddie and helping her with her hair, I'd greatly appreciate it."

"Of course."

She watched as Gray pulled on his coat, boots, and hat then tugged on his gloves before he lit a lantern and stepped outside with it.

Claire added wood to the stove and more to the fireplace, filled the kettle with water and set it to heat, then went to Maddie's room.

"Shall we braid your hair today, Maddie Mae?" she asked as Maddie tugged up the covers to make her bed. The child had already donned a pair of woolen pants and a warm flannel shirt. The little slippers on her feet looked like something for a doll rather than a child. Claire wondered if Gray had made them or purchased them from somewhere. When she'd asked how he got all his furnishings and animals, he'd said Luke Granger had helped him when he arrived in town.

Curiosity was about to eat her alive, but she knew Gray wouldn't tell her anything and neither would the Grangers.

Something about Gray niggled at the back of her mind, as though there was a memory trying to work its way free. It bothered her, but she couldn't think of why, or how, she might have previously seen Gray.

"I'm ready for you to comb my hair," Maddie said,

tugging Claire from her thoughts. Maddie held a brush in one hand and a comb in the other.

Claire sat on Maddie's bed then pulled the little girl onto her lap. With careful, gentle strokes, she once again worked the tangles out of the child's hair then braided it and tied the end with a piece of pink ribbon.

"I take it pink is your favorite color," Claire said as she finished the bow in the ribbon and set the brush aside.

"Yes. It's pretty!" Maddie snuggled against her. "I like pretty things. You're pretty, like a princess. Even Daddy says so."

Claire perked up at that bit of news. "Is that so?"

"Yep," Maddie said, then jumped down and raced into the other room.

Claire set the hairbrush and comb on Maddie's dresser, straightened the covers on the bed, then went to set the table for breakfast.

After eating the eggs and ham Gray fried along with leftover cinnamon buns she'd brought from Elsa, Claire bundled up in her coat and boots, slung her pack on her back, and stepped outside.

"We'll go with you, at least part of the way," Gray said, quickly helping Maddie on with her things.

"I don't want Maddie to catch a chill," Claire said as she strapped on her skis that Gray had left leaning against the side of the cabin beneath the porch so they wouldn't get lost in the snow.

With the sun sending streaks of pink and gold across the sky, it looked as though it would be a lovely day. Almost a foot of new snow covered the ground, though. Even if Fred did come looking for her, Claire doubted he'd be able to find the cabin with no tracks to point the way.

"I'll walk you to the glade," Gray said, closing the door behind him.

Claire handed him the rope tied to the little sled she'd used to haul out supplies. "You might as well pull Maddie on that. It'll be easier than carrying her."

Gray stepped inside, grabbed an old blanket and wrapped it around Maddie, then set her on the sled.

"I get to ride?" Maddie asked, looking up at Claire.

"You sure do, Maddie. At least for a little ways." Claire picked up her poles and pushed forward while Gray slogged through the knee-deep snow, pulling the sled. Maddie giggled and began chattering away as they made their way toward the glade. Claire could have been there in a third of the time it took with Gray trying to walk through the snow, but she didn't mind the company. They'd just entered it when a figure skied toward them from the other side.

"Hello, there!" Fred called, waving a ski pole in the air.

"Fred!" Claire said, smiling at her nephew. "What are you doing out so early?"

"Looking for you," he said. He skied up to her and gave her a hug, then looked to Gray and Maddie. "Are you all well?"

"We're fine," Claire said, glancing back at Gray and Maddie. "Gray insisted I stay once it started to snow. I'm so sorry, Fred. I hope I didn't worry you and Elsa too much."

He smiled. "We worried plenty, but assumed you have enough brains in your head to stay out of a blizzard." He leaned toward her and dropped his voice to a whisper. "I hope Gray behaved like a gentleman. I really don't want to go fetch my shotgun and Pastor Dodd."

Claire grinned. "No shotgun is needed." She glanced at Gray as he caught up to them. He held out a hand which Fred shook.

"Hi, Mr. Decker!" Maddie said, offering him a big

smile. "I get to ride Claire's sled!"

"You sure do. I bet Claire wouldn't mind a bit if you keep it."

"No, I wouldn't, that way your daddy can pull you home on it."

Gray looked to Claire. "Are you sure you don't mind?"

"Not at all. I'll retrieve it another day, unless you want to bring it by the house." Claire hoped he knew that meant she wanted to see him and Maddie again soon.

"We'll see," he said, then moved closer to Fred. "I apologize for keeping her, but it seemed best to not let her go out in the storm."

"You did the right thing, Gray. Thank you for keeping my auntie safe." Fred winked at Maddie then dug in his pocket and handed her a peppermint drop.

"Candy?" Maddie asked. At Fred's nod, her smile brightened. "Thank you, Mr. Decker!"

"You're welcome." Fred turned around and nodded at Gray. "If you don't mind, we better get on home."

"Take care and I'll see you later, Claire."

"Of that I have no doubt," Claire said, tossing a saucy grin over her shoulder.

Chapter Thirteen

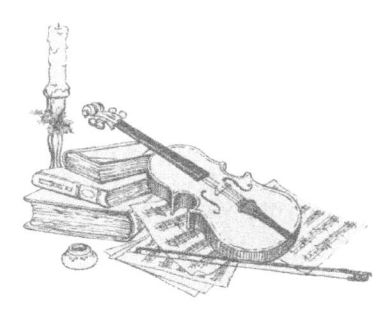

"It came!" Claire exclaimed as she raced inside the bakery, waving an envelope over her head.

The dozen customers still eating breakfast stared at her, but she ignored them as she hurried into the kitchen where Elsa was elbow deep in a lump of saffron-scented dough while Fred dried dishes and put them away.

"It came, it came, it came!" Claire said, flapping the missive at Elsa and then Fred as she danced around the counter where Elsa worked.

The two of them stared at her like she'd lost her mind, but Claire only smiled and waved the telegram again.

Fred set down the dish in his hand and snatched the paper from her. "What's this all about?"

Claire stopped dancing and beamed at Fred. "I

couldn't stop thinking about Gray's name. I don't know why, but something about it sounded so familiar. I sent a telegram to Ari asking if it sounded familiar to her. I just received her reply, but I'm too excited to open it. You read it."

Fred read the note then glanced at Elsa before he handed it back to Claire. "Why don't you read it aloud?"

Claire cleared her throat then looked to Elsa before she began reading.

Dear Claire,

The timing of your message couldn't have been any more serendipitous. Heath and I attended a lovely dinner at his sister's home yesterday. Hyacinth just happens to be dear friends with a charming woman named Victoria Carter Ness. She is a sister to Grayson Carter.

According to Victoria, her brother, his wife, and their infant daughter were killed in a house fire four years ago. They found the body of his wife, but never that of Grayson or the baby.

The Carter family has made the most exquisite violins for centuries. William Carter & Sons is in business here in Philadelphia, although there are no longer any sons to include in the business.

Grayson not only made beautiful violins, but also was a master of the instrument. He performed all across Europe and America before his death. How sad and tragic about his little family.

I'm curious what compelled you to inquire about him.

You were probably too young to remember, but father took us to see him perform once. The music he drew from the violin was magnificent.

We are all looking forward to spending Christmas in Hardman. We'll arrive on the twenty-third as

planned. Please give Fred and Elsa our love.
See you soon.
With much love,
Ari

Claire looked from Elsa to Fred, and then read the note through twice before she laid the sheet of paper on the counter. Fred pushed one of the chairs from the table beneath her before she sank onto the floor.

"I don't understand," she said. "If Grayson and his family were killed in a house fire, how can he be here, living in Hardman with Maddie? It makes no sense. Is the man in the woods an imposter? Did he really die in the house fire?"

"Claire, you need to leave this alone. If Grayson Carter is truly the man living in the woods, then you need to step back from this. If he wanted to be found, for anyone to know his whereabouts, they would." Fred knelt beside her and placed a hand on her shoulder. "Out of respect to his wishes, you can't keep delving into his past. You might inadvertently stir up something that's better left alone. If he truly did let others think he and Maddie died in a fire, he must have a very good reason for it. Trust that he knows what he's doing and leave it at that. If you want to keep on being friends with him, you've got to drop this and let it be."

"I agree with Fred, Claire. This is no one's business but Gray's," Elsa said.

"I know, but I just wanted to help. He seems so lonely and sad and broken." Claire sighed. "I thought, perhaps, I could somehow make a difference to him."

"Oh, Claire." Elsa wiped away bits of dough from her hands on a towel and hurried over to give her a warm, reassuring hug. "Don't you see how much you've helped him already? Why, for the first time in four years, he left his home to celebrate Thanksgiving with us. And he's allowed you to visit him not just once, but several times. You've been so good for Maddie, too. It's a wonderful thing you've done by extending your friendship, but you can't push him to share his past if it's something he wants to keep quiet."

"We don't even know for certain the Grayson who lives here is the same man who lived in Philadelphia. It's possible they have the same name and nothing else in common," Fred said, rising and leaning against the sink. "The best thing you can do is keep quiet about all this and wait for Grayson to say something, if he wants to. Just don't push or pry. Many of us have secrets in our past we prefer to stay there."

Claire hopped up and gave Fred a warm hug. "You have nothing in the world to be ashamed of, Fred. Besides, everyone who knows you thinks you're a fine, fine man." She kissed his cheek then stepped back. "I shall do my best not to seek out more information than Grayson is willing to share."

"Good girl," Fred said, patting her back then returning to the stack of dishes he'd been drying. "If you have nothing better to do, we could use a hand. Mrs. Smith is sick and wasn't able to come in to wash dishes today and Anna can't come after school because she has to practice for the Christmas program."

Claire hung up her coat, yanked on an apron, and started putting away the clean dishes. While she worked, her thoughts spun over and around Gray and who he really was, if he had run away from a life in Philadelphia, or if he was just a man who liked his privacy.

She knew Fred and Elsa were right about her minding her own business. But she didn't have to like it.

Afraid if she saw Gray anytime soon she'd say something to him she shouldn't, she stayed away from the woods for several days. She busied herself finishing her Christmas gifts and projects, helped Abby in her dress shop, and even spent an afternoon at Granger House helping Filly box up treats for families who needed a little extra cheer.

Nearly a week had passed and she was desperate to see Gray and hear Maddie's contagious giggles, so she decided to pay a visit to the cabin in the woods.

Claire helped clean up after the breakfast rush at the bakery and let Elsa know where she planned to head for the afternoon. She accepted the treats Elsa gave her to take, then hurried over to the mercantile.

She purchased a small child's sled, along with a tiny pair of ice skates and two bigger pairs, and almost ran home in her excitement.

Quickly changing into a skating outfit, she tugged on her boots, slipped on a warm coat and scarf, and packed the little sled with her things.

In no time at all, she was gliding down the trail on skis, thrilled with the glorious day and the prospect of seeing Gray and Maddie.

An azure sky dotted with clouds added a bit of cheer while the sun sparkled on the snow as though a fairy had spread iridescent dust with a heavy hand. Birds warbled and trilled from the trees. Claire grinned as she watched a doe and fawn bound through a stand of fragrant pines.

She headed to the glade, surprised when she encountered Gray and Maddie there. Maddie held a tin in her hands while Gray spread crumbs on a stump where he'd brushed away the snow. Birds darted about, no doubt eager for their treat, and a rabbit watched them speculatively from the safety of a bush several feet away.

"Are you leaving crumbs for the birds or the fairies?" she asked as she approached them.

Gray raised his eyebrows at her, although she could

see welcome in his eyes, while Maddie's face brightened with joy.

"Claire! We missed you!" Maddie thrust the tin at her father and bounded through the snow until Claire reached her.

She let her poles fall into the snow and picked up the little girl, lavishing her cool cheeks with kisses.

Maddie threw her arms around Claire's neck and gave her a tight hug. "You've been gone forever and ever."

Claire laughed and held her close. "Oh, surely not that long."

"Almost," Maddie said and leaned back, patting Claire's cheeks with her mitten-clad hands. "Did you bring more cookies? Did you bring any treats?"

"Madison Mae, you know better than to ask questions like that," Gray said, striding over to them with a scowl, although he looked as eager as Maddie for her to share the answer to the question.

Claire nodded. "I did bring a few things. And I have something fun for us to do after lunch, if you don't have other plans."

"I should finish some work, but I suppose an hour or two off won't hurt anything." Gray's voice sounded gruff, but he couldn't hide the interested light that snapped in his dark eyes. He lifted Maddie from Claire's arms, retrieved her ski poles from where she'd dropped them in the snow, and handed them to her. He set Maddie on the little sled Claire had left behind after her last visit and turned it around, heading toward his home.

"Been busy lately?" he asked without looking at her.

Claire gave him a long glance as he kept step beside her. Had he truly missed her, even a portion as much as she'd missed him? Or was he merely making conversation?

"There's much to do in preparation of Christmas," she said, unwilling to explain she'd been fearful of blurting out something she shouldn't. She stayed away until she felt in control of her ability to keep her mouth shut about the news Ari had sent.

"I suppose so. Are your sisters still planning to come for a visit?" he asked as they reached the cabin. He set Maddie on the porch and handed her the tin, then set about gathering an arm full of wood. Claire removed the skis and untied her bundle of surprises from the sled.

Together, the three of them strode into the cabin and for the strangest reason, Claire felt like she'd just come home.

Staggered by the realization that Gray and Maddie felt like home to her, she tried to set aside her feelings and focus on remaining lighthearted for the little girl.

"Comed see what Daddy and I made," Maddie said, grabbing her hand and tugging her in the direction of her bedroom.

Claire grinned over her shoulder at Gray and followed Maddie into her room. Sheets of paper had been cut into snowflakes and hung from fishing line on Maddie's window.

"Daddy and me made snow papers. Aren't they pretty?" Maddie asked, pointing to the snowflakes. Some were perfectly formed while others were lopsided and missing large chunks of paper. It was easy to see which ones Maddie had cut out herself.

Claire made a show of examining each one and offering compliments about them. "I think you and your daddy did a marvelous job of making snow papers." She stood back and admired them hanging in front of the window. The backdrop of snow and woods was something she'd love to paint, but she hadn't brought her sketchbook along today. Perhaps the next time she came to visit, she'd make time for a quick sketch of the scene.

"Let's take off our coats," Maddie said. The little girl yanked on her hand so Claire followed her back into the main room.

Gray had removed his coat and gloves, and stood at the stove, dropping sliced potatoes into a skillet of hot butter.

Claire helped Maddie remove her coat before she shrugged out of her own and hung it on a peg by the door.

"Elsa sent some things," Claire said, opening one of the two bundles she'd carried in. She set out a large jar full of potato dumpling soup, thick with carrots and smoky ham. Two loaves of light, golden bread, a jar of Swedish meatballs, a tin full of cookies and another of cinnamon buns soon lined the counter.

"I need to pay her for all the food she's sent. At this rate, she'll go out of business," Gray said, lifting the lid from the tin of cookies and snitching a cinnamon-laced cookie while Maddie wasn't looking. He ate it in two bites and turned back to the potatoes he fried. He added bits of venison roast along with slices of carrots and onions.

"Hope you don't mind leftovers for lunch."

Claire sniffed the air appreciatively. "Not at all. In fact, it smells delicious. If any of the girls in town find out you can cook, they'll start lining up at your door with invitations to join them at the altar at church."

Gray gave her a look that clearly expressed his disgust with that idea, making Claire laugh.

"If you're just going to be troublesome, I'll put you to work," he said, motioning for Claire to set the table.

Maddie shadowed her steps, so Claire asked the little one to set the forks and napkins on the table. While she did, Claire poured milk into glasses and set them on the table.

The way she felt so at ease, so comfortable at the

cabin with Gray and Maddie left her pondering her future. Could she really see herself there on a permanent basis?

Perhaps, but until Gray told her about his past, explained everything that had happened, she knew they couldn't have a future together.

"How about some of that good bread?" he asked, pointing to one of the loaves she'd set on the counter. "There's butter in the crock on the table."

Claire cut a few slices of the bread and set them on a plate on the table, noticing most of the oranges she'd used in the centerpiece had disappeared. She knew Maddie loved them. The next time she came out, she'd have to remember to bring more. The Bruner's had just gotten a fresh shipment of them in yesterday.

Gray set the skillet on the table and held out a chair for Claire while Maddie climbed into her chair.

"Thank you," Claire said, taking a seat and settling her skirts around her.

Gray took a seat between her and Maddie then bowed his head. After his brief prayer, they ate the filling meal while Maddie chattered nonstop about things she'd done and seen since Claire was last there.

"Have you ever skated?" Claire asked, glancing at Gray as he buttered his second slice of bread.

"My brothers and I used to skate in the winter, but that was a long time ago."

"How many brothers do you have?" Claire asked, unable to hold back the question.

Gray gave her a wary look. "Two."

She smiled. "I always wondered what it would be like to have a brother. Of course, I have Heath and Clark, but brothers-in-law aren't quite the same. Although, I must say, I rather feel like Fred is much more a brother than a nephew."

"He and Elsa both are quite fond of you," Gray

said, eating the last bite of his bread. "It's nice to have people who care about you."

"It certainly is." She took a sip from her glass of milk then looked at him again. "Do you think you'll come to Blake and Ginny's skating party on Saturday?"

"No."

"But, Gray, it would be such fun for you both, and a perfect way to introduce you to the community." Claire leaned forward. "If you won't do it for you, do it for a young one who needs to get out more and experience life."

Gray cast a quick glance at his daughter and shook his head. "No. Now, why don't you tell me more about the people of Hardman. I've learned about some of them from Luke and Filly, and the few I've met, of course, but I'd love to hear more. Is it true Arlan Guthry often quotes Ben Franklin and his wife does magic tricks at school?"

Claire knew he was trying to change the subject and for now she'd let him. "Those two tidbits are true. Alex is a wonderful teacher, well-loved by her students. She teaches in the morning and takes her son with her. Then Lila Grove, or sometimes even her husband, Tom, teaches in the afternoon. Lila is great fun. Have you heard of Arlan's brother, Adam? He and his wife, Tia, and their children live in Portland. Their little boy, Toby, is quite smitten with Pastor Dodd's daughter Erin. The two of them are already planning to wed when they grow up, and they are barely nine."

Gray grinned. "Didn't I hear the same of the Bruner's son and the girl who works for Elsa?"

"Yes. Percy has been in love with Anna since they started school. Anna is such a sweet girl, too. Percy, well, he's a good boy, but the grass will never grow under that one's feet. Every one jokes about when the wedding will take place. Each year at the Christmas program, Percy insists he and Anna play Mary and Joseph."

"That's interesting," Gray said, wiping his mouth on a napkin.

"Speaking of interesting, it would be positively fascinating if you'd bring Maddie to the skating party."

"No and no." He scowled at her.

"Will you at least think…"

"No," he said, cutting her off and rising to his feet. "You said you had something fun planned for this afternoon. I hope it isn't pestering me to death about the skating party."

Claire sighed. "No, it's not, but it does involve skates."

Both of his eyebrows inched upward. "Skates?"

"I thought Maddie might enjoy them, but I didn't even think about where we'd skate. Is there a place nearby?"

Gray stood at the sink, a dish in one hand and a soapy rag in the other as he stared at her. He turned around and rinsed the plate. "I might be able to figure out something. Will you watch Maddie for a little while?"

"Of course. I'll even take care of the dishes," Claire said, hopping up and carrying her dishes to the sink.

Gray dried his hands and shrugged into his coat. "I shouldn't be gone long. See if you two can stay out of trouble for that long."

Maddie asked Claire questions about her dress and where she'd left her britches and why her hair was pinned up instead of in a braid as Claire cleared the table and washed the dishes. She handed Maddie a rag and let the child wipe the crumbs off the table. Maddie stood on a chair and swished the rag back and forth, talking in a sing-song voice while Claire half-listened. She peered out the window, trying to figure out what Gray was about. She saw him walk by the house with a shovel in one hand and what looked like a broom missing most of its bristles in the other.

When he hadn't returned by the time she finished washing the dishes, she sat down in a chair with Maddie on her lap and combed the snarls out of the little one's tangled curls.

"Maddie Mae, I think the fairies come while you're sleeping and tie knots in your hair. What shall we do about it?"

"Set a trap!" Maddie said, giggling. "I want to catch a fairy, then I could make all the wishes I want and they'd all come true!"

"And what wishes do you have, little one?" Claire asked, gently working through a particularly nasty rat in Maddie's golden brown tresses.

"I wish we could go to town every day so I could play with my friend Maura and see you and Mrs. Decker and Mr. Decker," Maddie said, wiggling her legs and bouncing her fingers on the arms of the chair. "I wish I had a little sister, or even a brother, to play with. Or a puppy. I'd really like a puppy. And I wish I had cinnamon buns every day."

"Every day? What if you got a tummy ache from eating them?"

Maddie pushed out her tummy and patted it. "Then Daddy would make me tea and read me stories while I stayed in bed until I felt all better."

"You have a very nice daddy who takes good care of you, don't you?"

"Yes. He's the bestest daddy in the world." Maddie stopped wiggling and released a long breath. "I think my daddy is sad."

"Why do you say that, Maddie?" Claire wondered what had happened to give Maddie that idea. From what she'd observed, Gray did an excellent job of hiding his feelings, particularly from his impressionable daughter.

"Sometimes when he doesn't know I see him, he just looks sad. But he's always happy when you come to visit." Maddie started wiggling again. "I think you should stay with us all the time then my daddy would always be happy and me, too!"

Claire hugged the child and kissed the top of her head. "It would be fun to stay with you, but if I was always here, how would I bring treats like cookies and cinnamon buns?"

"Oh," Maddie said, growing silent and still again. As Claire finished combing the last section of her hair and started to braid it, Maddie clapped her hands. "I know. We should live with you in town! We can have cinnamon buns and cookies, and I can play with Maura and Cully anytime I want."

"My, but you are full of plans today, aren't you?"

"She's full of something," Gray said as he opened the door and stepped inside.

Claire hoped he hadn't overhead Maddie discussing how sad he seemed, but from the twinkle in his eye and the smile on his face, she assumed all was well. In fact, Gray looked nearly as excited as Maddie at the prospect of an afternoon adventure.

Not for the first time, Claire wished he'd shave off his abominable beard so she could clearly see his face. Regardless, she found him quite handsome and charming.

Claire's fingers flew as she finished braiding Maddie's hair since the child couldn't sit still. She quickly tied a ribbon on the end and gave Maddie a nudge forward. The child jumped off the chair and ran over to her father. "May we play outside now?"

"Just as soon as you and Claire put on your coats and things," Gray said, holding Maddie's coat for her to slip on.

Claire placed Maddie's brush and comb back in her room then pulled on her coat while Gray helped Maddie with her boots.

The little girl was fairly dancing by the time the three of them ventured outside. Maddie scurried down the steps and ran in circles in the yard, arms stretched wide, unable to contain her abundant energy.

Claire picked up the skates she'd left on the bench by the door and handed the largest and smallest pair to Gray.

"You didn't need to buy skates for us," he said, turning the silver blades over in his hands and studying them. "Let me repay you."

"Oh, it's fine, Gray. Don't give it a thought." She started down the steps, but Gray reached out and caught her upper arm in his hand, pulling her to a stop. "I mean it, Claire. I'm not destitute, by any means. I'd like to pay for all the things Elsa has sent and that you've given us."

She shook her head, finding it hard to speak when he moved down two steps so they stood nearly nose to nose. The light in his eyes flickered, like amber flames sparking to life. She started to lean toward him until she caught herself and pulled out of his grasp. "The things I've brought for you and Maddie are gifts. Simple gifts between friends. Don't make this into a thing."

He frowned. "A thing? What does that mean?"

Rather than answer, she hastened down the porch steps, held out a hand for Maddie to take and walked out of the yard.

She heard Gray's deep sigh behind her, then he was beside her, his hand on her back. "If you're going to march off, you might want to know where we're headed," he said.

She cast a sassy grin at him, then followed as he led the way to a shallow stream that ran through part of the pasture behind the barn. It wasn't deep or more than a half a dozen feet across at the widest point, but would provide a place they could play without worrying about the ice breaking or Maddie falling in. Gray had cleaned off a stretch of about thirty feet of the ice, leaving it free of snow.

"Are we gonna play with the horseys?" Maddie asked as the team Gray kept lifted their heads and watched them from where they stood in the distance.

"No, sweetheart. Claire brought ice skates. We'll fasten them on our feet, like she does the skis, and then we can slide on the ice."

"Oh, goodie!" Maddie clapped her hands.

Gray picked her up and held her feet out while Claire fastened on the skates. He set her down in the snow. "You stay right there until we get our skates on."

"Yes, daddy," Maddie said, fascinated with the shiny blades attached to the bottoms of her boots. She kept turning her feet this way and that to study the skates.

Gray removed his scarf and draped it over a fallen log he'd already cleared the snow from. "You can sit there to put your skates on." With perfect manners, he gave Claire a hand and helped her settle on the log then sat on the other end to put on his skates.

When they both were ready, they each took one of Maddie's hands and carefully stepped onto the ice.

"Do the horses drink from the stream?" Claire asked as they took a few tentative steps.

"Yes. I keep a section of the ice broken right behind the barn for them." Gray kept his eyes on his feet as he talked.

One of his feet veered left while the other went right and he almost fell before he righted himself.

Maddie giggled while Claire turned away to hide her smile. She released Maddie's hand and took a few gliding steps forward, spun in a circle, then skated backward to where Gray and Maddie both watched her.

"Do me! Do me! I want to do that!" Maddie exclaimed, grabbing Claire's hand as her feet slid out from beneath her.

Claire laughed and caught her, setting her upright.

"Here, Miss Maddie, you get in front of me and I'll help you," Claire said, positioning Maddie so she could push the little girl along on the ice and catch her if she started to fall.

Gray trailed behind them. From the scraping and clacking sounds, she assumed he hadn't yet recalled the finer points of skating. Instead of looking back to see if he'd fallen, she focused on Maddie.

The little girl's peals of laughter echoed around them, filling Claire's heart with joy as she skated to the edge of where Gray had cleared the ice, turned around and headed back. Gray's feet went out from under him and he tumbled down, landing on the bank of the stream with a thud.

"Daddy! You can't take a nap now," Maddie said, giggling.

Claire joined in her merriment and skated over to Gray. She would have offered him a hand, but he didn't look as though he'd accept it if she did. While he worked himself upright, she skated to the other end of the ice then turned Maddie around.

"Now, try it on your own, Maddie. Just slide one foot forward, and then the other," Claire said, staying close to the child, but letting her try on her own.

Maddie took a few uncertain steps, then began moving her feet in a glide rather than trying to walk on the ice.

She fell down twice, but popped back up with a grin and kept practicing.

"I think she's a natural," Claire said as she skated next to Gray. He'd given up moving and stood watching his daughter.

"She has her mother's grace," he said quietly, then looked at Claire. His gaze started at the little knit cap she wore on top of the hair she'd taken care pinning up in a popular style, over her skating outfit, down to her fur-lined boots, and back up to her face.

"You look beautiful, Claire, but I almost miss seeing those britches of yours."

A blush burned her cheeks, but she did her best to ignore it.

"If your daughter can learn to skate, so can you. I thought you said you skated as a boy?" Claire tossed Gray a challenging look.

"I did, but that was a long, long time ago."

She scoffed. "Unless you're far older than I know you to be, it wasn't that long ago. Since I can't push you around on the ice like I did, Maddie, we'll have to try an alternate method."

One eyebrow arched upward. "What do you have in mind, Miss Baker?"

She moved in front of him then held up her hands in a classic dance position. "Pretend we're going to waltz across the floor. Step and glide, that's all you need to do."

The moment his hand settled at her waist and the other twined their fingers together, Claire wanted to melt against him.

Instead, she kicked her chin up a notch, straightened her spine, and pushed herself backward. Gray took a hesitant step, scrambled to keep his footing, but kept going. She hummed her made-up song as they moved and kept time with the music.

They circled the ice three times before he relaxed and actually began skating instead of stumbling along.

Claire smiled and squeezed his shoulder where her hand rested. "Excellent, Gray. That's excellent."

Maddie was on the opposite end of the ice and paying them no mind as she sang a silly song about rabbits and goats. Claire gave the little girl a quick glance before she looked back at Gray.

When she did, he pulled her close against him and his breath warmed her face.

"Clarice Baker, whatever am I going to do with you?" His head lowered toward hers while his arms encircled her.

Claire felt dizzy and so light, like she might float up to the blue sky overhead. She couldn't have formulated a reply in that instant had her future existence hinged on it. Fortunately, the only thing she needed to focus on was his lips drawing ever closer to hers.

Chapter Fourteen

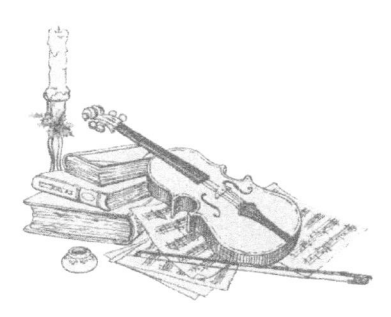

Gray knew he was playing with fire, setting himself up for heartache and Claire, too. At that moment though, he couldn't gather enough wits together to care.

The only thought penetrating the rapidly firing jolts in his brain was the fact he was finally, finally about to kiss Claire.

He'd dreamed about it, imagined what it might be like, considered how the experience would affect him.

Unwilling to rush something he'd spent so much time pondering, he slowly lowered his mouth to hers. His beard brushed against her chin before their lips connected. He expected hers to be cool, but they were warm. So warm and soft, and entirely inviting.

"Clarice," he whispered in a husky rumble before pulling her closer against him and tantalizing her mouth as he'd so often fantasized of doing.

Oh, she tasted like winter and sweetness mingled with hope and promises. It was the most decadent flavor he'd ever experienced in his life. Lost in the wonder of holding her, kissing her, being kissed in return, nothing else existed in that moment. Minutes or hours might have passed, because time seemed to stand still as she returned his ardent attention with demands of her own.

What might have happened next, he'd never know because one minute he was falling into the luxurious temptation of Claire and the next the two of them were skidding on the ice in a tumbled heap.

Maddie's giggles filled his ears and he opened his eyes to see the little mischief-maker sitting on the ice, clapping her hands in glee.

Claire, still wrapped in his arms as they came to a stop several feet away from Maddie, looked up at him with a smile although yearning still fogged her mesmerizing blue eyes.

"That child of yours has impeccable timing," she said, disentangling herself from him and rising to her feet with all the elegance of a queen.

Thoroughly discombobulated, Gray remained on his backside on the ice, watching Claire skate over to Maddie and then swing her around in her arms. The motion made her skirt bell around her and he caught a glimpse of frothy petticoats.

The woman never failed to amaze and surprise him. It had been nearly a week since she'd last ventured out to the cabin. That had been when a blizzard had left her trapped with him. Although Fred seemed good-natured about the whole thing, he'd begun to wonder if Claire had been shipped back to her sisters or Fred and Elsa had forbidden her to visit.

Even worse, he'd questioned if perhaps she'd been so distressed by having to spend the night at his place, she wanted nothing more to do with him.

Then he'd glanced up from helping Maddie feed her beloved birds, and there was Claire, looking like she'd come right out of one of the fashion magazines he knew she loved.

The sapphire blue outfit she wore was full enough she could still ski with it on. The particular shade of blue matched her beautiful eyes and made them seem bottomless, luminous. He'd wanted to rush to her, take her in his arms, and ravage her with kisses. But he hadn't. And he wouldn't.

Only he'd gotten a little carried away with her in his arms as she tried to help him skate. In fact, he used to be quite a good skater, but he wasn't nearly as interested in skating as he was in watching Claire move gracefully across the ice.

Of course, he was thrilled Maddie had taken right to it and was having such fun. But seeing Claire, observing her glide like a dancer, left him so rattled he could hardly stand upright let alone skate.

When she'd come to him with a smile and told him to think of it as waltzing with her, he wanted nothing more than to hold her the rest of the day and all night.

He'd had four years to grieve his wife and his losses. Four long years to think about what would happen if and when he met a woman who entranced and intrigued him. He knew he'd promised himself he would never fall in love again, but he battled to deny the love that filled his heart every time he saw Claire.

It was pure folly to even consider a romantic relationship with the woman, especially when she'd be returning to Philadelphia after Christmas. What would he do then? What would Maddie do?

His daughter was thoroughly infatuated with the woman. She'd talked about Claire constantly the past week. Actually, she'd talked about her since the first time they met. But the more time Claire spent with them, the more Maddie seemed to think Claire would always be there.

For Maddie's sake as much as his, he needed to cut things off with Claire. He hated to set aside their friendship, hated to even consider the possibility, but what would happen to Maddie when Claire left?

As he watched Claire spin around with Maddie and a look of absolute joy shining on his daughter's sweet little face, he realized it was far too late to protect Maddie's tender heart. He might as well allow her to spend as much time with Claire as possible because whether today was the last time they saw her or a month from now, Maddie was going to be shattered when Claire left for good.

Frustrated, with himself and circumstances beyond his ability to control, he forked his fingers through his hair, only then realizing he hadn't bothered to wear a hat. That woman-child with the vibrant eyes and teasing smile had him so flummoxed, he hardly knew up from down the past few weeks.

Claire, with her insistent, uplifting, encouraging spirit, had breathed life back into him, whether he wanted it or not.

"Come on, Daddy!" Maddie fluttered her little pink mitten-covered hand at him. "Come skate with us."

"Yes, Gray. Come join us," Claire said, smiling nearly as broadly as his daughter.

With effort, he rose to his feet, brushed off the seat of his denims and cautiously made his way over to the girls.

"Did you give us a shove, Maddie Mae?" he asked when he reached them.

The impish grin on her face gave her away, even before she bobbed her head. "You went splat," she said, slapping her hands together, although her mittens muffled the sound.

"I think I should splat you," Gray growled, raising his hands up like claws and making a silly face.

Maddie shrieked and scrambled to get away from him while Claire laughed. His daughter tangled her feet and would have fallen, but he swept her into his arms and tossed her in the air.

"Again, Daddy. Do it again!"

Gray obliged her demands, then kissed her cheek. "You're getting to be quite a bossy little thing, Maddie. Who taught you that?"

She giggled again and pointed to Claire. "The princess."

"Ah, of course." Gray tickled Maddie then set her on her feet. He glanced up and noticed the sky beginning to shift from blue to gray then looked to Claire. "Unless you want to spend another night at the cabin, you best be on your way home, little songbird."

Claire tossed a quick glance at the sky then frowned at the darkening clouds. "Oh, I didn't realize it looked like it might storm. I should be getting back," she said, skating over to the edge of the stream. Gray hurried to offer her a hand, then picked up Maddie and removed her skates, setting her down by Claire. He removed his, then pulled Claire up from the log where she'd sat and retrieved his scarf.

"Let's get you on your way before it starts to snow," he said, holding her hand as they started toward the cabin.

Maddie raced ahead of them, hopping and bobbing through the snow like a fox he'd watched trying to work through a deep drift.

"Thank you for the skates," he said, lightly squeezing Claire's hand as they neared the cabin. "It was kind of you to think of bringing them. Maddie had a wonderful time, and so did I."

Claire looked at him, her gaze resting on his mouth, as though she couldn't get their kisses out of her mind any better than he could. In fact, everything in him demanded he haul her into his arms and kiss her again.

But that would never do. Not with a storm brewing and Maddie intently studying their every move from where she swung back and forth while holding onto a porch post.

"Are you sure you won't come to the skating party? You know you'd be welcomed and Maddie could meet other children from Hardman." Claire grabbed her things and settled them on the little sled, then hurried to strap on her skis.

"I'm sure, Claire, but if you keep wearing me down, who knows what I might agree to," he said with a teasing grin.

She beamed at him then took the rope attached to the sled and tied it around her waist. Once the knot was secure, she motioned to Maddie to come close and gave her a big hug. "Be a good girl until I see you again."

"I will, Claire. Thank you for the skates. They're wonnerful!"

Claire kissed her rosy cheek. "I'm so glad you enjoyed them, sweetheart."

Gray swung Maddie into his arms to keep from reaching out to Claire and kissing her. He handed her the ski poles and stepped back as she pushed off. "Stay warm and I hope to see you soon!"

With a wave of one ski pole, she was gone, hurrying down the trail he knew had become familiar to her.

"Daddy?" Maddie asked, placing her hands on his cheeks and forcing him to look at her.

"What is it?" he asked, walking up the steps and opening the door to the cabin. The warmth enfolded them as he stepped inside and set Maddie on the floor.

"I like Claire. Do you think, if we asked nice, she'd stay with us?" Maddie gave him such an earnest, imploring look it made pain spear his chest.

Gray removed Maddie's coat, scarf, boots and mittens, setting them out to dry near the stove, then hung up his own.

He picked her up and carried her over to the rocking chair near the fireplace and settled into the smooth wood. With a gentle hand, he brushed the wayward tendrils that escaped the braid Claire had fashioned away from Maddie's face as she sat on his knee, waiting his response.

Finally, he cleared his throat and set the chair into motion. "I know you like Claire, sweetheart. I like her, too. But Claire can't stay with us all the time. She has her own life and things to do. And after Christmas, she'll go back home with her sisters. She won't be here to visit us anymore."

"But I want her to stay, Daddy. I love her." Maddie's lower lip quivered and tears pooled in her eyes. "Please, Daddy. Make her stay. I won't even ask for a puppy for Christmas. I'd rather have Claire."

"Me, too," he muttered to himself as he pulled Maddie against his chest and soothingly rubbed a hand over her back and shoulders as he rocked. "I'd rather have Claire, too."

Chapter Fifteen

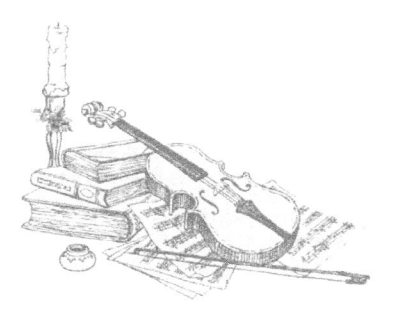

Claire sat on the end of a pew, waiting for the Sunday morning service to start. Beside her, Elsa smoothed a hand down the front of her skirt. Fred whispered something to Tom Grove as he and his wife, Lila, sat on the other side of him.

Yesterday, she'd had a lovely time at Blake and Ginny Stratton's annual skating party. It was a fun, lighthearted gathering the community attended. Children raced across the ice, courting couples went off in pairs, and the community band played lively tunes. Tables groaned beneath the assortment of cookies, pies, cakes, popcorn balls and candy while the spicy scent of apple cider filled the air.

If only she'd been able to talk Gray into coming and bringing Maddie. Then the day would have been perfect.

She glanced up from studying the appliquéd velvet scrolls on her dark blue gown as Pastor Chauncy Dodd stepped behind the ornately carved pulpit that was a gift from Blake Stratton a few years ago. He'd opened his bible when Claire felt a hand on her leg then a wriggly little body climbed onto her lap.

She snapped her gaze from Maddie to Gray as he motioned for her to scoot over so he could sit beside her.

Claire elbowed Elsa who was clearly astonished to see the reclusive man in church, and everyone shifted down to make room for him to take a seat.

Although whispers were kept to a minimum, everyone seemed interested in getting a gander at the newcomer and his daughter.

Chauncy smiled and nodded their way, then began the service. Maddie spent the entirety of it on Claire's lap. In spite of an occasional fidget, she sat quietly, alternating between looking around the church and smiling up at Claire.

Gray kept his gaze forward, fixed on the pastor until the closing hymn. When they stood to sing it, he started to take Maddie from her, but the little girl wrapped her arms around Claire's neck, making it clear she was not letting go.

Claire shrugged and patted Maddie's back while Gray held the hymnal. Claire knew the words by heart and the fact that Gray sang with his eyes closed made her think he did, too. Gray had a smooth, mellow singing voice that made her wonder if he'd had voice lessons at some point.

As the service ended, Gray glanced behind him, looking eager for a means of escape before people bombarded him with questions.

Claire turned her gaze to Fred and Elsa, and tipped her chin toward Gray. Fred nodded in understanding and hurried into the aisle with Elsa close behind him. The two of them bracketed Gray and headed for the door where Chauncy and Abby Dodd waited to greet everyone.

Tom and Lila Grove kept step with Claire as she made her way through the crowd, still holding Maddie. Many people stopped her to share a word of welcome, but Maddie tucked her face against Claire's neck and peeped out, overwhelmed by seeing so many people at once.

"And who is this young miss?" Chauncy asked, reaching out and touching Maddie's foot when Claire finally made it to the door.

"This is Madison Mae Carter, but we call her Maddie. She is acquainted with Maura Granger." Claire tried to catch a glimpse of the feisty little Granger girl, but had not yet located her.

"Maura and Cullen are both home sick with the sniffles today, but our two hooligans are running around here somewhere," Chauncy said, craning his neck, then waving his hand in the air.

Erin Dodd raced over, dark curls bouncing and blue eyes full of mischief. "Hello, Miss Baker," the child said with practiced politeness.

Claire bent down so Maddie was on eye level with Erin. "Erin Dodd, this is my special friend, Maddie."

"It's nice to meet you, Maddie," Erin said, smiling at the little girl. "Would you like to come outside to play with me?"

Shyly, Maddie nodded her head. Claire set her down and helped her on with her coat, tugged her knit cap over her curls, and made sure she had on her mittens before giving her a nudge toward the door with Erin.

"She's adorable," Abby said, watching Erin take Maddie's hand and lead her outside. "I met her father a few weeks ago. He came in to the dress shop to do a little Christmas shopping."

"Oh, that's wonderful," Claire said, distractedly. She hoped Gray wouldn't mind her keeping Maddie, then sending her off to play with Erin.

"Go on, Claire. We'll visit another time," Chauncy said with a knowing look.

She grinned and moved out of the way of the other church attendees as Tom gathered their coats. Soon, she stepped outside with Tom and Lila into the nippy December air. The leaden sky threatened snow, although none had started falling yet.

"We'll run on home to finish lunch preparations," Lila said, placing a hand on Claire's arm. "Please invite your friend to join us. We have plenty."

"Thank you, Lila. I don't know if he'll come, but I'll certainly ask." Claire had been planning to join the couple, along with Fred and Elsa for lunch today. While she'd been looking forward to dining with their friends, now all she wanted was to spend time with Gray and Maddie.

She caught sight of Erin introducing Maddie to a few other little girls. Assured Maddie was in good hands, Claire hastened in the direction of where Fred and Elsa spoke with Gray. Arlan and Alex Guthry caught up with her before she reached them.

"Good morning, Claire. How does this day find you?" Alex asked with a bright smile as she walked up to the group.

"Very well. How are you all today?" Claire looked around for Gabe and saw him being fawned over by some of Alex's older students.

"Excellent," Arlan said, pulling his wife a little closer to him. "If you haven't other plans today, you're all welcome to join us for lunch. Blake and Ginny are coming over, since Luke and Filly's little ones are sick."

"The invitation is much appreciated, but Tom and Lila have asked us to join them." Claire smiled at the couple. "Perhaps we can plan on it another time?"

"Yes, let's do. It would be fun to get everyone together when your sisters are here," Alex said, tossing her a teasing look. "I might even be persuaded to do a little magic for your brothers-in-law if you promise to sing for us."

"I think that can be arranged," Claire said, as they reached the group.

"What can be arranged?" Fred asked as she stepped beside him.

"A song in trade for a magic trick." Claire glanced at Gray. He looked like he was one step away from snatching Maddie and running back into his woods like Frankenstein's monster about to be chased by angry villagers.

She sidled closer to him and placed her gloved fingers on his hand as it nervously twirled the brim of his hat around and around. "Tom and Lila Grove invited you and Maddie to join us for lunch at their house. Lila, if you haven't yet met her, is a cousin to Luke Granger."

Gray didn't look at her as he continued watching Maddie play with a group of little girls, but he stopped spinning his hat around. "I suppose we could go, just this once."

Claire wanted to clap and cheer, but she merely nodded her head. "Shall we head over there?"

"Yes, let's get out of this cold," Elsa said, looping her arm around Fred's. "We'll run by the bakery and get the cake I promised to bring if you want to go ahead. It will just take a moment then we'll meet you there."

"Here that, Gray? There will be cake." Claire nudged him in the side when he appeared fixated on the fun Maddie was having with the children.

"I don't believe you've met my wife, Mr. Carter. Alex, Mr. Carter has done business with Luke for a while," Arlan said, reaching out a hand to Gray and forcing his attention away from Maddie.

Gray shook Arlan's hand. "It's nice to see you again, Mr. Guthry, and meet you, Mrs. Guthry." He tipped his head to Alex. "Did I hear you are a prestidigitator?"

Alex grinned. "Guilty as charged. And if you heard that from Luke, he probably worked the word into the conversation at least half a dozen times."

Gray chuckled. "That he did, ma'am. It's a rather catchy word to say."

Arlan snickered. "And seems to be among Luke's favorites for as often as he uses it."

"Oh, quit picking on the man," Claire said, giving Arlan an admonishing look. "There's worse things he could be guilty of."

"True," Arlan said, stepping away from Alex. "Don't be a stranger, Mr. Carter. It was good to see you here today, but if we're going to get home and serve lunch to Blake and Ginny, we better reclaim our son and go."

"Thank you, Mr. Guthry. And please, just call me Gray. My friends all do."

"Gray, it is, but only if you call us Arlan and Alex."

Gray smiled. "Thank you. And it was very nice to meet you, Mrs. Guthry. Your son is quite a handsome little fellow."

Alex beamed with motherly pride. "We like to think so, but I know we're biased. Enjoy your day."

Once the Guthry family walked away, Claire turned and watched as Erin gave Maddie a big hug. The two girls pressed their heads close together, giggling.

"Look what you've done," Gray said in a quiet tone.

Claire couldn't tell if he was pleased or upset, but then she noticed happiness shining in his eyes. "And what am I being blamed for now, Gray?"

"For dragging me out of the woods and forcing me to share my daughter with the world." He looked down at her with a broad smile. "The people are so welcoming and kind here. And just look at Maddie. She's having the time of her life."

"She's an easy girl to like, Gray." Claire reached out and took his hand between hers, giving it a squeeze. "You've done an excellent job of rearing a lovely child."

"Don't give me too much credit. She's only four. I've got a long, long way to go."

Claire laughed and tugged on his hand. "If you think we can pull Maddie away from her new friends, we should probably head over to Tom and Lila's place. I'm famished."

"Me, too." Gray caught Maddie's eye and motioned for her to join them. She gave Erin a hug, waved at the other little girls, then raced over to where they waited.

"Daddy! Did you see me? I made friends! They liked me!"

Gray swung her into his arms and gave her a kiss on her cheek. "I did see you, sweetheart. I'm so glad you had fun."

"Did you walk or drive into town?" Claire asked, glancing around.

"We walked. It's faster to cut through the woods and come out by Fred's house than driving the wagon all the way around. The snow's packed down so it was easy enough to walk on today. I pulled Maddie on the little sled and left it at Fred's place. I hope that isn't a problem."

"Of course not," Claire assured him. "That's perfectly fine."

Gray shifted Maddie from his right arm to his left as they started down the boardwalk toward the heart of town.

"Did you enjoy the service?" Claire asked.

"I did enjoy it. Pastor Dodd is a good speaker and I enjoyed his sermon very much." Gray glanced behind them, as though he expected someone to be following them.

"It's okay, Gray. I'm sure this is incredibly difficult for you after being away from groups of people for such a long time."

He nodded and swallowed hard, but followed her across the street. Claire pointed out Elsa's bakery and a few other businesses. She knew he did business at the mercantile and the bank with Luke, but didn't think he'd frequented any others in town, with the recent exception of Abby's dress shop.

They strolled down a side street to a two-story newly built home where circles of yellow glowed in the windows from lamps, offering a warm welcome.

"Fred helped Tom build this house after Tom and Lila wed. They've lived here a little more than a year, I think," Claire said as they walked through the gate in the yard's picket fence.

"Tom and Fred are good friends, aren't they?" Gray asked as they made their way up the walk and front porch steps.

"Yes. They were school chums for a while, then Fred had some problems. Once he got his life straightened out, he and Tom became close friends. I think it is safe to say they'd do anything to help each other now." Claire smiled when the door swung open and Tom beckoned them inside.

"Welcome, welcome! Come in out of the cold. Fred and Elsa just arrived a moment ago." Tom took their coats and hung them on the hall tree by the door. Claire admired the gleaming hardwood floors, flocked wallpaper, and gaslights on the walls.

"It's pretty here," Maddie whispered as Claire smoothed her flyaway hair after removing her little knit cap.

"I think it is, too," Claire said, smiling at the child, then taking her hand. "Shall we go wash up so we can eat?"

Maddie nodded and followed Claire to the bathroom where the little girl marveled over the big bathtub with ball and claw feet as well as the wonders of indoor plumbing.

"I wish we had a potty in our house," Maddie said as Claire helped her dry her hands. "I almost got stuck on the seat in the outhouse yesterday."

Claire hid a smile. "I bet that was scary."

"Oh, yes," Maddie said, holding Claire's hand as they started down the hall. "I thought I might fall in the hole and there are nasty monsters that live down there. I might have been eaten!"

"That would be a tragedy, Maddie Mae. I'm glad you're safe."

"Me, too," Maddie said emphatically as they walked into the dining room. Fred and Elsa were there, along with Tom's parents and their little daughter. Tom had been quite shocked to come home for the holidays two years ago to discover his mother expecting after him being the only child. But everyone loved little Jamie, although perhaps none quite as much as her father, who positively doted on the child.

Maddie immediately brightened at the sight of the toddler. Jamie seemed equally taken with Maddie when she squirmed for her father to set her down and raced over to Maddie, tugging on her hand.

Gray, who'd been standing with Fred, seemed to relax once he realized they'd not only been made welcome, but Maddie was having a wonderful time.

The group took seats around the dining room table and Tom said grace. The adults fell into an easy conversation.

"Did you read about the treaty with Columbia for the Panama Canal being signed this week and sent to the senate for ratification before they all leave for the holiday?" Tom asked.

"I did see that in your newspaper," Fred said, as he helped himself to another dinner roll and serving of buttered corn. "The treaty will give the United States the sole right to a hundred year lease, effectively making it last in perpetuity."

"I'm still not sure I understand what that means, exactly," Lila said, dabbing at her mouth with a napkin and looking from Fred to Tom.

"People have been trying to come up with a way to create a water passage across the Isthmus of Panama for hundreds of years. If they did, it would connect the Atlantic and Pacific Oceans, and save so much travel time. Right now, to make that trip, they have to sail around Cape Horn, a route that is both long and hazardous," Tom explained. "France attempted the task of creating a passage about twenty years ago, but their mistake was in trying to build a sea-level canal instead of a lock based canal. The frequent rains caused heavy landslides and they were plagued by yellow fever and malaria."

"Lock based? What's that?" Elsa asked.

Fred smiled at his wife. "A lock is a device used in a waterway to raise and lower boats when the water levels vary." He raised his hands and held them at two different heights, parallel to the table. "So if the Atlantic Ocean is here..." He wiggled his left hand. "And the Pacific Ocean is at this level..." He moved his right hand six inches higher than his left. "A lock provides a fixed chamber that adjusts the water level." He moved his hands so they were even.

"Oh, I understand," Elsa said. "And the United States wants control of it?"

"Yes," Tom said. "President Roosevelt pushed to purchase the French assets earlier this year. The first proposed treaty was rejected, but the new deal, thanks to the president throwing some military weight behind the Panamanian independence movement, looks promising."

"Won't it take a very long time to build the canal?" Claire asked, trying to fathom such a huge project.

Fred nodded. "It will most likely take a year or two before they even get started and then, I would think, another eight or ten years to finish the job."

"Considering how long people have been waiting for this, I'm sure it can't open a moment too soon," Claire said.

"While we're speaking of articles in my darling boy's newspaper, I was saddened to see Julia Grant passed away this week," Junie Grove said.

"I read that, too," Lila said, glancing at her mother-in-law. "From the details I've read, she was a respected First Lady."

"I believe she was," Junie said. "I remember reading something one time that said she often received callers at informal receptions, as long as the ladies wore hats and the men left their weapons at home."

"Wouldn't that be something to just appear at the White House for tea one day," Claire said, lifting her nose in the air with a haughty look on her face that made everyone laugh.

The conversation continued to flow with ease as they discussed the Christmas activities planned in Hardman, a new business in town, a family that had recently moved, and what treats Elsa would be serving at the bakery in the days before Christmas. Everyone carefully avoided asking Gray any questions that might make him uncomfortable. Claire had hoped Fred and Elsa would make sure the Grove family knew not to inquire about Gray's past.

After indulging in slices of Elsa's spice cake served with sweetened cream, no one seemed in a rush to hop up and leave.

The men volunteered to do the dishes while the women took the two little girls to the parlor where Jamie had an assortment of toys she shared with Maddie.

Claire loved watching Maddie crawl around the floor with Jamie as they pushed plush pull toys back and forth. Maddie seemed to favor a pink duck while Jamie liked a brown pony.

"She's absolutely beautiful," Junie Grove said as she and Lila sat together on the couch while Elsa and Claire settled into chairs across from them. All four of them watched the little girls play. "I've never seen such long, curly hair on one so young."

"Her father has quite a time keeping it tamed," Claire said with a grin, pleased Gray had gone to the effort of combing Maddie's hair and pulling it back in a bow. She wore the little sailor dress she'd seen Maddie in each time they came to town, and concluded that must be the child's only dress.

However, she assumed from what Abby shared that Maddie would be getting something new for Christmas. Perhaps Gray wouldn't mind if she purchased an outfit or two for Maddie. Excited at the prospect of dressing Maddie like a living doll, she planned to raid Abby's stock of children's clothes first thing tomorrow.

"Isn't that right, Claire?" Elsa asked as she and the others awaited her reply.

Claire blushed. "I let my mind wander and wasn't paying attention. My apologies."

Junie and Lila laughed while Elsa grinned and reached over to pat her hand.

"If you were distracted by thoughts of that handsome bearded man in the kitchen, I can't blame you," Lila said, giving her a teasing wink.

The blush on Claire's face deepened from pink to bright red. "I'm sure I don't know anything about that."

Elsa shook her head. "Clarice Baker! Don't you dare tell a fib, especially on Sunday."

She gave the other women a sheepish look, then grinned. "I might be slightly distracted by him."

"Have you wondered what he'd look like without that bushy beard?" Lila asked, earning a reproving look from her mother-in-law.

Then Junie raised her eyebrows and leaned forward conspiratorially. "But don't let him cut his hair. It makes him look like a knight from a fairy tale."

Amused by her friends, Claire leaned back and relaxed. Not long after that, the men joined them. Jamie rubbed her eyes and yawned widely.

"I think it's about nap time for our little miss, and we need to head on home anyway," Junie said, picking up her daughter and cuddling her close.

"You could put her down upstairs, Mama," Tom said, reaching to take his sister.

"No, we best get on home. I think it's gonna snow again today anyway," James said, holding Junie's coat then slipping his on. "It was nice to meet you, Gray. If you ever get out our way, stop by."

"Thank you, sir," Gray said as the couple bundled up their daughter. Once they left, he turned to Lila and Tom. "I best take Maddie and head for home, too. It's a long walk and I don't want to get caught out in the snow since it looks like it might start to fall at any moment."

"I can hitch up the wagon and give you a ride," Fred offered, taking a step toward the door.

"No. It's faster to walk past your place and I left Maddie's sled there, anyway." Gray pulled on his coat and held out Maddie's coat. "Come on, Maddie Mae. Time to go."

"But, Daddy, can't we stay just a little while

longer?" she asked, as she played with Jamie's toys.

"No, sweetheart. It's time to go."

Maddie looked like she wanted to argue, but she put the toy she was playing with back in the box in the corner then skipped over to where the adults stood in the entry. She stuck her arms in her coat without a word of protest. Claire was amazed, again, at how well she minded.

Lila dropped down on her knees to fasten Maddie's coat and wrapped the child's scarf around her neck. "I hope you'll come see me again sometime, Maddie. It was such fun to meet you."

"I like you. Your house is pretty, and you are too." Maddie threw her arms around Lila's neck and gave her a tight hug then eyed Tom until he hunkered down so she could give him a hug as well.

She hugged Fred and Elsa then grabbed Gray's hand, ready to leave.

"I'll walk with you back to the house," Claire said, quickly tugging on her coat and gloves and plopping her hat on her head.

"That's not necessary, Claire. Stay and enjoy the afternoon." Gray opened the door and stepped outside. "Thank you, again, for your hospitality," he said to Tom and Lila, tipped his head to Fred and Elsa, and started to close the door, but Claire grabbed the knob before it clicked shut.

"Gray, wait!" she said, rushing to catch up to him since his long strides had carried him across the street before she even made it down the porch steps.

He stopped and watched as she bustled across the street. "Go back inside, Claire. I don't want to ruin your afternoon."

"How could you possibly ruin it when seeing you has been the best part of my day?" she blurted, taking both of them by surprise.

To hide her embarrassment, she took Maddie's other hand so the child walked between the two of them.

Gray gave her a studying glance, but remained silent as they walked past the church and headed toward Fred and Elsa's home.

"Can I run, Daddy?" Maddie asked.

"Yes, but stay where I can see you. Don't run too far ahead," Gray said in warning. He chuckled as Maddie took off running, or as best as she could in the tracks through the snow. She spun around in circles, arms wide, and her giggles carried back to them.

"She's just wonderful, Gray. You should be very proud of her."

"I am, for many reasons," he said, then glanced down at Claire. "But I want her to stay sweet and humble."

"I have a feeling she will." Claire moved a little closer to him. "I'm so glad you came to church today. It wasn't as bad as you feared, was it?"

"No. It was nice to be there and it did my heart a world of good. I try to have a little Sunday school lesson with Maddie each week, but it was pleasing to hear a pastor deliver a sermon." He sighed and gazed ahead as Maddie hopped on one foot for a while, then switched to the other. "What really hit me, though, was watching Maddie make friends so easily with the other little girls. She needs to be around children her own age, to interact with them. I, um… I think perhaps we'll plan to attend the Christmas Eve festivities."

Unable to stop herself, Claire clapped her hands together then gave Gray an impulsive hug, pulling back quickly before she begged him to kiss her right there on the street.

"That is fantastic news! My sisters and brothers-in-law will be here. You'll get to meet Ari and Heath, and Bett and Clark. They're all marvelous, of course.

Heath's sister is friends with your sister. Victoria, isn't that her name?"

At his shocked look, Claire wished she'd kept from blathering on like a fool. Gray glared at her then began marching along the pathway. She had to run to catch up to him. Only by darting in front of him and grabbing onto his arm did she get him to stop.

He looked like he wanted to throttle her as he jerked his arm from her grasp and glowered at her. "How could you talk about me, Claire, when I specifically asked you not to? What have you done?"

"When you finally told me your name, it sounded familiar, but I couldn't place why. I asked Ari if it meant anything to her and she recalled someone named Grayson Carter being a concert violinist before he perished in a fire along with his wife and newborn baby." Claire took his hand in hers. "I didn't mean anything by it, Gray. Honest. Our father took us to watch you perform once. You were superb. I see now where Maddie gets her talent."

"She's far, far better than I ever dreamed of being," he said with a faraway look in his eyes. He remained silent for a moment before he expelled a long breath. "Who else knows?"

"Just Fred and Elsa. They won't tell anyone. I didn't tell Ari that you're here. All she knows is that I was curious about the name." Claire wanted to banish the wounded look he wore, but had no idea how. She really should have minded her own business, but it was a little late to worry about it now.

Gray took his hand from hers, stuffed both hands in his pockets, and slowly continued walking. "As you know, I played the violin. My father and brothers and I crafted violins, carrying on a tradition that has been in our family for generations. Neither of my brothers was interested in performing, but I loved it, even more than making violins. Papa made sure I received the training I needed to have a career as a concert violinist. And I was good. When I was nineteen, I was in Virginia performing and looked out in the crowd. A beautiful girl with hair that looked like spun gold happened to be sitting three rows back from the stage and caught my eye. I was immediately smitten, and Laura felt the same. Although she was barely seventeen, we wed a month later and she traveled with me whenever I performed. When I wasn't on stage or practicing, I worked with my father and brothers making violins."

He fell silent for a moment and watched as Maddie attempted to roll snow into a ball for a snowman. Claire thought he might end the story there, but he cleared his throat and continued.

"When Laura had Maddie, I was elated. She seemed like such a miracle to both of us and came at a time when we needed a boost of hope. Six months prior, my oldest brother died of a stomach malady that came seemingly out of nowhere. Three months before Maddie was born, my other brother drowned in a boating accident, only he was a strong swimmer and the water was only eight feet deep. Twice, someone shot at me as I was leaving after a performance, once I was nearly plowed over by a runaway team of horses, and someone tried to cut me with a knife when I was walking down the street, but in the jostling crowd, they didn't do any vital damage."

"My word, Gray! Did you tell the police? Did they capture whoever attempted to harm you?" Claire asked, gaping at him in disbelief.

He shook his head. "The police couldn't connect the deaths of my brothers to the attempts on my life. They claimed what happened to Cliff and Warner were tragic accidents. They also decided whoever was trying to kill me was most likely an overzealous fan."

"But what do you think?" Claire questioned as they neared Fred's house.

"That someone killed my brothers and wanted me dead."

"Who would do such a thing?"

"If I knew the answer to that, I wouldn't have spent the last four years hiding in the woods with my daughter." Gray shrugged. "I might never know the truth, but being here has kept Maddie safe."

Claire motioned for him to follow her inside the kitchen. Maddie scampered inside. After removing her coat and boots, Claire set the little girl at one end of the kitchen table with crayons and paper, and a glass of milk, then made cups of tea for her and Gray.

"What happened to your wife?"

Gray's jaw tightened and he took a long sip of the hot tea. "Strange things had happened at our house right around the time Maddie was born. Perhaps I was paranoid, but I worried one of the staff might have been the guilty party, so I dismissed everyone except for the woman who was my nanny when I was a boy. My mother died when I was six, and Nanny Roth took such good care of us. I knew I could trust her with Maddie and Laura. I was scheduled to give a performance and told Laura I'd cancel, but she insisted I go. When I left the house, she was sitting in the parlor, rocking Maddie while Nanny Roth worked on knitting a blanket. I can't think it was anything but the hand of God that urged me to cut the performance short and make haste back to the house. I returned to find flames glowing in the windows across the front of the house and the front door barred from the inside."

"Oh, Gray. No." Claire reached out and placed her hand over his. He turned his over so her palm rested against his and entwined their fingers.

"I rushed around to the back of the house and inside

the kitchen. That's when I heard two loud pops and thought it must be glass bursting from the fire. I raced into the hall only to find Laura and Nanny both shot in the head. I thought I heard footsteps above me and ran up the stairs, desperate to get to Maddie's nursery, hoping against hope I'd find her there. A figure, all dressed in black, loomed in the hallway in front of me, but something downstairs exploded and blew up through the floor. The man fell and I leaped past the gaping hole in the floor to reach the nursery. Poor Maddie was screaming for all she was worth but unharmed."

He grew quiet and sipped his tea before he continued. "Laura knew of my concerns. I'd even tried to talk her into taking the baby and leaving town for a while. Her parents were both deceased, but she had an aunt in New York she could have visited. Although she refused to go, she did prepare traveling cases for us in the event we needed to leave on a moment's notice. I wrapped up Maddie, grabbed our cases, and managed to make it downstairs. I thought the man who'd fallen was most likely dead, but he was nowhere to be seen when I ran out of the house. Fearful he'd keep coming after me and Maddie, I headed for the train station, purchased a ticket, and found myself on the way to Oregon. When the train stopped in Heppner, I heard someone talking about Hardman being such a nice community. So I got off the train, bought a wagon full of supplies, and here we are. I made two promises to myself then. One was that I would never put another woman's life in danger through association with me. I won't ever wed again. Not ever. The second was that I'd never play the violin again. If I hadn't been on stage that night, Laura and Nanny might very well be alive right now."

Claire felt as emotionally drained as Gray had to be by the telling of his story. The poor man had been through so much. He'd somehow survived the grief of having his wife and beloved nanny murdered, as well as his brothers.

"What of your father? Is he well? And your sister? Was she never in danger?"

Gray swirled the now tepid tea around in his cup. "Papa is alive and well. Victoria's husband works with him. To my knowledge, no one ever tried to harm them."

"The violins. How do you make them if you won't play them? Don't you need to tune them, test the sound of them?"

"Maddie. She wasn't even yet two the first time she picked up a violin. Instead of the horrific noise one might expect, she played. I taught her everything I know about the instrument and she plays each one for me before I ship it."

"You send the violins to your father to sell?" Claire asked, trying to piece together the puzzle that was Gray.

"Not exactly. Papa collects the orders then sends them to his trusted attorney, Roberts. The attorney sends them to me. When the violins are complete, I ship them to Roberts and he makes sure they are delivered. No one at Papa's shop knows I make them."

"But your father knows you are alive?"

Gray nodded. "Yes, he knows. I contacted him, through Roberts, as soon as I arrived in Hardman. No one else knows, though. Not even Victoria. She was never any good at keeping secrets and Papa and I thought it best Victoria and her husband not know." He looked up at Claire and offered her a weak smile. "So there you have it, Clarice, my sad, sorry tale of why I live like a recluse in the woods, always looking over my shoulder."

"But Gray, don't you think if someone was going to come after you, they would have done it by now."

"Perhaps, but if he had no idea how to find me, he might just be waiting for a clue that will lead him here.

I'm fairly certain whoever it was that night is aware that I did not perish in the fire."

"You can't live your whole life in hiding, Gray." Claire tipped her head toward the other end of the table where Maddie hummed and colored. "Think of her."

"I am. That's why I reluctantly agree with you. It's time for me to become part of this community, even if I plan to keep my past a secret. If I don't, I can't keep Maddie safe." Gray stood and looked at the clock on the wall. "It's far past time for me to head home. It'll be dark by the time we get there if I don't hurry."

"Take one of our lanterns with you, just in case."

Gray nodded and pulled on his coat while she helped Maddie on with hers. She filled a tin with cookies Elsa had brought home the previous day from the bakery and handed it, along with a lantern, to Gray.

Maddie bounded down the steps and hopped onto the sled, clearly ready to go.

Gray set the tin of cookies on her lap, then turned back to Claire as she stood shivering on the porch. He cupped her chin and kissed her cheek. "Thank you for listening to my story and for relentlessly nagging me to death."

Claire swatted his arm, but smiled as he kissed her lightly on the lips then hurried to grab the rope attached to the sled.

"Come visit soon," Maddie called as Gray broke into a trot on the trail.

"I will! I promise!" Claire waved until they were out of sight.

She rushed back inside, stoked the fireplace in the parlor, and curled onto the couch, sobbing into her handkerchief at all the pain and loss Gray had endured. She cried for all the love she longed to give him but couldn't since he'd declared he'd never again wed.

Broken dreams, shattered hearts, and lost years

weighed heavy on her as emotions overtook her.

When her tears abated, she vowed to do everything she could to bring him and Maddie as much happiness as possible before she had to return to Philadelphia.

Chapter Sixteen

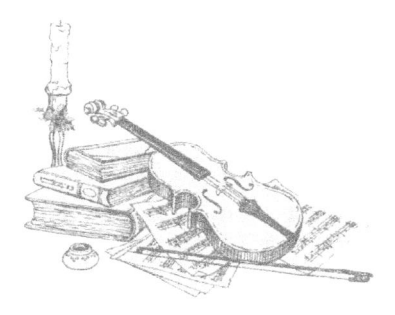

"This one, Daddy! It's our tree!" Maddie exclaimed, pointing to the pink ribbon tied to a branch.

"So it is," Gray said, grinning at his daughter as she hopped off the little sled and ran around the tree.

Since the day was pleasant with the sun shining brightly overhead, Gray decided to go cut down their tree and bring it home. He'd hoped Claire would come for a visit, but so far there had been no sign of her.

Perhaps she'd been put off or frightened by what he'd shared with her yesterday. He hadn't meant to reveal all the secrets of his past, but she had a way of digging it out of him whether he wanted her to or not.

Claire was the only person who knew the whole story of what had happened to him, to his family. He hadn't even told his father everything. And Luke and

Filly Granger just knew bits and pieces. He'd encountered the friendly banker within minutes of arriving in Hardman. He didn't know if it was the screaming infant he held in his arms or the look of utter despair on his face that led Luke to invite him to Granger House for a meal. He ended up staying with the generous couple for nearly a month while he purchased a piece of property, built a cabin with help from Luke, and prepared to disappear into the woods with Maddie.

It felt good to share the burdens he'd carried through four long years of solitude. He just hoped in the telling he hadn't pushed Claire away.

The sensible part of his brain told him to let her go and leave well enough alone. But his heart, that unpredictable wild thing in his chest that had started beating madly the first time he'd seen Claire, begged for him to forget about his ridiculous vow to never wed again and claim the gorgeous girl for his own.

Warring with himself was accomplishing nothing beyond giving him a headache, so he decided he and Maddie needed an adventure. He'd planned to cut down their tree Christmas Eve morning, but now seemed like a perfect time. If his wishes were granted, Claire would be at the cabin waiting for them when they returned.

He took a saw from the pack he'd carried and dropped down to his knees so he could better reach the trunk. It didn't take long before the tree wobbled. If someone had told him even five years ago he'd become proficient at sawing down trees, cooking, and building things other than violins, he would have thought they'd lost their grip on sanity. Here he was, though, able to not only care for himself alone in the woods, but also raise his daughter.

"Get behind me, Maddie, so I know you're safe," he cautioned, then sawed a few more strokes. The tree cracked and fell with a whoosh in the snow.

"You did it, Daddy! You cut down our tree!" Maddie clapped and cheered. "Now we can take it home?"

"We sure can, sweetheart." Gray set the tree on Maddie's sled then picked her up and settled her on his shoulders.

She tapped him on the head. "You forgot your hat again, Daddy."

"So I did." He looked up at her and grinned as he walked toward the cabin, pulling the sled with their tree. "Should I borrow your hat? Do you think I'd look good in pink?"

Maddie giggled and shook her head. "No, silly! My hat's too small and pink is for girls."

"Oh, of course. I must have forgotten," he said, grinning at her again.

It didn't take long to reach the cabin. Gray set Maddie on the porch then lifted the tree from the sled. He bounced it a few times to shake out the snow and any loose needles, then he carried it onto the porch and leaned it against the door.

"We'll need a bucket and some dirt," he said, turning toward the barn. "You stay right here, Maddie."

"Okay, Daddy," she said, leaning closer to the tree and sniffing the aromatic fragrance.

Gray hurried out to the barn and shoveled a few scoops of dirt into a large bucket and filled a second bucket then returned to the house. Maddie sang to the tree and gently rubbed a branch, as though it was a pet. He really needed to track down a puppy for her for Christmas. If he'd been thinking, he should have asked James, Tom, and Fred yesterday. Between the three men, he was sure one of them would know where he could find a dog.

He set the buckets inside the cabin then carried in the tree with Maddie dancing around, too excited to stand still.

"It's bee-you-ti-full, Daddy! The best tree in the whole world!"

Gray smiled as he set the tree in the larger bucket. He pumped a pitcher full of water and poured it in, then added the dirt from the second bucket, tamping it down. When he stepped back and the tree remained upright, he let out a breath of relief.

The tree was about his height and he'd placed it in front of the window farthest away from the fireplace. He didn't want it to dry out. Besides that, if Claire came to visit, she'd be able to see it as she approached the cabin.

Missing her, wanting to see her, talk to her, Gray decided to go visit Claire. She might have some ideas for decorations and go shopping with them at the Bruner's Mercantile. He could hardly wait to see the look on Maddie's face when they stepped into the store. A picture of her eyes wide with wonder and little mouth forming a perfect O drew out his smile.

Under normal circumstances, he would have taken the time to tame Maddie's wild hair, changed her into her dress, and drove the wagon, but for today, he'd leave her in pants with her hair twisted into a messy braid since he planned to walk to Fred's place on the trail. One thing he definitely intended to purchase today was a pair of skis. He'd seen how quickly Claire could cover the ground on the trail in them and wanted to be able to close the distance between her home and his in as little time as possible.

He wondered if Bruner's might have child-sized skis, too. He'd heard from Luke and also Fred that there wasn't a piece of wood in the world Blake Stratton couldn't turn into something amazing. Maybe he'd ask the man to make a pair for Maddie. He knew she'd have great fun with them and it would make it easier for her to get around on the snow, too.

Thoughts and possibilities filled him with anticipation as he pulled on his coat again.

"Are you going out to work, Daddy?" Maddie asked, shifting her gaze away from the tree to him.

"No, sweetheart. We're going to go visit Claire. How does that sound?"

"Wonnerful!" Maddie raced across the room and grabbed her coat, trying to shove her arms into the sleeves, yank on her boots, and tug on her mittens all at the same time.

"Slow down, Maddie Mae. We've got plenty of time, so let's get you bundled up first." Gray helped her with her coat, wrapped her scarf around her neck and pulled on her hat then he slid her feet into her boots. After she jerked on her mittens, he took her hand in his and hurried out the door, then raced back in to get a blanket to wrap Maddie in so she'd stay warm on the way to see Claire as she rode on the sled.

Maddie chattered excitedly as they made their way through the glade and turned onto the path that would take them to Hardman. Two months ago, it had been a trail made by deer that was barely visible in the woods. But after Claire's many visits, it was easy to see.

Almost as easy to spot as his feelings for the beautiful, fascinating, big-hearted girl.

With Christmas magic in the air and the hope of things to come, he was ready to move beyond his pain and grief to explore the possibility of a future with Claire.

He wouldn't ever be able to return to Philadelphia with her, but perhaps, just perhaps, she'd be willing to stay in Hardman with him.

If she would accept his affections and become his bride, he'd see about building a house in town in the spring. Once Maddie started school in the fall, he couldn't very well live miles from town and expect his little daughter to traipse through the woods twice a day. No, that wouldn't do at all.

He rather liked the idea of building a house somewhere in the vicinity of Fred's place. It was close enough to town to be an easy walk, but far enough out that he wouldn't feel neighbors closing in on every side. He'd noticed a place that looked abandoned just down the road from Fred.

If it was for sale, he'd definitely consider purchasing it, contingent on Claire being interested in his attentions and the request he intended to make to court her.

Buoyed by the dreams he hoped would become reality, Gray didn't notice the figure looming in the trees until he heard a pop and felt fire sear his shoulder as a bullet found it's mark. Terrified of what might happen to his daughter, Gray swept Maddie into his arms and raced behind the cover of a nearby grouping of trees.

"You can't hide there forever, Carter. Might as well give up now," the man hollered. "There's no one around to save you and I'm not leaving until you and the brat are dead. And if you thought that wild hair and bushy beard is a disguise, think again. I'd recognize you anywhere."

Gray thought the voice sounded familiar, but he couldn't place it. How had the killer found him in Hardman? Had he somehow tracked him down through Claire's message to her sister? Why, now that he'd finally decided to start living again, did this have to happen?

"Daddy?" Maddie clung to him, tears rolling down her cheeks. "I'm scared."

"I know, baby, but I'll keep you safe."

"Daddy, what's that?" Maddie asked, leaning back as blood soaked through the wool of his coat and dripped into the snow.

The coward had shot him in the back. He had to do something, quickly, before he lost too much blood to protect Maddie. Glancing around, he realized they weren't all that far from Fred's place. If he could distract the gunman, Maddie might be able to get away.

"Maddie, I want you to do exactly as I say. Do you understand?" he asked, setting her on her feet and dropping to one knee in front of her. He clasped her arms in his hands and looked square into her precious, beloved face.

"Yes, Daddy," she whispered, nodding her head and sniffling.

"I want you to stay right here. I'm going to go over to where that man is hiding and keep him busy while you run to Claire's house. When I yell for you to run, I want you to run as fast as you can. When you get there, tell Claire there's a bad man in the woods and to bring the sheriff. Can you do that, Maddie? Can I count on you?"

Maddie nodded and sniffled again, wiping her nose on her mitten then lifting her little chin. "I can do it, Daddy. I'll run fast as anything."

"I know you will, sweetheart. I love you so much, Maddie. Don't ever forget that." Gray pulled her against him and hugged her as though he'd never hold her again, never hear her giggles or see her eyes light with joy. He kissed her cheeks, tasting the salt of her tears, before he let her go. "Stay here, Maddie Mae. And listen for me to tell you to run. Understood?"

"Yes. I love you, Daddy."

Gray gave her one last look then silently worked his way through the woods until he made his way around to where the shooter stood with a rifle pointed in the direction of the trees where he'd left Maddie.

Without a weapon for defense and a wound that burned like the devil himself had inflicted it, Gray picked up a fallen branch and swung it, catching the man upside the head.

"Run, Maddie! Run!" Gray shouted and swung the branch again, hitting the man on the backs of his knees, knocking him to the ground. The gun dropped into the snow and the two of them scrambled for it.

Gray threw himself on top of it before the shooter could grab it. Using his elbows and toes to push himself forward, he tried to get away, but the man grabbed his legs and drew him back.

With a mighty kick, he heard his assailant bellow in pain followed by a loud crack. He rolled over to see blood spurting from the villain's nose and smeared all over his face. A face he knew all too well.

Chapter Seventeen

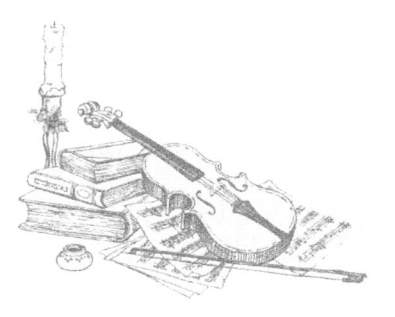

The crisp morning air added a rosy hue to Claire's cheeks as she stood in front of the dress shop, waiting for Abby to arrive first thing Monday morning. After Gray explained what had happened to him, the reasons he stayed in the woods with Maddie made sense.

However, she was glad he was ready to finally move beyond his fear of someone finding them and join in their community. She knew he'd enjoy it and Maddie would love having friends.

The fact Gray made it clear they had no future together wasn't something Claire was going to let bother her. In fact, she'd decided to look at it as an obstacle to overcome instead of the end of her dreams where that handsome, intriguing, thoroughly frustrating man was concerned.

She planned to pay Maddie and Gray a visit right after lunch, but this morning, she had shopping to do, starting with clothes for a certain little girl.

Claire waved when Abby stepped onto the boardwalk with her son holding tightly to her hand as he toddled along beside her.

"What are you doing here so early?" Abby asked as she hurried toward Claire.

When she reached the door of her shop, Claire swept Owen into her arms and kissed his cheeks, making him chortle with glee while his mother unlocked the door and motioned her inside.

"Down, Cwaire. Down!" Owen demanded the moment they stepped into the shop.

"Let's take your coat off first," Abby said, barely managing to remove his coat as he impatiently lunged forward.

"He's a determined little thing," Claire teased when Owen yanked free of his coat and raced to the corner where Abby kept toys. He picked up a toy train and began scooting it across the floor, making rumbling noises.

Abby hung up her coat and Owen's. "Is this a social call or are you in need of a dress?" she asked as she removed her hat and hung it on a rack in her back room next to the coats.

Claire removed her coat and set it on the counter than smiled at Abby. "I'd like to purchase clothing for a little girl."

Abby cocked an eyebrow. "Might that little girl be the one who clung to you at church yesterday?"

Claire nodded.

"She's adorable. Dressing her would be like dressing a doll."

"She is adorable," Claire said, thinking of how cute Maddie would look in the gown Abby had on display.

She walked over to it and fingered the lace on the sleeve of the pale blue gown. "I think the dress she wore yesterday may be the only one she has. I wanted to get her a few things for Christmas."

Abby moved beside her. "I normally wouldn't share this information, but her father purchased her a beautiful pink dress, along with a new red coat and muff. I'm sure he plans to give them to her for Christmas."

"Well, a girl can never have too many dresses. What else do you have in her size?"

Abby showed her the selection she had on hand and Claire settled on a dress the color of lilacs with purple embroidery down the front and along the hem. Delicate lace edged the wrists and collar.

"She'll absolutely love this. Maddie is quite fond of talking about fairies and princesses. I think this might make her feel like one," Claire said, holding out the little dress and admiring Abby's excellent craftsmanship.

"I have no idea if Mr. Carter bought her anything elsewhere. Would you like me to wrap this up for you?"

"Yes, please." Claire walked over to a stack of handkerchiefs and selected one with dainty violets embroidered along the edge. She added a tiny beaded handbag and a miniature lace parasol to her purchases. Maddie would have no use for it, but she'd love it just the same.

"Do you have a hat that would match the coat he purchased?"

Abby shook her head. "I do, but I won't sell it to you because he bought one with the coat."

Claire grinned at her friend. "Very well, then. I suppose the dress will be it today."

"When Erin was just a little older than Maddie, we purchased a child's size tea set for her. She spent hours and hours playing with it, and still does. She and Maura Granger have quite the tea parties from time to time."

Abby handed Claire the dress she'd wrapped in pink paper and tied with pink ribbon.

"That's a fabulous idea. She'd love to have a tea party when I go out to their place to visit, I'm sure. I'll see if the mercantile has any." Claire paid Abby for the gown, gave Owen a kiss on his cheek, then hurried out the door.

She entered the mercantile and smiled, inhaling a deep breath of the scents of furniture polish, kerosene, oranges, spices, and leather. There was nothing quite like those mingled aromas and she took another deep breath.

Due to the early hour, the mercantile was not yet busy. Aleta bustled around with a feather duster while George stocked canned goods on the shelves.

Claire eyed a basket full of oranges near the counter and planned to purchase several. Her gaze roved over the colorful displays full of Christmas cheer. Boxes of candies, jars of peppermints, and spools of red and green ribbon all bore testament to the rapidly approaching holiday.

With her sisters arriving on the train tomorrow, Claire knew she wouldn't have much time to spend with Gray and Maddie before Christmas, but she hoped to talk them into joining them Christmas Day for the big meal Elsa planned to serve. Maybe she'd even convince Gray to stay in town Christmas Eve and eat supper with them.

Glad she had gifts for her family wrapped and ready to tuck beneath the tree, she could focus her attention on putting together some fun surprises for Maddie and her father. Would Gray mind her buying the little girl a few things? She hoped not. He hadn't seemed too upset in the past when she brought things to them, but she didn't want to push him too much.

Now that she knew who he was, who he'd been, she realized he was most likely a very wealthy man in his own right from the performances he'd given, not to mention the fine violins he created.

She wondered how he'd feel about marrying a wealthy woman. Would he care one way or the other?

"Good morning, Claire! What brings you in the store so early in the day?" Aleta asked, setting her feather duster behind the counter and giving her a welcoming smile.

"I wanted to purchase a few more Christmas gifts. Do you have anything that would fit a four-year-old girl?" Claire asked, glancing back toward the ready-made clothing.

Aleta's smile broadened. "If you're thinking of shopping for a certain little girl who sat with you at church yesterday, I can tell you her father bought several things for her for Christmas, including underclothes, stockings, nightgowns, shirts and pants, a wool coat, boots, the cutest little leather shoes, a doll, and a clip for her hair. Oh, and I think there was a storybook, too."

Claire's eyes widened at the assortment of gifts Gray purchased for his daughter. For one who'd lectured her about not spoiling Maddie, he certainly had bought a wealth of gifts for her. Then again, he might not have intended to be back in town until spring and wanted to make sure she had plenty of clothes to make it through the winter months ahead.

She'd noticed Maddie's coat was getting too small and her boots would soon be pinching her toes. It made sense Gray would buy her bigger sizes to replace the things she'd soon outgrow.

The doll and storybook, though, made her smile.

"Do you have any tea sets for children?" Claire asked.

"Certainly. Right this way," Aleta said, leading her down an aisle to where three lovely tea sets sat on a shelf.

"This one," Claire said, selecting a delicate set painted with tiny pink roses. "She'll love this one."

"Wonderful. I'll take that up to the counter for you. Is there anything else I can help with?" Aleta picked up the tea seat and looked at Claire.

"Not at the moment. I think I'll just look around a bit." Aleta gave her a quick nod then rushed to the counter as a customer walked in with a shopping list in hand.

In no rush, she browsed around the store. She stopped at the fabric and notions section and chose three ribbons in pink, lavender, and red for Maddie. As she meandered back toward the front of the store, a display of razors and shaving soap caught her eye. Would Gray see the gift of a razor as a joke or be offended? As much as she'd love to see him with a clean-shaven face, she thought the gift a little too intimate to give him. Besides, she'd finished the gift she'd been working on for weeks Saturday morning before the skating party. It was wrapped and ready to present to him on Christmas Day.

The bell above the door jangled and Claire glanced that way as Luke Granger strode inside. He waved at Aleta then made a beeline for the bottles of perfume.

Claire followed him, aware he hadn't seen her, and spoke just before he reached out for a bottle of heliotrope perfume.

"She won't like that scent," she said, startling Luke so badly, he jumped slightly before spinning around and glaring at her.

"What in the dickens are you trying to do to me, Claire Baker?" he asked.

She laughed softly and pointed to the perfume bottles. "Prevent you from purchasing one Filly won't like."

"Who says I'm buying perfume for Filly?" Luke cocked an eyebrow upward. The look on his face dared her to comment.

She accepted the dare. "If you're buying perfume for someone other than your wife, I'll run through town screaming at the top of my lungs that Luke Granger is a lying, cheating, low-down skunk."

He scowled at her and looked around to see if anyone was listening to their conversation. Assured no one paid them any mind, he pointed to the display. "I was planning to get a bottle for Mother. Filly mentioned at breakfast this morning she thought we needed to find a little extra something to give her for Christmas. She's quite upset that Ginny and Blake left yesterday afternoon to head to England to see his family. They won't be back until February."

"Oh, that's right. I forgot all about them leaving. I'm sure Dora will miss having Ginny close by." Claire looked at the selection of fragrances and handed Luke a bottle of violet-scented perfume. "I believe that is the fragrance Dora prefers." She selected a second bottle of a soft, floral scent and gave it to him with a smile. "And Filly will love that one."

He gave her a pleased smile. "Thank you for helping. Want to pick one out for Maura, too?"

Claire studied the bottles and chose one with a very light scent. "You might want to pour half of that in another bottle and dilute it with water."

"Good idea, otherwise she's likely to douse herself with enough to choke a mule."

Claire grinned and walked with Luke to the counter.

"I failed to ask what you're doing out and about so early this morning. You're either at home or helping Elsa at this time of day."

"Elsa has all the help she needs today. I was doing a little Christmas shopping before I spend the afternoon with friends," Claire said, standing beside Luke as he paid Aleta for the perfume. The storekeeper tucked the bottles into boxes and wrapped them with foil paper.

"The one in green paper is Filly's, and the red one is Maura's," Aleta said, as though she knew for whom the gifts were intended.

Luke took the three packages and tipped his head to them both. "Enjoy your day." He smirked at Claire. "And stay out of trouble."

"You take the fun out of everything, Luke Granger," Claire said, affecting a pout, before she grinned and waved as he left the store.

"Anything else?" Aleta asked as she rang up Claire's purchases.

"I think that should do it," she said, paying the woman and accepting the packages she handed to her.

She was just walking out of the store when a small trunk, painted with a woodland fairy scene caught her eye. "Is that trunk for sale?" she asked, stepping back to the counter.

"Which one?" Aleta asked, stepping around the counter.

Claire pointed to the trunk tucked beneath a table with a keg of nails in front of it.

"Oh, that Alice! She wants that trunk and has hidden it a dozen times since it came in." Aleta lowered her voice. "What that little sneak doesn't know is that I ordered two of them and already hid one for her upstairs."

"I'd like to purchase that one, if I may."

Aleta nodded. "Of course." She caught her husband's eye. "George! Would you come dig this little trunk out of hiding? Alice has been at it again, but Miss Baker would like to purchase it."

A few minutes later, Claire left the store with a promise from George to have Percy deliver the trunk, filled with her purchases, as soon as he got out of school for the day.

Pleased with her purchases and imagining how much Maddie would love the trunk, she hurried home and changed into her britches, a warm woolen shirt, and her boots. She didn't bother braiding her hair, leaving it pinned up. After yanking on her coat, wrapping a warm scarf around her neck and ears, she tugged on her gloves and hurried outside.

Quickly strapping on her skis, she grabbed her poles and pushed away from the yard, eager to see Gray and Maddie.

Would he welcome her, now that he'd revealed his entire past? Would he act hesitant around her, or uncomfortable?

She hoped not, because she fully intended to win his heart. And whether he knew it or not, he'd already claimed hers.

Claire had just skied around a bend when she saw a little figure running toward her, wild curls flying behind her. For Maddie to be out here alone was unthinkable.

Had something terrible happened to Gray? Was he injured? What would drive Maddie to run through the woods alone?

Claire raced toward her, sending prayers heavenward.

Chapter Eighteen

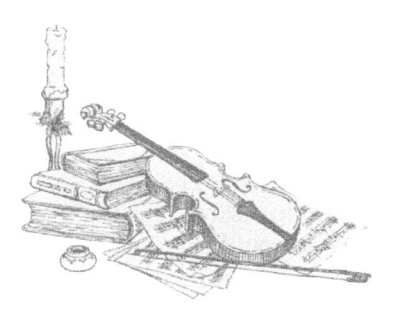

"Claire!" Maddie screamed, waving her little hands above her head. "Help, Claire! Help!"

Claire skied as though her life depending on reaching Maddie as quickly as possible. She slid to a stop, dropped the poles and pulled Maddie into her arms as the child collapsed against her.

"What's wrong, darling? What's happened? Where's your daddy?" Claire looked down the trail, expecting Gray to be running after his daughter.

"There's a bad man," Maddie sobbed. "He hurt my daddy. Daddy told me to find you and to tell you to get the sheriff."

"Then let's go," Claire said, dropping the pack she'd carried on her back into the snow. "Climb on my back, Maddie, and hang on tight."

THE CHRISTMAS MELODY

The little girl obeyed without question, holding so tightly, she nearly choked Claire, but she didn't take time to worry about it. She snatched up her ski poles, turned around and raced back toward home. She sailed past Fred's house and continued right into town, stopping only when she reached the sheriff's office. Rather than remove her skis, she lifted a pole and banged it against the door.

"What in thunderation is all the racket out here?" the sheriff asked, opening the door.

At the sight of Claire with Maddie, he hurried down the steps and gave her his full attention. "What's happened, Miss Baker?"

"I found Maddie in the woods. She said a bad man hurt her father and he sent her to get the sheriff."

"Let me get my horse and we'll be on our way." The sheriff took off running down the street in the direction of the livery.

"Maddie, is your daddy on the trail to my house or somewhere else?"

"On the trail," Maddie said, as Claire swung her down and set her on the boardwalk someone had shoveled clear of snow. "We were coming to get you so we could decorate our Christmas tree. Daddy was so happy. Then the bad man hurt my daddy."

Maddie started crying again and Claire picked her up, holding her on one hip as she struggled to ski up the street. She hurried to the bank and rapped on the door with a ski pole. Luke was quick to pull it open, giving her a startled glance.

"What's wrong?" he asked.

"Something's happened to Gray. The sheriff is getting his horse. Can you take Maddie to stay with Filly?" she asked, starting to hand the child over to Luke.

Maddie latched onto Claire with strength beyond

what a small child should possess. "No. I wanna go with you. I need to help my daddy!"

"Sweetheart, your daddy would want you to be warm and safe until the sheriff catches the bad man who hurt him. Will you please stay with Filly and Cullen? They'll take good care of you."

Maddie gave her a long look, then slowly nodded her head.

"That's a good girl," Claire said, kissing Maddie's cheek then handed her to Luke.

"I'll run her over to the house and be along shortly."

"Thank you, Luke. I appreciate it," Claire said, turning around and speeding through town. She reached the livery as the sheriff led his horse outside with Fred beside him on Festus, his trusty mount.

"You stay here, Claire," Fred said, as he swung into the saddle.

"I'm going, Fred, and nothing or nobody can convince me to stay," she gave her nephew a defiant look then headed off toward his house. The horses passed her as they raced through the snow, but she wasn't far behind.

About halfway to the glade, drops of blood stained the snow bright crimson.

"My word," Claire whispered and wondered what had happened when the splashes of red grew bigger.

"No!" they heard someone shout and the sound of a gunshot echoed through the trees.

"That way! Over there!" the sheriff said as he and Fred jumped off their horses and ran on foot in the direction of the shot.

Claire hastily removed her skis and hurried after them, afraid of what she would find. She rounded a large grouping of trees to see two men in the snow, red seeping from their wounds into the pristine coat of white on the ground.

One appeared unconscious while the other looked at her in relief.

"Gray!" Claire rushed to his side, dropping to her knees and cradling his face between her hands. She kissed his cold lips and pulled back, grateful he was still alive. "You'll be okay. Promise me you'll be okay."

"I don't think I'll be departing my life here on earth today, but I'd sure like to get the bullets dug out of my side and shoulder. They hurt like blazes." Gray gave her a weak smile.

"Who's this fella?" the sheriff asked, toeing the other man with his boot.

"That man murdered four people that I know of, and attempted to kill me on numerous occasions, including today," Gray said, glancing over at him. "His name is Wendell Ness. He's married to my sister."

"What?" Claire glanced from Gray to the man sprawled beside him. "Victoria's husband was the one who killed your brothers, your wife, and your nanny?"

"That's what he admitted to as he attempted to kill me a few minutes ago. You can get the full story out of him when he comes to. I knocked him a good one with the butt of his rifle. Only problem was that it discharged and nicked my side," Gray said, grinning at Fred. "I don't suppose you could help me up?"

"I'd be happy to," Fred said, reaching down to give Gray a hand while Claire supported his wounded side. He swayed as soon as he was upright, but Fred brought his horse over and mounted, then pulled Gray up behind him. "I'll get him to the doc, if you want to stay with the criminal, Sheriff."

"I'll just truss this one up like a Christmas goose while he's not going to put up any fight and haul him to the jail. You go on with Fred, Miss Baker. I won't be far behind." The sheriff gave her an encouraging smile as he fastened a pair of handcuffs on the criminal's wrists.

Claire ran back to where she left her skis, fumbled with the buckles in her distraught state, and finally got them on. As she skied toward town, she noticed the pack she'd dropped in the snow and lifted it without even stopping.

Luke caught up to her a few minutes later.

"You might go help the sheriff with his prisoner," she hollered at him and kept going. Since Luke didn't say anything, she glanced back to see him riding in the direction she'd just come.

Fred was just helping Gray inside the doctor's office when she caught up with them. In no time, she was beside Gray, helping support him as the doctor directed them to an examination room.

"Two bullet wounds, one in the shoulder and one in the side," Fred said, since Gray had passed out.

"We best get 'em dug out of there, then." The doctor took a look at Claire and shook his head. "You go on, Miss Baker. I've got enough help without you here."

Reluctantly, she backed from the room and took a seat in the waiting room. She paced the floor, wrung her hands, prayed, paced some more, and jumped when Fred's hand settled on her shoulder.

"The bullets are out and he's going to be just fine. He's just weak from losing all that blood, but Doc said he'll likely make a quick recovery."

"Oh, that's wonderful news," Claire said, giving Fred a hug.

He held her and patted her back comfortingly.

"Thank you, Fred, for your help."

"I'm more than happy to give it. I'll run over to the jail to see if the sheriff needs a hand. Are you going to check on Maddie?" Fred asked, standing at the door.

"I'm sure she's worried. I'll pop over there, then come back to sit with Gray."

Fred pointed to her coat. "You might change before you go, or you're likely to scare Maddie half to death."

Claire glanced down at her coat, smeared with Gray's blood. She took it off and tossed it on a chair, then followed Fred outside.

"You can't be out here without a coat," he said, starting to remove his to give her.

"I'll grab one from Abby's shop on my way to Granger House," she said, breaking into a jog and heading down the street.

People gaped at her, dressed as she was in britches and boots, but she paid them no mind. She raced into Abby's shop. The woman stared at her open-mouthed for a moment before she hastened over to her.

"What's happened?" Abby asked, placing an arm around her waist.

"Gray was shot. Blood on coat. Need a new one," Claire said, afraid if she spoke in complete sentences, she'd lose the tenuous hold she had on her emotions and burst into tears.

Abby yanked a beautiful blue coat off a rack and held it for Claire. She slipped her arms into the satin-lined sleeves. In any other circumstance, she would have admired the soft velvet and furry ruff around the collar. For now, she just needed something to keep her warm.

"I'll pay you later. Thank you."

"You're welcome. If you need anything else, let me know. Chauncy and I will be praying for Mr. Carter's recovery."

Claire squeezed her hand. "Thank you, Abby."

She hastened out the door and ran most of the way to Granger House. After tapping on the kitchen door, she let herself inside, but no one was there. She wandered down the hall toward the sound of voices in the parlor and found Filly in a rocking chair near the fire with Maddie curled up in her arms and Cullen standing at her knee, patting Maddie's leg.

"Maddie owie," Cullen said as Claire entered the room. "Maddie sad."

Claire gently brushed a hand over the toddler's head then lifted Maddie into her arms. The child clung to her, sobbing.

"How long has she been like this?" Claire asked Filly over Maddie's head.

"Since Luke left her. I thought she might cry herself to sleep, but the tears just keep coming." Filly placed a hand on Maddie's back. "She's about to break my heart."

"Mine, too," Claire said, blinking back her own tears. "Maddie, darling, you must stop crying. Your daddy is going to be just fine. He's at the doctor's office right now, resting. He'll be fine, I promise."

Maddie didn't appear to hear a word Claire said. She took a seat on the couch and tried to push Maddie back, but the child wouldn't loosen her hold.

"Madison Mae Carter, you listen to me," Claire said in a commanding tone. "Your daddy is going to be fine. He's going to be fine. If you want to go see him, you need to stop crying."

Maddie hiccupped, sniffled twice, then raised her head. "Daddy isn't deaded?"

"No, your daddy will be fine, sweetheart. He just needs some time to get better." Claire brushed curls away from Maddie's face. "If you stop those tears and wash your face, I'll take you to see him."

"Really?" Maddie asked, looking uncertain, as though she couldn't quite yet believe she hadn't been left an orphan.

"Really. Come on, let's go wash your face, and maybe even tame that mane of hair a bit," Claire offered Maddie a warm smile.

Maddie nodded and allowed Claire to take her to

the bathroom where they washed her face and hands then finger combed her hair.

Filly was in the kitchen with Cullen when Claire and Maddie entered it.

"Would you mind terribly if I bring her back in a little while?"

"Not at all, Claire. Whatever you need, please just let us know," Filly said, giving her a hug, then cupping Maddie's chin in her hand. "When you come back, we'll have hot chocolate and those cookies you love so much."

Maddie merely bobbed her head in agreement, clinging tightly to Claire's hand as they left. All the way to the doctor's office, the little girl remained silent. When they stepped inside, Luke was just walking out the door.

"He'll be fine," he said, patting Maddie on the shoulder. "Would you like me to take her back to the house?"

Claire glanced down at Maddie's little face, pinched with worry. "I'll bring her by in a bit."

Luke nodded once then left.

Claire took a deep breath and led Maddie down the hall to the room where Gray recuperated from surgery. He wasn't yet awake, but his color was no longer ashen and he took in strong, regular breaths.

"Daddy?" Maddie whispered, clinging to Claire as they stood in the doorway.

Claire hunkered down and wrapped her arms around Maddie. "The doctor had to do surgery on your daddy and it made him sleepy, but he's okay. See how his chest goes up and down, that means he's just sleeping, sweetheart. You can talk to him if you like."

Maddie took a step forward, then glanced back at Claire. "You come, too."

Claire stood and held Maddie's hand. Together, they approached Gray's bed. Maddie leaned forward and pressed a kiss to her father's cheek. "I love you, Daddy. Get all better so we can decorate our tree."

Maddie gave her father's cheek another kiss then moved back, obviously ready to go.

Claire picked her up and carried her outside, heading back toward Granger House. She'd only taken a few steps that direction when a sleigh full of faces she recognized came into view. Her sisters waved, full of laughs and smiles.

"What in the world are you doing dressed like that and who is this beautiful child?" Ari asked as her husband stepped out of the sleigh and swung her onto the boardwalk in front of Claire.

"Oh, Ari!" Claire struggled to hold onto her emotions. "This is Maddie, Gray's daughter and it's just... Oh, it's been…"

"Give me that precious girl," Bett said, taking Maddie from Claire. "I'm Aunt Bett, Claire's sister. Did I hear your name is Maddie?"

Assured Maddie was in good hands, Claire allowed Ari to enfold her in a hug. Heath wrapped his arms around both of them, offering strength and warmth.

Claire couldn't stop the tears that rolled down her cheeks or the emotion that left her knees weak.

"What on earth has transpired?" Ari asked when Claire's tears subsided. Heath handed her a pristine handkerchief.

She mopped at her tears then gave her family a watery smile. "Let's go to the bakery. I need one of Elsa's bracing cups of tea."

When they were all seated and Maddie was occupied in the kitchen with Elsa and the promise of milk and cookies, Claire told them what little she knew of what happened with Gray and his brother-in-law.

"This is my fault," Claire said, taking a shuddering breath. "I should never have asked if you were familiar with Gray's name. He trusted me to keep it a secret and I failed miserably."

Ari and Bett exchanged looks. "We're as much to blame as you. After you inquired about Grayson and we happened to share dinner with his sister, we went to call on her one day to find out more about his disappearance. Poor Victoria really and truly thought he'd perished in the fire that claimed his wife."

"Tell her what else happened," Heath said, giving his wife a pointed look.

"Well, it was the strangest thing. A few days after that, Victoria's husband came by our house. We all found him odd from the start, but that's neither here nor there," Ari said. "Anyway, he asked a dozen questions about you and Hardman, and how long you'd been here, and how hard it was to reach Hardman. It wasn't a day later that I went to find your latest letter and it had disappeared. I turned the house upside down trying to find it, and it was just gone. We assume Mr. Ness appropriated it, seeking information about Grayson."

"We had no proof he'd taken the letter, but it made us suspicious, just the same," Heath said, placing a hand on his wife's slender shoulder. "I decided to drop by the Carter & Sons office only to find Victoria there, upset because her husband hadn't come home the previous evening. With a bit of sleuthing, it was discovered Ness purchased a train ticket headed west."

"So we made haste to get here, hoping to arrive before he did. It appears we're a bit too late to be of any assistance," Bett said, offering Claire an apologetic look. "I'm sorry for the part we played in Grayson being assaulted by that horrid man. I can't even fathom what he's done to that family."

"I don't understand the reason behind his actions," Ari said. "Why would he kill his wife's family? What possible purpose could it serve?"

"I will answer that question," an elderly man said as he walked inside the bakery.

Heath and Clark both rose and shook his hand, then pulled another chair up at the table for him.

"Claire, this is William Carter, Grayson's father," Heath said in introduction.

"Mr. Carter, what a wonderful surprise to see you here. Welcome to Hardman," Claire said, suddenly aware of her britches and boots and hair that had fallen out of its pins hours ago.

"I wish I'd journeyed here under better circumstances, but it's nice to meet you, Miss Baker." The man took the seat Heath indicated.

Ari hopped up and breezed into the kitchen, returning with a cup of steaming cider and a warm cinnamon bun, placing them in front of Mr. Carter.

"Thank you, my dear," he said, taking an appreciative sip of the cider. "I never approved of my daughter's husband. He's a money-grubbing, lazy wastrel. My daughter refused to listen to reason, charmed by Wendell and his empty promises. She married him and then begged me to allow him to work with us in the family business."

Mr. Carter scoffed and took another sip of his cider. "Wendell failed, quite spectacularly, at every job we gave him to do. By that time, all three of my sons had joined me as partners in the business. If something had happened to me, they would have inherited the business equally. Victoria understood that was the way things had been done for centuries and she also knew her husband was not earning his keep. There wasn't a single job we could give him to do that he didn't botch, so I created a position that basically kept him out of our way while he hobnobbed potential clients."

"But how did he go from doing that to murdering your family?" Claire asked, realizing only after she spoke how blunt she sounded.

"He was jealous of my sons, of the work they accomplished, the inheritance that awaited them. Somewhere in his convoluted mind, he decided if he could eliminate my boys, then I'd leave everything to Victoria, and it would be his. He had no idea how much money we made in a year, or how much work was truly involved in keeping the business going, but he wanted it all for himself." Mr. Carter sighed. "Victoria is beside herself that her husband is behind the deaths of her brothers and poor, sweet Laura, as well as our beloved nanny. She's staying with my sister in Boston for the holiday where she can get away from everything for a while."

"But how did you find out what Ness had planned?" Heath asked.

"When Victoria said her husband had disappeared, I couldn't help but wonder if he'd somehow discovered Grayson's whereabouts. I've always known where my son had placed himself in exile, but that was a secret I would have taken to my grave. At all costs, he and I wanted to protect Maddie. I'd questioned Wendell's motives many times over the years, pondered if perhaps he wasn't the criminal who brought so much pain to my family. For the sake of my daughter, though, I refused to believe it. However, as soon as she said he'd not come home I knew trouble was afoot. I packed my bag and left immediately. We must have been on the same train, in different cars."

"If we'd known you were traveling to Hardman, we would have given you a ride from Heppner, sir," Clark said.

"I appreciate that young man." Mr. Carter took a bite of the cinnamon bun and a look of pleasure passed over his face. "That is delicious."

"How did you happen to come to the bakery, sir?"

Claire asked.

"The first stop I made when I arrived in town was the sheriff's office. I was quite pleased to see Wendell behind bars where he belongs. The sheriff assured me he'll spend the rest of his days in prison. From there, I visited Grayson at the doctor's office. Fine gentleman, the doctor. He suggested I check the bakery to find the girl who rescued my granddaughter and saved my son." Mr. Carter wiped his mouth on a napkin. "Is it possible I might meet Maddie?"

"Oh, of course!" Claire jumped up and went into the kitchen where Maddie sat at the table on Anna Jenkins' lap, eating a cookie and coloring.

"Maddie, there's someone very special here who'd like to meet you," Claire said, kneeling in front of the child. "Would you come with me?"

"Who is it?" Maddie asked, sliding off Anna's lap and taking Claire's hand.

"Your grandfather. He's your daddy's father."

"My daddy's daddy?" Maddie asked as they walked through the kitchen.

"Mr. Carter, this is Madison Mae Carter, your granddaughter," Claire said, offering Maddie an encouraging smile when the little one held back, suddenly shy.

The elder man's chair scraped back as he stood from the table and walked around the table to where Maddie stood, leaning against Claire's legs.

"Oh, Maddie, my dear, I'd recognize you anywhere. You look like your father with your mother's beautiful hair." Mr. Carter knelt in front of the child. "I'm your grandfather."

"Hello, grandfather," Maddie said, reaching out to touch his face. "You don't have hair like my daddy. Your face is soft and smooth."

"So it is," the older man said, tears glistening in his

eyes. "May I give you a hug, child?"

Maddie nodded and wrapped her arms around his neck.

Claire blinked back the tears that stung her eyes then met the gazes of her sisters, knowing a Christmas miracle had happened that day. A family torn apart by tragedy was about to be reunited.

Chapter Nineteen

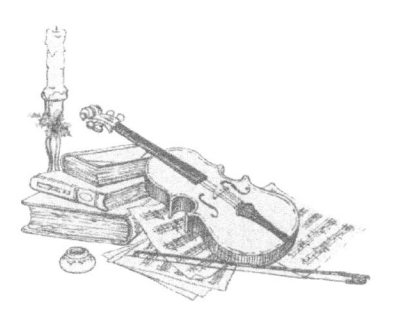

Gray dreamed his body was on fire, burning in the flames that consumed the home he and Laura had built and filled with hopes and dreams. He envisioned her as the last time he'd seen her, lifeless on the entry floor next to a woman who'd been like a mother to him.

Tormented by the images, by the pain, he tried to pull himself from such a dark place.

The soft, sweet voice of his daughter pierced through the anguished musings in his mind. He heard her say she loved him and struggled to make his way back to her, to tell her he loved her too.

Although she didn't speak, he sensed Claire was there, too. Her fragrance wafted around him, bringing a rush of longing and comfort. His mind quieted and he rested.

Slowly, he awakened, aware of a searing pain in his shoulder and one only slightly less horrid clawing at his side. It took him a moment to recall what had transpired earlier that day when he'd looked into the face of his sister's husband and seen only a crazed monster. To think Wendell had been the one who killed his brothers. He'd poisoned Cliff and hired someone to tip over Warner's boat then rendered him unconscious in the water, resulting in his death. Wendell had gleefully confessed to every nightmarish thing he'd done to Gray's family, from hiring someone to shoot and stab him, to the death of Laura and Nanny.

Wendell hadn't expected him to return home quite so soon. He'd planned to kill them all, set the house on fire, and drag Gray's body outside, making it look like he'd shot himself. Only Gray had arrived home early and managed to save Maddie.

Had his daughter gotten away? Was she well? Had Claire found her?

Thoughts of Claire, of how tenderly she'd kissed him, how she'd raced to help him heedless to her own safety, settled in his mind. Wanting to see her, to thank her, he opened his eyes and sucked in a gasp.

A man he never thought to see this side of heaven sat beside the bed, looking as though he was deep in prayer.

"Papa?" Gray asked, blinking his eyes twice to make sure he wasn't dreaming.

"Grayson," his father said, reaching out and taking his hand between his. "Oh, my son."

Tears welled in his father's eyes and Gray felt the sting of emotion burning up his throat. "It's so good to see you, Papa. What are you doing here?"

His father smiled and released his hand. He removed a white linen square from his pocket and dabbed at his eyes and nose, then cleared his throat.

"I've often wondered over the years if Wendell was involved in underhanded schemes. Your sister came to me the other day, distraught because her husband hadn't come home and had all but disappeared. He'd been to visit the Baker girls, inquiring about the youngest daughter being here in Hardman. When I heard about that, I knew he was on his way to find you. I didn't think a telegram would do any good, so I boarded the first train heading West and thought I'd come to your rescue. Only, I arrived a little too late."

"I'm so glad you came, Papa. It's been far too long since I've seen you." Gray squeezed his father's hand. "I've dreaded this day for four years, but now that it's come. I'm glad it's over."

"Wendell will spend the rest of his life behind bars and you'll never again have to worry about someone trying to cut your life or Maddie's short."

"Is Maddie well? Have you seen her?" Gray asked, trying to push himself up. A wave of nausea rolled over him and he settled back against the pillows.

"The doctor said you needed to stay still and rest, so you best follow his orders," William Carter said, giving Gray a pointed look. "My first stop was the sheriff's office. He said I'd find you here. The doctor thought Maddie was most likely with the Baker girls at the bakery."

Gray gave his father a questioning glance. "Claire's sisters have arrived. I didn't think they were due in until tomorrow."

"Well, it appears reinforcements are filling the town, even if we've missed all the excitement," William said with a grin and rose to his feet. He brushed a hand over Gray's head in a gesture that was familiar from childhood days. "You really do look like you live in some primitive dwelling in the woods. I would hardly have recognized you."

Gray lifted his good hand to his face and rubbed his jaw. "I've gotten so used to all this fur, I might freeze my face if I finally shave it off."

His father chuckled. "What does Miss Claire think of that beard?"

Gray felt heat climb up his neck.

His father's chuckles increased. "I see. Well, I believe I'll go in search of her and meet my granddaughter."

"She'll be excited to meet you, Papa." Gray felt his eyelids grow heavy and fought to keep them open. His father patted his head, as though he was a little boy instead of a man grown.

"Just rest for now, Gray. I'm pleased beyond words you will make a full recovery. I love you, son."

"I love you, too, Papa. Thank you for coming."

Gray's eyes drifted shut before his father left the room.

The next time he awakened, he knew Claire was there. Her tantalizing fragrance filled his nose and her presence soothed his spirit.

He opened his eyes and looked into her beautiful face.

"Hello," she whispered, taking his hand in hers and bringing it to her lips, kissing the tips of his fingers.

"Claire," he said, uncertain how to express the depths of his gratitude for all she'd done for him, for Maddie. Suddenly overwhelmed by the enormity of it all, a lump clogged his throat and he found it impossible to speak.

Claire must have sensed his turmoil, because she leaned forward and brushed her fingers across his brow then trailed them through his hair. "Maddie is just fine, Gray. My family arrived earlier today and she's in real threat of being hugged and kissed to death by Ari and Bett. Heath and Clark have taken quite a shine to her, too. But they are going to have to do battle with your father to claim much of her attention or affection. Dora and Greg Granger offered to allow them all to stay at their place, but Fred has invited them all to stay at his house. He and Elsa have plenty of room and Ari and Bett love being on the farm. When I left them at the bakery, Fred promised to show Heath how to milk the cow and Clark volunteered to feed the hog. Your father was busy showing Maddie how to dance a jig. Maybe he should give up making violins and consider a career as a dancer and entertainer."

Gray smiled, grateful she chose to joke and lighten the heaviness of the situation. "You are an angel, Claire. Maddie and I, we wouldn't have... I wouldn't be..."

Claire placed her fingers on his lips and silenced him, then followed it with a tender kiss. "Don't tax yourself, Gray. You need to rest so you can heal quickly and get back on your feet in time to celebrate Christmas. Don't forget, you promised to bring Maddie to all the Christmas Eve festivities and I'm holding you to it."

"Clarice Baker, I love you," he said, unable to hold in his feelings for this girl a moment longer. "I've loved you since the day you spied on Maddie as she played in the glade. You're amazing and independent, strong and giving, smart and crazy, and I love you."

"I love you, too, Gray, more than anything in this world." Claire kissed him again then stood. "Doc said not to stay too long once you awakened. Sleep is what you need, but I'll be back soon."

It was then Gray noticed Claire still had on her britches and boots. Her hair was a mess, having fallen out of the elaborate updo she'd no doubt fashioned that morning. She looked tired, yet so lovely.

"You're beautiful, songbird. More beautiful than a dream," he said, drifting back to sleep once more.

Chapter Twenty

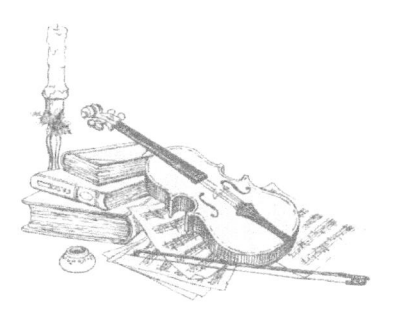

"Where do you think you're going?" Claire asked Christmas Eve morning.

Gray stood at the door, gingerly pulling on a new coat and wrapping a warm scarf around his neck.

"There are things I need from the cabin for Christmas," he said, glancing at his father who tugged on his gloves. "Papa will go with me."

"I forbid it!" Claire said, moving in front of the door in an attempt to keep him from leaving.

Gray merely kissed her cheek and nudged her out of the way. "I promise we'll be back in plenty of time for the Christmas carnival. We don't want to miss the magic show."

"I don't know that I've ever witnessed the splendor of prestidigitation," William said with a broad smile.

Claire laughed and moved out of their way. "You've been talking to Luke Granger."

The older man nodded. "Indeed, I have." He patted Claire on the arm as Gray opened the door. "I promise we'll take good care of him."

"We? Who else is going?" Claire asked, following them outside Fred's house where they all were staying.

Fred drove a sleigh up near the door and stopped. Heath and Clark sat beside him.

"I should have known," Claire said, fisting her hands on her waist and glaring at her brothers-in-law. "At least don't let him try to lift anything!"

"We'll make him behave," Heath said, waving to her as Gray and William climbed in the sleigh and Fred snapped the reins.

Claire rubbed her hands on her arms in the nippy December air and hurried back into the house. Bett had gone to visit Abby Dodd and Ari had taken Maddie to the bakery since it was a fun place to be on Christmas Eve with people popping in and out.

Alone in the big house, Claire looked for something to keep her hands busy as she waited for Gray. The dishes had been all washed, dried, and put away. The beds were all made, the rooms tidy. They'd even decorated a tree yesterday and hung it with Elsa's heirloom ornaments as well as new keepsakes Ari and Bett had brought along as gifts.

Maddie had squealed with delight at the sight of the tree when it was decorated. Claire could only imagine her joy and excitement when they returned home after Christmas Eve services this evening and lit the hundred tiny candles on the tree. In the morning, there would be gifts to open, but Claire thought the best gift of all was having Gray alive and near.

He hadn't made any more declarations of love, not that they'd spent a moment alone in the past two days, but she rather hoped he'd tell her again that he loved her.

Perhaps he'd just been under the influence of pain and whatever medication the doctor had given him to ease it.

Conflicted and tormented by her thoughts, she yanked on her coat and gloves, slapped on a hat, and left the house, determined to find something to occupy her mind and time.

Elsa could probably use help at the bakery, or she could go to Granger Mansion where the Christmas carnival would start in a few hours and see if anyone there might need an extra hand.

Quickly deciding Elsa probably had enough people underfoot this morning, especially with Percy Bruner dogging Anna's every step, she turned down a side street and strode to the impressive home Dora and Greg Granger owned.

The first time the Christmas carnival was held there, the couple had not yet moved in, so the house with its large rooms stood empty.

In following years, though, the tradition continued. Greg hired strong young men to move furniture out of the way during the festivities. There were games for the children, an auction of handmade items crafted by the Hardman School students, a delicious luncheon, and a magic show provided by Alex Guthry.

As she hurried up the walk, Claire thought about last Christmas Eve when Fred had swept Elsa off her feet and down the aisle, marrying her before the festivities began. Oh, it had been so romantic and sweet to watch her nephew fall in love with the beautiful baker.

Claire knew romance fairly floated in the air in Hardman during the holiday season. Luke and Filly Granger had wed in November, but she could think of several couples who'd entered wedded bliss between Christmas Eve and New Year's Day.

How she longed to be counted among them as Grayson Carter's bride. Claire felt selfish for wanting him all to herself when he'd just had two days with his father after years apart. She couldn't even imagine how she'd feel if she had to spend that much time away from Ari and Bett, even Heath and Clark. She loved them all dearly and would miss them completely if they'd had to endure such a long separation.

Pulling her thoughts together, she rang the bell and waited. It didn't take long for Greg Granger to open the front door, festooned with a pine wreath and a fluffy red bow.

"Warmest greetings of the season, Claire," Greg said, stepping back and motioning her inside the house. The smell of ham and yeasty rolls filled the air, along with spices and apples from the large pot of cider she knew was simmering on the stove.

"Good morning, Mr. Granger. I wondered if perhaps an extra pair of hands might be useful."

"Of course. Come on back to the kitchen. Filly and her helpers are there." He hung her coat on a rack near the door. Greg led the way through the house to the kitchen where Filly and several other women Claire knew laughed as they prepared food for the feast they'd set out at noon.

"More help has arrived, Filly!" Greg said, over the noise of clanging pans and friendly chatter.

"Hello, Claire!" Filly wiped her hands on a dishtowel and gave her a hug. "What brings you by so early? I assumed you'd be busy with your sisters and Gray."

"Gray talked the men into taking him to the cabin for Christmas things, whatever that means. Bett has gone shopping and Ari took Maddie to the bakery." Claire accepted the apron Mrs. Kellogg handed to her.

"Leaving you alone and needing to keep busy?"

Filly asked with a knowing smile.

"Exactly. I can't cook, as you well know, but I can chop or peel or set out dishes." Claire looked around the room. "Put me to work, ladies."

An hour later, Claire sent Maura Granger to the bakery to let Ari and Elsa know where to find her. Maddie and Maura wanted to play, so Maura returned accompanied by Maddie and Ari.

Claire watched as her sister took charge of the children, engaging them in activities to keep them occupied. Noting the special glow on her sister's face, Claire rushed over to her and engulfed her in a hug.

"What was that for, not that I'm complaining, mind you," Ari said with a laugh.

"How could you not tell me? Does Bett know?" Claire asked, hugging her again.

"Know what?" Ari asked.

"Don't play coy with me. When is the baby due?" she pulled back and glared at her sister.

Ari's face softened and her hands settled on her stomach. "We just found out a few days before we left, so no one knows except Bett and Clark. I meant to tell you, but things have been a little hectic since we arrived."

"Congratulations," Claire wrapped her sister in another hug. "I'm so happy for you and Heath."

"We are happy, too, and so looking forward to the arrival of a little one. I thought it might be good to practice with the children here, since there are so many of them of varying ages." Ari glanced over to where Maura and Maddie played with a set of blocks. "Maddie is amazing. You'll make a great mother to her, Claire."

"Only if her father gets around to proposing. I'm not so sure he's interested." Ari's laughter made Claire scowl at her. "I don't see anything humorous about it."

Ari patted her on the shoulder. "You are the only

one who can't see how infatuated Grayson is with you. He positively dotes on you. Give him time to heal and then I'm sure he'll be ready to court you properly."

"He can skip the courting properly part and get right down to business." Claire shot her sister a saucy grin. "I wouldn't mind at all."

Ari shook her head, but couldn't contain her laugh. "You're a loon, Clarice Baker."

"So I've been told."

Bett arrived with Abby Dodd and then the guests began to stream inside. It was nearly time to kick off the festivities and the men still hadn't returned.

Claire had just set a bowl of mashed potatoes on the dining room table when she caught a glimpse of Fred and Elsa in the other room.

She started their way, but the bustling crowd kept her from reaching them. Ahead of her, she saw Heath speaking to Luke Granger, so she knew the men had returned, but Gray was nowhere to be seen.

Unable to make headway into the front parlor where most everyone had gathered, she worked her way down the hall to the kitchen.

She heard the Hardman Community Band begin to play and grinned at the sound of Arlan's trumpet. Back and forth she scurried with the other women helping in the kitchen to refill bowls, pour drinks, and fill baskets with bread while the musicians filled the house with cheerful carols.

The music stopped then the sound of a lone violin began to play. Goose bumps rippled over her skin and she shoved the bowl of fried apples she held into Filly's hands then raced from the room and down the hall.

In the parlor, Maddie stood on top of a table someone had moved near the Christmas tree and played from her little heart. Eyes closed, Maddie brought the sounds of snowfall, of magic and reindeer, of tradition and holiday dreams to life. Silence reined throughout the house as Maddie played, everyone in awe of the larger-than-life music created by this tiny, talented girl.

When she finished, Maddie ducked into a curtsey, grinned at her father, and leaped off the table into her grandfather's arms.

Applause was so loud, it made Claire's ears hurt, but she rushed forward until she held Maddie in her arms.

"That was amazing, Maddie Mae. I could hear the snowflakes falling in your song."

"Oh, good! Did you smell the tree, and hear the carols?" Maddie asked, patting Claire's cheeks.

"I did. It was wonderful!" Claire kissed her nose. "Did your daddy bring you your violin?"

"Yes. He and Grandpapa brought it from the cabin. I'm gonna go play with Maura."

Maddie ran off the moment Claire set her down, still dazzled by the child's unbelievable talent.

"I think everyone enjoyed hearing her play," a familiar voice said from behind her.

Claire spun around and looked into a stranger's face, until she realized Gray had shaved off his beard.

"Oh, my," she whispered, caught off guard by his handsome face. He had a strong, square chin, with the slightest hint of a cleft right in the center of it. Now she knew where Maddie got the little dimple in her chin. His lips were full and so enticing. And his freshly shaved skin, so taut and smooth, begged for her kiss.

His hair had been trimmed, but it was still far longer than how the other men in town wore theirs. She wouldn't admit as much, but she was thrilled he hadn't cut it. So many times, she'd imagined running her fingers through it and hated to see him chop it all off before she had the chance.

"Gray, you look..." She stumbled to find the

appropriate words to say. In her typical fashion, she blurted out the first thing that popped into her head. "Good enough to kiss."

The spark she'd seen flickering in his eyes burst into a full flame. His eyes fairly smoldered as he cupped her elbow and guided her through the crowd. At the front door, he hesitated as he stared at the dozens of coats. Claire snatched hers and slipped it on along with her scarf and gloves while Gray worked a dark wool coat over his injured shoulder, favoring his side.

"Come with me," he said, taking her hand and opening the door. He led her away from the house and down the street. It wasn't until they were on the outskirts of town, near the schoolhouse that he slowed and then stopped.

Quiet settled around them with a peaceful welcome after the cacophony of noise at the carnival.

"Claire," Gray whispered, pulling her against him as though he intended to hold her there forever. "My beautiful Clarice."

"Gray, what has gotten into you? We should get back to the gathering. Maddie will…"

Gray silenced her with a quick kiss. "Maddie will be fine until we return. Between your sisters, Fred and Elsa, and my father, she has plenty of supervision." He took a step back, as though he wanted to memorize every detail of her face, and smiled. "You are a vision, Claire. You look like a Christmas holly berry."

Claire glanced down at her red brocade velvet coat. She wore a burgundy gown with a full layered chiffon skirt. As the breeze blew, it whipped the fabric around Gray's legs, entangling them together.

If only he'd be as willing to entangle their lives and their hearts.

With a groan, he pulled her into his arms again and kissed her with such unrestrained longing, such tender passion, she marveled the snow around them didn't melt and flood the town.

When he finally raised his head, he ran his fingers across her just-kissed lips. "You are perfection, beautiful songbird."

He took a rolled scroll of parchment from his coat pocket and handed it to her.

"What's this?" Claire asked.

"Open it," Gray said, clearly eager for her to read it.

She removed the red ribbon wrapped around the parchment and handed it to him. He tucked it in his pocket and gave her an encouraging nod. "Go on."

Slowly, she unrolled the parchment to find music notes. It was a piece of music. Then she recognized the words penned beneath the notes. "My song? You wrote it down, created a Christmas melody for my song?"

"Your song has been in my heart since I first heard the tune. Papa thinks it's quite good and has a friend who'd most likely be eager to publish it. I rather hope you'll sing it tonight at the Christmas service. Pastor Dodd has agreed to add it to the program if you're willing. If it wasn't for my injury I'd accompany you, but Maddie could handle the task."

"You mean you'd play for me, if you could?" Claire asked, rolling up the parchment and staring at him, confused. "You said you'd never play again."

"I did say that, but I'm now revoking my rash statement. I'd like to take back the other one, too." He raised her hand and kissed her fingers, even though she wore a glove. "Clarice Baker, I love you with all my heart. You've filled my whole world with joy and excitement, and selfless love. Not only that, but you've given Maddie a taste of what it's like to have a mother. If you are so inclined, I'd be honored beyond words if you'd consider allowing me to pay court to you."

Claire shook her head and tucked the parchment

back in Gray's pocket. "I won't allow you to pay court to me Gray. Not when I already know I'll love you from now through all eternity. I won't court you, but if you ask, I'd happily marry you."

He smiled and kissed her again, kissed her until her knees felt weak and she clung to him for support.

"Well, then, Claire, would you do me the great honor of becoming my wife? If you aren't opposed, perhaps a wedding could be arranged with haste before your sisters and my father return to Philadelphia."

"Yes, yes, and yes!" Claire pulled his head down and kissed him, then smiled against his lips. "I love you, Gray. I love you so much!"

"I should tell you, you're about to make Maddie's Christmas wish come true. She told me if you would stay with us always, she wouldn't even ask for a puppy for Christmas."

Claire laughed and wrapped her arms around him, kissing him again. "And you and Maddie are making all my dreams come true."

Happy chatter filled Fred and Elsa's parlor as the three Baker girls, their men, young Maddie, and William Carter gathered there to toast the newlywed couple with cups of spicy cider.

"To many happy years ahead," William Carter said, lifting his cup.

"And to a lifetime of love and joy," Heath added.

"And a house full of feisty children, just like Claire," Ari added with a teasing grin.

Gray groaned, but kissed Claire's cheek. He could hardly believe she'd agreed to become his bride.

One moment he'd been hoping she'd agree to being

courted and the next, they were hurrying back to find her sisters and announce their plans to wed the day after Christmas.

Christmas Eve, Maddie had played her violin while Claire sang the Christmas song she'd composed, a song full of love and hope that he knew the world would enjoy hearing, too.

Later that evening, when they had a few stolen moments alone, Claire had presented him with a portrait she'd painted of Maddie playing the violin in his workshop.

Light streamed around his daughter in what appeared to be a heavenly aura while he stood in the background, eyes closed, with a blissful expression on his face. Claire had masterfully caught the joy of Maddie's song in the painting, as well as the fact the child stood on a table, playing in the midst of a violin workshop.

Awed by the woman's talent, he knew he'd treasure the painting always.

Christmas Day had been filled with laughter and joy as they exchanged gifts. Through a friend of Fred's, they'd found a puppy for Maddie. The brown and white fuzzy pup was immediately given the name Bear. The poor thing had been packed around everywhere with Maddie. She even tied a blue ribbon around his neck and carried him in a basket to their wedding ceremony at the church earlier that afternoon.

Now, Gray looked at his gorgeous wife. His heart filled with gratitude for the blessings in his life. He was no longer in exile. No longer alone. No longer lost in the torment of grief and unresolved misery.

And it was all because of Claire.

He set aside his cup of cider, gave Maddie a hug and whispered in her ear to be a good girl for her aunties and that he'd see her in the morning, then without a bit of ceremony, led Claire to the door.

"Going somewhere?" Fred asked with a teasing grin.

"Yes, I'm taking my bride away for the evening and if anyone needs us, we'll be at the apartment over the bakery, which Elsa so kindly offered for our use."

"We're so happy for you, Claire," Ari said, while she and Bett both gave her warm hugs. "We'll see you for breakfast."

Claire nodded then bent down and hugged Maddie and Bear, since the child had picked up the puppy again. "Be a good girl, Maddie Mae. We'll see you in the morning."

"I'm going to play checkers with Uncle Heath. Uncle Clark cheats," she said, giving the man a dark glare.

"I do not cheat!" Clark declared as the rest of them laughed.

Gray settled Claire's coat around her shoulders, grabbed his, and hurried outside before anyone stopped them.

"What is your rush?" Claire asked as he hastened her down the walk and headed toward town.

"The rush, my darling, delightful, delectable girl, is to get you alone." Gray gave her a rakish wink. When they were out of sight of the house, he stopped and pulled her into his arms, kissing her long and slow. "Admittedly, it's not so much of a rush, as a need to be alone with you, uninterrupted."

"That's nice," Claire said, gazing up at him with moonlight bathing her face in silver. If he hadn't already been thoroughly infatuated with her, he would have been at that moment.

"Oh, how I love you, my little songbird. Shall we get out of this cold and you can sing me a song from your heart."

"But only if you play the melody," she teased with an inviting warmth in her eyes. "I love you, Gray. Forever, with all my heart."

Spice Cake

I love the smell of spice cake baking in the oven. It just fills the house with the most delicious scent that makes me think of my grandma. I hope you enjoy this old-fashioned recipe!

Spice Cake
2 1/2 cups all-purpose flour
2 teaspoons baking powder
1 teaspoon baking soda
1/2 teaspoon salt
2 teaspoons ground cinnamon
1 teaspoon ground ginger
1 teaspoon ground nutmeg
1 cup vegetable oil
1 ¾ cup packed brown sugar
1 cup applesauce
4 large eggs
2 teaspoons vanilla extract
1 cup grated apple
Cream Cheese Frosting
8 ounces cream cheese
1/2 cup butter
4 cups powdered sugar
1 teaspoon pure vanilla extract

Preheat the oven to 350°F and grease a 9x13 inch baking pan.

Whisk dry ingredients together and set aside.

Mix the oil, brown sugar, applesauce, eggs, vanilla extract in a large bowl. Add the dry ingredients and mix until blended. Stir in the grated apple until combined.

Spread batter into the prepared pan. Bake for 40-50 minutes. The cake is done when a toothpick inserted in the center comes out clean.

Remove the cake from the oven and set on a wire rack.

To make the frosting, bring cream cheese and butter to room temperature. Mix together on medium speed in a large bowl, then add sugar and vanilla. Mix for about two minutes, until frosting is smooth. Spread on cake and refrigerate at least thirty minutes before serving.

Author's Note

Thank you, dear reader, for coming along on another adventure in Hardman. There are times I so wish I could see the town I imagine in these stories. Wouldn't it be fun to shop at Bruner's Mercantile, or gaze in the window at the displays in Abby's dress shop, or stop by the bakery for one of Elsa's cinnamon buns?

I hope you enjoyed this story about hope and love. I don't know about you, but little Maddie just stole my heart.

There are a few tidbits of real life incorporated into this story.

The mention of the robbery at the Helix mercantile really happened in the autumn of 1902. I found mention of it in a newspaper archive. The thieves broke in, used tools they found in the store to blow up the safe, only to discover it held $29 dollars. So they stole jewelry, and the store owner's coat, and fled. The county sheriff was determined to catch the criminals, so he boarded a train headed toward Baker City with one of his deputies and the two of them kept watch to see if any fires were visible along the tracks, since it was dark out. Sure enough, they caught sight of a fire, had the train stop and walked up to the robbers, catching them by surprise. The thieves were hauled back to jail without any fuss and incarcerated.

The scene of Claire shooting her bow and arrows was inspired by several images I found of Victorian women who belonged to archery clubs. I had no idea the clubs existed for women, but loved the idea of the outdoorsy girls of the day having something like that to participate in.

Oh, and I must tell you about the skis Fred brought home. During my growing up years, we lived on a hill. When it snowed, my dad would take down a section of the fence around the pasture behind our house and we could sled down it to our heart's content (the hike back up the hill was a killer, but we had such fun!). At the bottom of the hill was a ginormous drainage ditch, another fence, and then our pond where we skated if it froze over.

One year, my brother unearthed an old pair of wooden skis. He was good at ice skating and skateboarding, so of course he had no problem strapping on those old skis and giving them a go on our sledding hill.

In fact, he made it look like such fun, I begged and pleaded for a turn. I was probably about six or seven at the time. Not old enough to know better! I don't know where the rational adults were at the time, but my brother strapped me on the skis, got me centered at the top of the hill, then gave me a big push.

Between my very short life flickering before my eyes and the very real possibility of slamming into the drainage ditch, or worse, the fence on the other side of it, I closed my eyes and hoped I wouldn't die. Then I vowed I'd never again put skis on my feet.

Since I somehow survived the experience, I have not once been skiing. But it sure seemed like a fun thing for Claire to enjoy.

I do plan on there being another Hardman Holidays story next holiday season. If you have any suggestions for future characters, be sure to let me know.

Special thanks to my editors and proofreaders. Thank you Shauna, Katrina and Leo for your excellent help with the book and to Melanie for your help with the book blurb. You all are so appreciated!

Wishing you a bright and beautiful holiday and a blessed new year!

Thank you for reading *The Christmas Melody* I'd be so grateful if you'd share a review so other readers might discover this heartwarming holiday series. Even a line or two is appreciated more than you can know.

Read the rest of the books in the
Hardman Holidays series!
The Christmas Bargain
The Christmas Token
The Christmas Calamity
The Christmas Vow
The Christmas Quandary
The Christmas Confection

Also, if you haven't yet signed up for my newsletter, won't you consider subscribing? I send it out a few times a month, when I have new releases, sales, or news of freebies to share. Each month, you can enter a contest, get a new recipe to try, and discover news about upcoming events. When you sign up, you'll receive a free short and sweet historical romance. Don't wait. Sign up today!

And if newsletters aren't your thing, please follow me on BookBub. You'll receive notifications on pre-orders, new releases, and sale books!

For more sweet Christmas romances, don't miss out on the Rodeo Romance series!

Rodeo Romance Series
Hunky rodeo cowboys tangle with independent sassy women who can't help but love them.

The Christmas Cowboy (Book 1) — Among the top saddle bronc riders in the rodeo circuit, easy-going Tate Morgan can master the toughest horse out there, but trying to handle beautiful Kenzie Beckett is a completely different story.

Wrestlin' Christmas (Book 2) — Sidelined with a major injury, steer wrestler Cort McGraw struggles to come to terms with the end of his career. Shanghaied by his sister and best friend, he finds himself on a run-down ranch with a worrisome, albeit gorgeous widow, and her silent, solemn son.

Capturing Christmas (Book 3) — Life is hectic on a good day for rodeo stock contractor Kash Kressley. Between dodging flying hooves and babying cranky bulls, he barely has time to sleep.

The last thing Kash needs is the entanglement of a sweet romance, especially with a woman as full of fire and sass as Celia McGraw.

Barreling Through Christmas (Book 4) — Cooper James might be a lot of things, but beefcake model wasn't something he intended to add to his resume.

Chasing Christmas (Book 5) — Tired of his cousin's publicity stunts on his behalf, bull rider Chase Jarrett has no idea how he ended up with an accidental bride!

Racing Christmas (Book 6) — Brylee Barton is racing to save her family's ranch. Shaun Price is struggling to win her heart. . . again.

Hopeless romantic Shanna Hatfield spent ten years as a newspaper journalist before moving into the field of marketing and public relations. Sharing the romantic stories she dreams up in her head is a perfect outlet for her love of writing, reading, and creativity. She and her husband, lovingly referred to as Captain Cavedweller, reside in the Pacific Northwest.

Shanna loves to hear from readers. Connect with her online:
Blog: shannahatfield.com
Facebook: Shanna Hatfield's Page
Shanna Hatfield's Hopeless Romantics Group
Pinterest: Shanna Hatfield
Email: shanna@shannahatfield.com

Made in the USA
Monee, IL
27 September 2021